MURANO

N

Cimitero

ISOLA DI
S. MICHELE

L A G U N A

Ospedale Civile

SS Giovanni
e Paolo

BORGOLOCO
S. LORENZO

CAMPO SANTA
MARIA FORMOSA

RIO DI SAN
LORENZO

San Lio

CALLE DEI
FABBRI

Questura

San
Lorenzo

PONTE
DEI GRECI

C O

San
Zaccaria

PIAZZA
SAN
MARCO

C A S T E L L O

Basilica di
San Marco

CAMPANILE
DI SAN MARCO

RIVA DEGLI SCHIAVONI

BACINO DI
SAN MARCO

ISOLA DI
S. GIORGIO
MAGGIORE

↓Lido

About Face

Donna Leon

About
Face

Atlantic Monthly Press
New York

First published in 2009 in the United Kingdom by William Heinemann,
The Random House Group Limited, London

Endpaper map by ML Design, London

Published simultaneously in Canada
Printed in the United States of America

ISBN-13: 978-0-8021-1896-7

Atlantic Monthly Press
an imprint of Grove/Atlantic, Inc.
841 Broadway
New York, NY 10003

Distributed by Publishers Group West
www.groveatlantic.com

09 10 11 12   10 9 8 7 6 5 4 3 2

For Petra Reski-Lando
and Lino Lando

Che ti par di quell'aspetto?

What do you think of that face?

Così fan tutte

—Mozart

1

He noticed the woman on their way to dinner. That is, as he and Paola paused in front of the window of a bookstore, and he was using the reflection to adjust his tie, Brunetti saw the woman's reflection as she passed by, heading towards Campo San Barnaba arm in arm with an older man. He saw her from behind, the man on her left. Brunetti first noticed her hair, a blonde as light as Paola's, braided into a smooth bun that sat low on the back of her head. By the time he turned around to get a better look, the couple had passed them and was nearing the bridge that led to San Barnaba.

Her coat – it might have been ermine, it might have been sable: Brunetti knew only that it was something more expensive than mink – fell to just above very fine ankles and shoes with a heel too high, really, to be worn on streets where patches of snow and ice still lay.

Brunetti recognized the man but failed to recall his name: the impression that came was the vague memory of wealth and importance. He was shorter and broader than the woman and he was more careful about avoiding the patches of ice. At the bottom of the bridge, the man took a sudden sidestep and braced his hand on the parapet. He stopped, and the woman's momentum was arrested by the anchor of his arm. One foot still in the air, she began to pivot in the direction of the now motionless man and swung farther away from the still-curious Brunetti.

'If you felt like it, Guido,' Paola said from beside him, 'you could get me the new biography of William James for my birthday.'

Brunetti looked away from the couple and followed the direction of his wife's finger towards a thick book at the back of the window display.

'I thought his name was Henry,' he said, straight faced.

She yanked at his arm, pulling him closer. 'Don't play the fool with me, Guido Brunetti. You know who William James is.'

He nodded. 'But why do you want a biography of the brother?'

'I'm curious about the family and about anything that might have made him the way he was.'

Brunetti remembered that, more than two decades before, he had felt the same urgency about the newly met Paola: inquisitive about her family, her tastes, her friends, anything at all that could tell him more about this wondrous young woman whom some beneficent agency of fate had allowed him to bump into among the shelves of the university library. To Brunetti, this curiosity seemed a normal enough response to a warm and living person. But to feel it about a writer who had been dead for almost a century?

'Why do you find him so fascinating?' he asked, not for the first time. Hearing himself, Brunetti realized he sounded just like what her enthusiasm for Henry James had so often reduced him to being: a petulant, jealous husband.

She released his arm and stepped back, as if to get a better look at this man she found herself married to. 'Because he understands things,' she said.

'Ah,' Brunetti contented himself with saying. It seemed to him that this was the least that could be expected of a writer.

'And because he makes us understand those things,' she added.

He now suspected that the subject had been closed.

Paola must have decided they had spent more than enough time on this. 'Come on. You know my father hates people to be late,' she said.

They moved away from the bookstore. When they reached the bottom of the bridge, she stopped and glanced up at his face. 'You know,' she began. 'You're really very much like Henry James.'

Brunetti did not know whether to be flattered or offended. Over the years, fortunately, he had at least ceased to wonder, upon hearing the comparison, whether he needed to reconsider the foundations of their marriage.

'You want to understand things, Guido. It's probably why you're a policeman.' She looked thoughtful after saying this. 'But you also want other people to understand those things.' She turned away and continued up the bridge. Over her shoulder, she added, 'Just as he did.'

Brunetti allowed her to reach the top of the bridge before calling after her, 'Does that mean I'm really meant to be a writer, too?' How nice it would be if she answered yes.

She dismissed the idea with a wave of her hand, then turned to say, 'It makes you interesting to live with, though.'

Better than being a writer, Brunetti thought as he followed after her.

Brunetti glanced at his watch as Paola reached up to ring the bell beside the *portone* of her parents' home. 'All these years, and you don't have a key?' he asked.

'Don't be a goose,' she said. 'Of course I have a key. But this is formal, so it's better to arrive like guests.'

'Does that mean we have to behave like guests?' Brunetti asked.

Whatever answer Paola might have given was cut off as the door was opened by a man neither of them recognized. He smiled and pulled the door fully open.

Paola thanked him and they started across the courtyard towards the steps that led to the *palazzo*. 'No livery,' Brunetti said in a shocked whisper. 'No periwigs? My God, what's the world coming to? Next thing you know, the servants will be eating at the high table, and then the silver will start to disappear. Where will it all end? With Luciana running after your father with a meat cleaver?'

Paola stopped in her tracks and turned to him, silent. She gave him a variation on the Look, her only recourse in his moments of verbal excess.

'*Sì, tesoro*?' he asked in his sweetest voice.

'Let's stand here for a few moments, Guido, while you use up all of your humorous remarks about my parents' place in society, and when you've calmed down, we'll go upstairs and join the other guests, and you will behave like a reasonably civilized person at dinner. How does that sound to you?'

Brunetti nodded. 'I like it, especially the part about "reasonably civilized".'

Her smile was radiant, 'I thought you would, dear.' She started up the steps to the entrance to the main part of the *palazzo*, Brunetti one step behind.

Paola had accepted her father's invitation some time before and explained to Brunetti that Conte Falier had said he wanted his son-in-law to meet a good friend of the Contessa.

Though Brunetti had come, over the years, to accept without question his mother-in-law's love, he was never sure of just where he stood in the Conte's estimation, whether he was viewed as a jumped-up peasant who had stolen in and made off with the affections of the Conte's only child or a person of worth and ability. Brunetti accepted the fact that

4

the Conte was entirely capable of believing both things simultaneously.

Another man whom neither of them recognized stood at the top of the steps and opened the door to the *palazzo* with a small bow, allowing its warmth to spill out towards them. Brunetti followed Paola inside.

The sound of voices came down the corridor from the main *salone* that looked across the Grand Canal. The man took their coats silently and opened the door of an illuminated closet. Glancing inside, Brunetti saw a single, long fur coat hanging by itself at the end of one of the racks, isolated either by its value or by the sensibilities of the man who had hung it there.

The voices lured them, and they started towards the front of the house. As Brunetti and Paola entered, he saw their host and hostess standing in front of the centre window. They were facing towards Brunetti and Paola, allowing their guests the view to the *palazzi* on the other side of the Grand Canal, and Brunetti, once again seeing their backs, recognized them as the man and woman who had passed them on the street; either that, or there existed another thickset, white-haired man who had a tall blonde companion with black stiletto-heeled shoes and hair pulled back into an elaborately woven bun. She stood a bit apart, gazing out the window and appearing from this distance not to be engaging with the others.

Two other couples stood on either side of his parents-in-law. He recognized the Conte's lawyer and his wife; the others were an old friend of the Contessa's who, like her, engaged in good works, and her husband, who sold armaments and mining technology to Third World countries.

The Conte glanced aside from what looked like a flourishing conversation with the white-haired man and saw his daughter. He set his glass down, said something else to the man, and stepped around him to come towards Paola and

Brunetti. As his host moved away, the man turned to see what had drawn his attention, and the name came to Brunetti: Maurizio Cataldo, a man said to have the ear of certain members of the city administration. The woman continued to look out of the window, as if enchanted by the view and unaware of the Conte's departure.

Brunetti and Cataldo, as often happened in the city, had never been introduced to one another, though Brunetti knew the general outline of his history. The family had come from Friuli, Brunetti thought, some time early in the last century, had prospered during the Fascist era, and had become even richer during the great boom of the sixties. Construction? Transport? He wasn't sure.

The Conte reached Brunetti and Paola, kissed them each twice in greeting, and then turned back to the couple with whom he had been talking, saying, 'Paola, you know them,' and then to Brunetti, 'but I'm not sure you do, Guido. They're eager to meet you.'

This was perhaps true of Cataldo, who watched them approach, eyebrows raised and chin tilted to one side as he cast his eyes from Paola to Brunetti with open curiosity. As for the woman, her expression was impossible to read. Or more accurately, her face expressed pleasant, permanent anticipation, fixed there immutably by the attentions of a surgeon. Her mouth was set to spend the rest of its time on earth parted in a small smile, the sort one gives when introduced to the maid's grandchild. Though the smile was thin as an expression of pleasure, the lips that made it were full and fleshy, a deep red most usually seen on cherries. Her eyes were crowded by her cheekbones, which swelled up on either side of her nose in taut, pink nodes about the size of a kiwi fruit cut longitudinally. The nose itself started higher on her forehead than it was normal for noses to start and was strangely flat, as though someone had smoothed it with a spatula after placing it there.

6

Of line or blemish there was no sign. Her skin was perfect, the skin of a child. The blonde hair gave no sign that it differed from spun gold, and Brunetti had learned enough about fashion to know that her dress cost more than any suit he had ever owned.

This, then, must be Cataldo's second wife, *'la super liftata'*, some distant relative of the Contessa about whom Brunetti had heard a few times but whom he had never met. A quick search through his file of social gossip told him that she was from the North somewhere and was said to be reclusive and, in some never explained way, strange.

'Ah,' the Conte began, breaking into Brunetti's thoughts. Paola bent forward and kissed the woman, then shook the man's hand. To the woman, the Conte said, 'Franca, I'd like you to meet my son-in-law, Guido Brunetti, Paola's husband.' And then to Brunetti, 'Guido, may I present Franca Marinello and her husband, Maurizio Cataldo.' He stepped aside and waved Brunetti forward, as though he were offering Brunetti and Paola the other couple as a Christmas gift.

Brunetti shook hands with the woman, whose grasp was surprisingly firm, and the man, whose hand felt dry, as if it needed dusting. *'Piacere,'* he said, smiling first into her eyes, and then into the man's, which were a watery blue.

The man nodded, but it was the woman who spoke. 'Your mother-in-law has spoken so well of you all these years; it's a great pleasure finally to meet you.'

Before Brunetti could think of a response, the double doors leading to the dining room were opened from inside, and the man who had collected the coats announced that dinner was served. As everyone made their way across the room, Brunetti tried to remember anything the Contessa might have told him about her friend Franca, but he could summon only that the Contessa had befriended her years ago when she came to study in Venice.

The sight of the table, laden with china and silver, exploding with flowers, reminded him of the last meal he had had in this house, only two weeks before. He had stopped by to bring two books to the Contessa, with whom, in the last years, he had begun to exchange them, and he had found his son there with her. Raffi had explained that he had come to pick up the essay he had prepared for his Italian class and which his grandmother had offered to read.

Brunetti had found them in her study, sitting side by side at her desk. In front of them were the eight pages of Raffi's essay, spread out and covered with comments in three different colours. To the left of the papers was a platter of sandwiches, or rather what had once been a platter of sandwiches. While Brunetti finished them, the Contessa explained her system: red for grammatical errors; yellow for any form of the verb *essere*, and blue for errors of fact or interpretation.

Raffi, who sometimes bridled when Brunetti disagreed with his view of history or Paola corrected his grammar, seemed entirely persuaded that his grandmother knew whereof she wrote and was busy entering her suggestions into his laptop; Brunetti listened attentively as she explained them.

Brunetti was pulled back from this memory by Paola's muttered, 'Look for your name.' Indeed, small hand-printed cards stood propped in front of each place. He quickly found his own and was comforted to see Paola's to his left, between himself and her father. He glanced around the table, where everyone seemed to have found his or her proper place. Someone more familiar with the etiquette of seating at dinner might have been shocked at the proximity of wives to their husbands: it is to be hoped that their sensibilities would have been calmed by the fact that the Conte and Contessa faced one another from the ends of the rectangular table. The Conte's lawyer, Renato Rocchetto, pulled out the Contessa's

8

chair and held it for her. When she was seated, the other women took their places, followed by the men.

Brunetti found himself directly opposite Cataldo's wife, about a metre from her face. She was listening to something her husband said, her head almost touching his, but Brunetti knew that would merely delay the inevitable. Paola turned to him, whispered *'Coraggio'*, and patted his leg.

As Paola took her hand away, Cataldo smiled at his wife and turned towards Paola and her father; Franca Marinello looked across at Brunetti. 'It's terribly cold, isn't it?' she began, and Brunetti braced himself for yet another one of those dinner conversations.

Before he could find a suitably bland answer, the Contessa spoke from her end of the table: 'I hope no one will mind if we have a meatless dinner this evening.' She smiled and looked around at the guests and added, in a tone that suggested both amusement and embarrassment, 'What with the dietary peculiarities of my own family and because I let it go until too late to call each of you to ask about yours, I decided it would be easiest simply to avoid meat and fish.'

' "Dietary peculiarities?" ' whispered Claudia Umberti, the wife of the Conte's lawyer. She sounded honestly puzzled, and Brunetti, who sat beside her, had seen her and her husband at enough family dinners to know she understood that the only dietary peculiarity of the extended Falier family – Chiara's off and on vegetarianism aside – was an insistence on ample portions and rich desserts.

No doubt wanting to save her mother the awkwardness of being caught in an open lie, Paola spoke into the general silence to explain, 'I prefer not to eat beef; my daughter Chiara won't eat meat or fish – at least not this week; Raffi won't eat anything green and doesn't like cheese; and Guido,' she said, leaning towards him and placing a hand on his arm, 'won't eat anything unless he gets a large portion.'

9

Everyone at the table obliged with gentle laughter, and Brunetti kissed Paola's cheek as a sign of good humour and sportsmanship, vowing at the same time to refuse any offer that might be made of a second helping. He turned to her and, still smiling, asked, 'What was that all about?'

'I'll tell you later,' she said and turned away to ask a polite question of her father.

Apparently having decided not to comment on the Contessa's remarks, Franca Marinello said, when Brunetti's attention returned to her, 'The snow on the street's a terrible problem.' Brunetti smiled, quite as if he had neither noticed her shoes nor been listening to that same remark for the last two days.

According to the rules of polite conversation, it was now his turn to make some meaningless remark, so he did his part and offered, 'But it's good for the skiers.'

'And the farmers,' she added.

'I beg your pardon?'

'Where I come from,' she said, in an Italian that displayed no trace of local accent, 'we have a saying, "Under the snow is bread. Under the rain is hunger."' Her voice was pleasantly low: had she sung, she would have been a contralto.

Brunetti, urban to the core, smiled apologetically and said, 'I'm not sure I understand.'

Her lips moved upward in what he was coming to recognize as her smile, and the expression in her eyes softened. 'It's supposed to mean that the rain simply runs away, doing only temporary good, but the snow lies on the mountains and melts away slowly all summer long.'

'And thus the bread?' Brunetti asked.

'Yes. Or so the old people believed.' Before Brunetti could comment, she went on, 'But this snowfall was a freak storm here in the city, only enough to close the airport for a few hours; no more than a few centimetres. In Alto Adige, where I come from, it hasn't snowed at all this year.'

10

'So it *is* bad for the skiers?' Brunetti asked with a smile, picturing her in a long cashmere sweater and ski pants, posed in front of a fireplace in some five-star ski resort.

'I don't care about them, only the farmers,' she said with a vehemence that surprised him. She studied his face for a moment, and then added, '"Oh, farmers: if only they recognized their blessings."'

Brunetti all but gasped, 'That's Virgil, isn't it?'

'*The Georgics*,' she answered, politely ignoring his surprise and everything it implied. 'You've read it?'

'At school,' Brunetti answered. 'And then again a few years ago.'

'Why?' she inquired politely, then turned her head aside to thank the waiter placing a dish of *risotto ai funghi* in front of her.

'Why what?'

'Why did you reread it?'

'Because my son was reading it in school and said he liked it, so I thought I should have another look.' He smiled and added, 'It was so long since I read it at school that I no longer had any memory of it.'

'And?'

Brunetti had to think before he answered her, so rarely was he presented with the opportunity to talk about the books he read. 'I have to confess,' he said as the waiter set his risotto in front of him, 'all that talk about the duties of a good landowner didn't much interest me.'

'Then what subjects do interest you?' she asked.

'I'm interested in what the Classics say about politics,' Brunetti answered and prepared himself for the inevitable dimming of interest on the part of his listener.

She picked up her wine, took a small sip, and tipped the glass in Brunetti's direction, swirling the contents gently and saying, 'Without the good landowner, we wouldn't have any of this.' She took another sip, and set the glass down.

Brunetti decided to risk it. Raising his right hand, he waved it in a small swirling circle that encompassed, should one be inclined so to interpret it, the table, the people at it, and, by extension, the *palazzo* and the city in which they sat. 'Without politics,' he said, 'we wouldn't have any of this.'

Because of the difficulty her eyes had in widening, her surprise was registered in a gulp of laughter. This grew into a girlish peal of merriment that she attempted to stifle by putting one hand over her mouth, but still the helpless giggles emerged, and then they turned into a fit of coughing.

Heads turned, and her husband withdrew his attention from the Conte to place a protective hand on her shoulder. Conversation stopped.

She nodded, raised a hand and made a small waving gesture to signify that nothing was wrong, then took her napkin and wiped her eyes, still coughing. Soon enough the coughing stopped and she took a few deep breaths, then said to the table in general, 'Sorry. Something went down the wrong way.' She covered her husband's hand with her own and gave it a reassuring squeeze, then said something to him that caused him to smile and turn back to his conversation with the Conte.

She took a few small sips from her water glass, tasted the risotto, then put down her fork. As if there had been no interruption, she looked across to Brunetti and said, 'It's Cicero I like best on politics.'

'Why?'

'Because he was such a good hater.'

Brunetti forced himself to pay attention to what she said rather than to the unearthly mouth out of which the words emerged, and they were still discussing Cicero when the waiters took away their almost untouched plates of risotto.

She moved on to the Roman writer's loathing of Cataline and all he represented; she spoke of his rancorous hatred of Marc'Antonio; she made no attempt to disguise her joy that

Cicero had finally won the consulship; and she surprised Brunetti when she spoke of his poetry with great familiarity.

The servants were removing the plates from the next course, a vegetable loaf, when Signora Marinello's husband turned to her and said something that Brunetti could not hear. She smiled and gave her attention to him, and she continued speaking to him until the dessert – a cream cake so rich as to atone fully for any lack of meat – was finished and the plates had been taken away. Brunetti, called back to the conventions of social intercourse, devoted his attention to the wife of Avvocato Rocchetto, who informed him of the latest scandals involving the administration of Teatro La Fenice.

'. . . finally decided not to bother to renew our *abbonamento*. It's all so terribly second-rate, and they will insist on doing all that wretched French and German rubbish,' she said, almost quivering with disapproval. 'It's no different from a minor theatre in some tiny provincial French town,' she concluded, sweeping the theatre to oblivion with a wave of her hand and taking French provincial life along with it. Brunetti reflected upon Jane Austen's suggestion that a character 'save his breath to cool his tea', and thus resisted the temptation to observe that Teatro la Fenice *was*, after all, a minor theatre in a tiny provincial Italian town and so no great things should be expected of it.

Coffee came, and then a waiter moved around the table pushing a wheeled tray covered with bottles of grappa and various *digestive*. Brunetti asked for a Domenis, which did not disappoint. He turned in Paola's direction to ask her if she wanted a sip of his grappa, but she was listening to something Cataldo was saying to her father. She had her chin propped on her palm, the face of her watch towards Brunetti, and so he saw that it was well after midnight. Slowly, he slid his foot along the floor until it came up against something hard but not as solid as the leg of a chair. He gave it two slight taps.

Not more than a minute later, Paola glanced at her watch and said, '*Oddio*, I've got a student coming to my office at nine, and I haven't even read his paper yet.' She leaned forward and said down the table to her mother, 'It seems I spend my life either doing my homework or having to read someone else's.'

'And never getting it done on time,' the Conte added, but with affection and resignation, making it clear that he was not speaking in reproach.

'Perhaps we should think about going home, as well, *caro*?' Cataldo's wife said, smiling at him.

Cataldo nodded and got to his feet. He moved behind his wife and pulled her chair back as she rose. He turned to the Conte. 'Thank you, Signor Conte,' he said with a small inclination of his head. 'It was very kind of you and your wife to invite us. And doubly so because we had a chance to meet your family.' He smiled in Paola's direction.

Napkins were dropped on to the table, and Avvocato Rocchetto said something about needing to stretch his legs. When the Conte asked Franca Marinello if they would like him to have them taken home in his boat, Cataldo explained that his own would be waiting at the *porta d'acqua*. 'I don't mind walking one way, but in this cold, and late at night, I prefer going home in the launch,' he said.

In staggered pairs, they made their way back through the *salone*, from which had already vanished all sign of the drinks that had been served there, and towards the front hall, where two of the evening's servants helped them into their coats. Brunetti glanced aside and said softly to Paola, 'And people say it's hard to find good staff these days.' She grinned but someone on his other side let out an involuntary snort of laughter. When he turned, he saw only Franca Marinello's impassive face.

In the courtyard, the group exchanged polite farewells: Cataldo and his wife were led towards the *porta d' acqua* and their boat; Rocchetto and his wife lived only three doors away; and the other couple turned in the direction of the Accademia, having laughed off Paola's suggestion that she and Brunetti walk them to their home.

Arm in arm, Brunetti and Paola turned towards home. As they passed the entrance to the university, Brunetti asked, 'Did you enjoy yourself?'

Paola stopped and looked him in the eye. Instead of answering, she asked, coolly, 'And what, pray tell, was *that* all about?'

'I beg your pardon,' Brunetti answered, stalling.

'You beg my pardon because you don't understand my question, or you beg my pardon because you spent the evening talking to Franca Marinello and ignoring everyone else?'

The vehemence of her question surprised Brunetti into bleating out, 'But she reads Cicero.'

'Cicero?' asked an equally astonished Paola.

'*On Government*, and the letters, and the accusation against Verres. Even the poetry,' he said. Suddenly struck by the cold, Brunetti took her arm and started up the bridge, but her steps lagged and slowed him to a halt at the top.

Paola moved back to get perspective on his face, but kept hold of his hand. 'You realize, I hope, that you are married to the only woman in this city who would find that an entirely satisfactory explanation?'

Her answer forced a sudden laugh from Brunetti. She added, 'Besides, it was interesting to watch so many people at work.'

'Work?'

'Work,' she repeated, and started down the other side of the bridge.

When Brunetti caught up with her, she continued unasked, 'Franca Marinello was working to impress you with her intelligence. You were working to find out how someone who looks like her could have read Cicero. Cataldo was working to convince my father to invest with him, and my father was working to try to decide whether he should do it or not.'

'Invest in what?' Brunetti asked, all thought of Cicero banished.

'In China,' she said.

'*Oddio*,' was the only thing Brunetti could think of to say.

2

'Why in God's name would he want to invest in China?' Brunetti demanded.

That stopped her. She came to a halt in front of the firemen's dining hall, windows dark at this hour and no scent of food spilling into the *calle*. He was honestly puzzled. 'Why China?' he repeated.

She shook her head in a conscious imitation of complete befuddlement and looked around, as if seeking sympathetic ears. 'Please, would someone tell me who this man is? I think I see him in the morning sometimes, beside me in bed, but this can't be my husband.'

'Oh, stop it, Paola, and tell me,' he said, suddenly tired and in no mood for this.

'How can you read two newspapers every day and not have any idea of why a person would want to invest in China?'

He took her arm and turned her towards home. He saw no sense in standing on a public street and discussing this, not when they could do it while heading for home, or in their bed. 'Of course, I know all that,' he said. 'Soaring economy, fortunes to be made, stock market gone wild, no end in sight. But why would your father want any part of it?'

He felt her pace grow slower; fearing a pause for further rhetorical flourishes, he kept moving, forcing her to keep up with him. 'Because my father has the ichor of capitalism flowing in his veins, Guido. Because, for hundreds of years, to be a Falier has been to be a merchant, and to be a merchant is to make money.'

'This,' Brunetti observed, 'from a professor of literature who maintains she has no interest in money.'

'That's because I'm the end of the line, Guido. I'm the last person in our family who will carry the name: our children have yours.' Her steps slowed, as did her voice, but she did not stop. 'My father has made money all his life, thus permitting me, and our children, the luxury of not having to take an interest in making it.'

Brunetti, who had played what must have been thousands of games of Monopoly with his children, was sure that the capitalist gene had run true to form in them and that they already had the interest, perhaps even the ichor itself.

'And he thinks there's money to be made there?' Brunetti asked, and then quickly added, if only to prevent her from again demanding how he could ask such a question, 'Safe money?'

She turned to him again. 'Safe?'

'Well,' he said, hearing himself how silly that had sounded, 'Clean money?'

'At least you accept that there's a difference,' she said with the bite of her years of voting Communist.

He said nothing for a while. Suddenly he stopped and asked, 'What was all that about, what did your mother call it, "dietary peculiarities"? And all that nonsense about what the kids wouldn't eat?'

'Cataldo's wife is a vegetarian,' Paola said. 'And my

mother didn't want to call attention to her, so I decided that I should be the one to – as you police people say – "take the fall".' She squeezed his arm.

'And thus the fiction of my appetite?' he could not prevent himself from asking.

Did she hesitate an instant? Regardless, she repeated, tugging his arm and smiling at him, 'Yes. Thus the fiction of your appetite.'

Had Brunetti not warmed to Franca Marinello because of their conversation, he might have remarked that she hardly needed dietary peculiarities to draw attention to herself. But Cicero had intervened to change Brunetti's opinion and he had come, he realized, to feel protective of the woman.

They passed in front of Goldoni's house, then the sudden left and right and down towards San Polo. As they walked out into the *campo*, Paola stopped and gazed across the open space. 'How strange to see it empty like this.'

He loved the *campo*, had loved it since he was a boy, for its trees and its sense of openness: SS Giovanni e Paolo was too small, the statue in the way, and soccer balls were prone to end in the canal; Santa Margherita was oddly shaped, and he'd always found it too noisy, even more so now that it had become so fashionable. Perhaps it was the lack of commercialization that made him love Campo San Polo, for only two sides of it held shops, the others having resisted the lure of Mammon. The church, of course, had succumbed and now charged people to enter, having discovered that beauty brought more income than grace. Not that there was all that much to see inside: a few Tintorettos, those Tiepolo Stations of the Cross, a bit of this and that.

He felt Paola tugging at his arm. 'Come on, Guido, it's almost one.'

He accepted the truce her words offered, and they made their way home.

*

Unusually, his father-in-law phoned Brunetti at the Questura the next day. After thanking him for the dinner, Brunetti waited to see what was on the Conte's mind.

'Well, what did you think?' the Conte asked.

'Of what?' Brunetti asked.

'Of her.'

'Franca Marinello?' Brunetti asked, hiding his surprise.

'Of course. You sat opposite her all evening.'

'I didn't know I was supposed to be interrogating her,' Brunetti protested.

'But you did,' the Conte answered sharply.

'Only about Cicero, I'm afraid,' Brunetti explained.

'Yes, I know,' the Conte said, and Brunetti wondered if it was envy he heard in his voice.

'What did you talk about with the husband?' Brunetti inquired.

'Earth-moving equipment,' the Conte said with singular lack of enthusiasm, 'and other things.' After the briefest of pauses, he said, 'Cicero is infinitely more interesting.'

Brunetti remembered that his own copy of the speeches had been a Christmas gift from the Conte and that the dedication on the title page stated that it was one of the Conte's favourite books. 'But?' he asked in response to his father-in-law's tone.

'But Cicero,' the Conte answered, 'is not much in demand among Chinese businessmen.' He considered his own observation and then added, with a theatrical sigh, 'Perhaps because he had so little to say about earth-moving equipment.'

'Do Chinese businessmen have more to say?' Brunetti prodded.

The Conte laughed. 'You really can't lose the habit of interrogation, can you, Guido?' Before Brunetti could protest, the Conte went on, 'Yes, the few I know are very interested in it, especially bulldozers. So is Cataldo, and so is his son – he's

20

the son from his first marriage – who runs their heavy equipment company. China's gone crazy with a building boom, so their company's got more orders than they can handle, which means he's asked me to go into a limited partnership with him.'

Over the years, Brunetti had learned that circumspection was the appropriate response to anything his father-in-law might divulge about his business interests, so he did no more than mutter an attentive 'Ah.'

'But you can't be interested in that,' the Conte said, quite accurately as it happened. 'What did you think of her?'

'May I ask why you're curious?' Brunetti said.

'Because I sat next to her at dinner a few months ago, after meeting her here for years and never really talking to her, and the same thing happened to me. We started talking about a story that had been in the paper that day, and then suddenly we were talking about the *Metamorphoses*. I don't remember how it happened, but it was delightful. All those years, and we'd never talked, well, never about anything real. So I suggested Donatella put you across from her while I talked to the husband.' Then, with remarkable self-awareness, the Conte added, 'You've been forced to sit with so many of our dull friends all these years: I thought you deserved a change.'

'Thank you, then,' Brunetti said, choosing not to comment on the Conte's assessment of his friends. 'It was very interesting. She's even read the argument against Verres.'

'Oh, good for her,' the Conte all but chirped.

'Did you know her before?' Brunetti asked.

'Before the marriage or before the facelift?' the Conte inquired neutrally.

'Before the marriage,' Brunetti said.

'Yes and no. That is, she's always been more Donatella's friend than mine. Some relative of Donatella's asked her to keep an eye on her when she came here to study. Byzantine history, of all things. But she had to leave after two years.

Family trouble of some sort. Her father died, and she had to go home and find a job because the mother had never worked.' Vaguely, he added, 'I don't remember all the details. Donatella probably does.'

The Conte cleared his throat and then said, sounding apologetic, 'Hearing all this, it sounds like the plot summary of a bad television series. You sure you want to hear it?'

'I never watch television,' said a falsely virtuous Brunetti, 'so I find it interesting.'

'All right, then,' the Conte said and continued. 'The story I've heard – and I don't remember whether it was Donatella or other people who told me – is that she met Cataldo while she was modelling – furs, I think – and the rest, as my granddaughter is in the annoying habit of saying, is history.'

'Was divorce part of the history?' Brunetti asked.

'Yes, it was,' the Conte answered ruefully. 'I've known Maurizio a long time, and he is not a patient man. He offered his wife a settlement, and she accepted.'

The instinct developed over decades of prodding reluctant witnesses suggested to Brunetti that something was not being said here, and so he asked, 'What else?'

There was a long silence before the Conte answered. 'He was a guest at my table, so I don't like to say these things about him, but Maurizio is also said to be a vindictive man, and this might have encouraged his wife to accept the terms he offered.'

'I'm afraid I've heard this story before,' Brunetti said.

'Which one?' the Conte asked sharply.

'The same one you've heard, Orazio: the old man who meets the sweet young thing, leaves his wife, marries her *in fretta e furia*, and then perhaps they don't live happily ever after.' Brunetti himself did not like the sound of his own voice.

'But it's not like that, Guido. Not at all.'

'Why?'

'Because they *are* living happily ever after.' The Conte's voice held the same longing it had when he spoke of being able to spend an evening discussing Cicero. 'Or at least that's what Donatella tells me.'

After some time, the Conte asked, 'Are you troubled by her appearance?'

'That's a delicate way of phrasing it.'

'I've never understood it,' the Conte said. 'She was a lovely thing. No real reason for her to do it, but women today have different ideas about . . .' the Conte said, letting the sentence wither.

'It happened years ago. They went away, ostensibly on a vacation, but they were gone a long time: months. I can't remember who told me.' The Conte paused, then said, 'Not Donatella.' Brunetti was glad he said this. 'At any rate, when they came back, she looked the way she looks now. Australia – I think that's where they said they had been. But a person doesn't go to Australia for plastic surgery, for God's sake.'

Brunetti spoke without thinking, 'Why would anyone do that?'

'Guido,' the Conte said after some time, 'I've given that up.'

'Given what up?'

'Trying to understand why people do things. No matter how hard we try, we'll never get it right. My father's driver always used to say, "All we have is one head, so we can think only one way about anything."' The Conte laughed, and then said with sudden briskness, 'That's enough gossip. What I wanted to know was whether you liked her or not.'

'Only that?'

'I hardly thought you were going to run off with her, Guido,' he laughed.

'Orazio, believe me: one woman who reads is more than enough for me.'

I know what you mean, I know what you mean.' Then, a bit

23

more seriously, 'But you still haven't answered my question.'

'I liked her. A great deal.'

'Did she strike you as an honest woman?'

'Absolutely,' Brunetti answered instantly, not even having to think about it. But when he did, he said, 'Isn't that strange? I know almost nothing about her, but I trust her because she likes Cicero.'

Again, the Conte laughed, but in a softer voice. 'It makes sense to me.'

The Conte seldom displayed such interest in a person, so Brunetti was led to ask, 'Why are you curious about whether she's honest or not?'

'Because if she trusts her husband, then maybe he's worth trusting.'

'And you think she does?' Brunetti asked.

'I watched them last night, and there was nothing false about them. She loves him, and he loves her.'

'But loving isn't trusting, is it?' Brunetti asked.

'Ah, how good to hear the cool tones of your scepticism, Guido. We live in such sentimental times that I sometimes forget my best instincts.'

'Which tell you what?'

'That a man can smile and smile yet be a villain.'

'The Bible?' Brunetti asked.

'Shakespeare, I think,' the Conte said.

Brunetti suspected the conversation was over, but then the Conte said, 'I wondered if you could do me a favour, Guido. Discreetly.'

'Yes?'

'You have information there, far better than I sometimes have, and I wondered if you could get someone to have a look around to see if Cataldo is anyone I would want to . . .'

'Trust?' Brunetti asked provocatively.

'Never that, Guido,' Conte Falier said with adamantine certainty. 'Perhaps better to say whether he's someone I would want to invest with. He's in a terrible hurry for me to decide, and I don't know if my own people can find . . .' The Conte's voice drifted away, as if he could not think of the words to express the precise nature of his interest.

'I'll see what I can do,' Brunetti said, realizing that he was curious about Cataldo but not wanting, just then, to try to figure out why.

He and the Conte exchanged pleasantries, and the conversation ended.

He glanced at his watch and saw that he would have time to speak to Signorina Elettra, his superior's secretary, before going home to lunch. If anyone could have a discreet look into Cataldo's business dealings, it was surely she. He toyed for a moment with the idea of asking her to check, while she was about it, for whatever she could find about Cataldo's wife, as well. He felt a flush of embarrassment at his desire to see a photo of what she had looked like before the . . . before the marriage.

To enter Signorina Elettra's office was to be reminded that it was Tuesday. An enormous vase of pink French tulips stood on a desk in front of her window. The computer which she had allowed a generous and grateful Questura to supply her with some months before – consisting of nothing more than an anorexic screen and a black keyboard – left ample room on her desk for an equally large bouquet of white roses. The coloured wrapping lay neatly folded in the bin used only for paper, and woe to the member of staff who forgot and stuffed paper carelessly in the regular garbage. Paper; cardboard; metal; plastic. Brunetti had once heard her on the phone with the president of Vesta, the private company which had been awarded – he turned his thoughts away from consideration of the factors that might have affected that choice – the contract to collect garbage in the city, and he still recalled the exquisite politeness with which she had called to his attention the many ways a police investigation or, worse, one from the Guardia di Finanza, could impede the easy running of his company and how expensive and troublesome could be the unexpected discoveries to which an official financial investigation often led.

After that conversation – but surely not as a result – the garbage men had altered their schedule and begun to moor their 'barca ecologica' in front of the Questura every Tuesday and Friday mornings after picking up paper and cardboard from the residents in the area of SS Giovanni e Paolo. The second Tuesday, Vice-Questore Giuseppe Patta had ordered them to leave when he saw the boat moored there and had been outraged at the brutta figura of policemen seen carrying bags of papers from the Questura to a garbage scow.

It had taken Signorina Elettra no time at all to lead the Vice-Questore to see the tremendous publicity advantage to be gained from introducing an eco-iniziativa that was the product, of course, of Dottor Patta's wholehearted commitment to the ecological health of his adopted city. The following week, La Nuova sent not only a journalist but a photographer, and the next day's front page carried a long interview with Patta and above it a large photo. Though it did not show him actually carrying a bag of rubbish out to a garbage scow, it did show him at his desk, one hand placed assertively on a stack of papers, as if to suggest he could resolve the cases they documented by sheer force of will, and then diligently ensure that the papers were disposed of in the proper recycling receptacle.

As Brunetti entered, Signorina Elettra was just emerging from her superior's office. 'Ah, good,' she said, when she saw Brunetti at the door. 'The Vice-Questore wants to see you.'

'About?' he asked, all thought of Cataldo and his wife forgotten for the moment.

'There's someone in with him. A Carabiniere. From Lombardia.' The Most Serene Republic had ceased to exist more than two centuries before, but those who spoke its tongue could still, with a single word, express their suspicion of those bustling, upstart Lombards.

'Just go in,' she said, moving closer to her desk to allow him free passage to Patta's door.

He thanked her, knocked, and entered at Patta's shout.

Patta sat at his desk, to one side the same stack of papers that had served as props in the photographs in the news-papers: for Patta, any large pile of papers could be only decorative. Brunetti noticed a man seated in front of Patta's desk; when he heard Brunetti come in, he started to get to his feet.

'Ah, Brunetti,' Patta enthused, 'this is *Maggior* Guarino. He's from the Carabinieri in Marghera.' The man was tall, about a decade younger than Brunetti, and very thin. He had an easy, lived-in smile and thick hair already greying at the temples. His dark eyes were deep-set and gave him the look of a man who preferred to study what went on around him from some safe, half-hidden place.

They shook hands and exchanged pleasantries, then Guarino moved aside to allow Brunetti to slip past him to the other chair in front of Patta's desk.

'I wanted you to meet the *Maggiore*, Brunetti,' Patta began. 'He's come to see if we can be of any help to him.' Before Brunetti could ask, Patta sailed on. 'For some time, there's been growing evidence of the presence, especially in the North-east, of certain illegal organizations.' He glanced at Brunetti, who had no need to ask for clarification: anyone who read a newspaper – anyone, in fact, who had ever had a conversation in a bar – knew about this. To content Patta, however, Brunetti raised his eyebrows in what he hoped was a semblance of interested interrogation, and Patta explained, 'Worse – and this is why the *Maggiore* is here – there is increasing evidence that legitimate businesses are being taken over, specifically the transportation industry.' What was that story by the American writer, about the man who fell asleep and woke up after decades? Had Patta perhaps been hibernating in a cave somewhere while the Camorra moved north, and had he awoken to discover it only this morning?

Brunetti kept his eyes on Patta and pretended to pay no attention to the reaction of the man next to him, who cleared his throat.

'*Maggior* Guarino's been involved with this problem for some time, and his investigations have led him to the Veneto. As you might realize, Brunetti, this concerns all of us now,' Patta continued, voice filled with the shock of the new. As Patta spoke, Brunetti tried to figure out why he had been asked to join them. Transportation, at least the kind that moved on road or rail, had never been a concern of the police in Venice. He had little direct experience with land transport, criminal or otherwise, nor could he remember that any of the men in his squad had, either.

'. . . and so I hoped that, by introducing you two, some synergy could be created,' Patta concluded, using the foreign word and again giving evidence of his ability to be fatuous in any language he used.

Guarino started to answer, but, seeing Patta's not very discreet glance at his watch, seemed to change his mind and said, 'You've already been too generous with your time, Vice-Questore: I can't in conscience ask you to give us any more of it.' This was accompanied by a large smile, which Patta returned affably. 'Perhaps the Commissario and I,' Guarino said, with a nod in Brunetti's direction, 'should talk about this together, and then get back to you to ask for your input?' When Guarino used the English word, it sounded as though he knew what it meant.

Brunetti was amazed at the speed with which Guarino had acquired the pitch-perfect manner for addressing Patta and at the subtlety of his suggestion. Patta would be asked to give an opinion, but only after other men had done the work: thus he was to be spared both effort and responsibility and would still be able to take credit for any progress achieved. This for Patta would surely be the best of all possible worlds.

'Yes, yes,' Patta said, as if the Major's words had suddenly forced him to reflect upon the burdens of office. Guarino stood, followed by Brunetti. The Major made a few more remarks; Brunetti went to the door and waited for him to finish, then they left the office together.

Signorina Elettra turned to them as they emerged. 'I hope your meeting was successful, Signori,' she said pleasantly.

'With an inspiration such as that presented by the Vice-Questore, Signora, it could have been nothing but,' Guarino said in a dead level voice.

Brunetti watched as her attention turned to the man who had spoken. 'Indeed,' she answered, giving Guarino her brightest look. 'I'm so pleased to discover another person who finds him inspiring.'

'How could one fail to, Signora? Or is it Signorina?' Guarino asked, injecting into his voice curiosity, or was it astonishment, that she might still be unmarried.

'After the current head of our government, Vice-Questore Patta is the most inspiring man I've ever encountered,' she answered, smiling, but responding to only the first of his inquiries.

'I can well believe it,' Guarino agreed. 'Charismatic, each of them in his own way.' Turning to Brunetti, he asked, 'Is there a place where we can talk?'

Brunetti nodded, not trusting himself to speak, and they left the office. As they climbed the stairs, Guarino asked, 'How long has she worked for the Vice-Questore?'

'Long enough to fall completely under his spell,' Brunetti answered. Then, at Guarino's look, 'I'm not sure. Years. It seems as if she's always been here, though she hasn't.'

'Would things fall apart if she weren't?' Guarino asked.

'Yes, I'm afraid so.'

'We have someone like her in the office,' the Major answered. 'Signora Landi: the formidable Gilda. Is your Signora Landi a civilian?'

'Yes, she is,' Brunetti answered, wondering that Guarino had failed to notice the jacket that had hung oh-so-negligently on the back of her chair. Brunetti knew little of fashion, but he could spot an Etro lining at twenty paces, and he knew that the Ministry of the Interior was not in the habit of using it in their uniform jackets. Guarino had apparently overlooked the clue.

'Married?'

'No,' Brunetti answered, then surprised himself by asking, 'Are you?'

Brunetti had moved ahead of the other officer, so he did not hear his answer. He turned back and said, 'Excuse me?'

'Not really,' Guarino said.

Now, what in hell was that supposed to mean? Brunetti asked himself. 'I'm afraid I don't understand,' he said politely.

'We're separated.'

'Oh.'

Inside Brunetti's office he led his guest over to the window and showed him what view there was: the eternally about-to-be-renovated church and the completely restored rest home.

'Where does the canal go?' Guarino asked, leaning forward and looking to the right.

'Down to Riva degli Schiavoni and the *bacino*.'

'You mean the *laguna*?'

'Well, the water that will take you out to the *laguna*.'

'Sorry to sound like such a country bumpkin,' Guarino said, 'I know it's a city, but it still doesn't feel like one to me.'

'No cars?'

Guarino smiled and grew younger. 'Well, it's partly that. But the strangest thing is the silence.' After a long moment, he saw that Brunetti was about to speak but added, 'I know, I know, most people in cities hate the traffic and the smog, but the worst is the noise, believe me. It never stops, even late at night or early in the morning: there's always a machine at work somewhere: a bus, or a car, a plane coming in to land, or a car alarm.'

'Usually the worst we get,' Brunetti said with an easy laugh, 'is someone walking under your window and talking late at night.'

'They would have to talk very loud to bother me,' Guarino said and laughed.

'Why?'

'I live on the seventh floor.'

'Ah,' was the only thing Brunetti could think of to say, so unusual to him was the reality of such a thing. In the abstract, he knew that people in cities lived in tall buildings, but it seemed inconceivable that they would hear any noise on the seventh floor.

He waved Guarino to a chair and sat down himself. 'What is it you want from the Vice-Questore?' he asked, feeling that they had spent enough time on preliminaries. He pulled open his second drawer with his foot, then propped his crossed feet on it.

The casual gesture seemed to relax Guarino, who went on. 'A bit less than a year ago, our attention was called to a trucking company in Tessera, not far from the airport.'

Brunetti was immediately alert: a month ago, the attention of the entire region had been called to a trucking company in Tessera.

'We first got interested when the name of the company turned up in the course of another investigation,' Guarino continued. This was a routine lie Brunetti himself had used countless times, but he let it pass unremarked.

Guarino stretched out his legs and glanced back at the window, as if the view of the façade of the church would help him tell his story in the clearest way. 'Once our attention had been called to this company, we went to talk to the owner. Been in the family for more than fifty years; inherited from his father. It turned out he'd been having problems: rising fuel costs, competition from foreign haulers, workers who went on strike whenever they didn't get what they wanted, need for new trucks and equipment. The usual things.'

Brunetti nodded. If this was the same trucking company in Tessera, then the ending had not been one of the usual things. With a candour and resignation that surprised Brunetti, Guarino said, 'So he did what anyone would do: he started to cook the books.' Almost with regret, he added, 'But he wasn't very good at it. He could drive and fix a truck and make out a schedule for pick-ups and deliveries, but he was not a bookkeeper, so the Guardia di Finanza smelled something wrong the first time they took a look at his records.'

'Why did they investigate his records?' Brunetti asked.

Guarino raised his hand in a gesture that could mean anything.

'Did they arrest him?'

The *Maggiore* looked at his feet, then flicked a hand at his knee, wiping away a speck invisible to Brunetti. 'It's more complicated than that, I'm afraid.' This seemed obvious to Brunetti: why else would Guarino be there, talking to him?

Slowly, and with some reluctance, Guarino said, 'The person who told us about him said he was transporting things we were interested in.'

Brunetti cut him off by saying, 'There are a lot of things being shipped around that we're all interested in. Perhaps you could be more specific.'

Ignoring Brunetti's interruption, Guarino went on, 'A friend of mine in the Guardia told me what they had found, and I went to talk to the owner.' Guarino glanced at Brunetti and then away. 'I offered him a deal.'

'In return for not arresting him?' Brunetti asked unnecessarily.

Guarino's look was as angry as it was sudden. 'It's done all the time. You know it.' Brunetti watched the *Maggiore* decide to say what he would immediately regret saying. 'I'm sure you do it.' Guarino's look softened at once.

'Yes, we do,' Brunetti said calmly, then added, to see how Guarino would react, 'And it doesn't always work out the way it's planned.'

'What do you know about this?' the other man demanded.

'Nothing more than what you've just told me, *Maggiore*.' When Guarino said nothing, he asked, 'And then what happened?'

Guarino took another swipe at his knee, then forgot about it and left his hand there. 'He was killed in a robbery,' he finally said.

The details began to seep into Brunetti's memory. Because Tessera was closer to Mestre than to Venice, Mestre had been given the case. Patta had outdone himself in seeing that the Venice police did not get dragged into the investigation, claiming lack of manpower and jurisdictional uncertainty. Brunetti had spoken of it at the time to friends in the Mestre police, but they said it looked like a botched robbery with no leads.

'He always went in early,' Guarino continued, still not bothering to give the dead man's name, an omission which irritated Brunetti. 'At least an hour before the drivers and the other workers. They shot him. Three times.' Guarino looked across at him. 'You know about it, of course. It was in all the papers.'

'Yes,' Brunetti said, not mollified: Guarino had been a long time about it. 'But I never read more than what was in the papers.'

'Whoever did it,' Guarino went on, 'had already searched his office, or went through it after they killed him. They tried to open a wall safe – failed – went through his pockets and took whatever money he had on him. And his watch.'

'So it looked like a robbery?' Brunetti asked.

'Yes.'

'Suspects?'

'No.'

'Family?'

'Wife, two grown children.'

'They involved with the company?'

Guarino shook his head. 'The son's a doctor in Vicenza. The daughter's an accountant and works in Rome. The wife's a teacher, due to retire in a couple of years. With him gone, it all fell apart. The business didn't survive him by a week.' He saw Brunetti's raised eyebrows. 'I know it sounds incredible, in the age of the computer, but none of our people could find a list of orders, or routes, or pick-ups and deliveries, not even a list of drivers. He must have kept everything in his head. All of the records were a mess.'

'So what did the widow do?' Brunetti asked blandly.

'She had no choice: she closed it down.'

'Just like that?' Brunetti asked.

'What else could she do?' Guarino answered, almost as if he were pleading with Brunetti to have patience with the woman's inexperience. 'I told you, she's a teacher. Elementary school. She didn't have a clue. It was one of those one-man businesses we're so good at running.'

'Until that one man dies,' Brunetti said ruefully.

'Yes,' Guarino said and sighed. 'She wants to sell it, but no one's interested. The trucks are old, and now there aren't any clients. The best she can hope for is that another company will buy up the trucks and she'll be able to find someone to take over the lease for the garage, but she'll still end up selling it all for nothing.' Guarino stopped speaking, almost as if he had given all the information he was prepared to give. He had not said a thing, Brunetti realized, about whatever might have passed between the two of them during the time they knew one another and, in a certain sense, worked together.

34

'Am I correct in assuming,' Brunetti asked, 'that you discussed something other than the fact that he was cheating on his taxes?' If not, then there was no reason for the man to be here, though he hardly had to point this out to Guarino.

Guarino measured out a single word. 'Yes.'

'And that he gave you information about something other than his tax situation?' Brunetti found his voice growing tight. For God's sake, why couldn't the man just tell him what was going on and ask him whatever he wanted? For surely he had not come here to chat about the lovely silence of the city nor the charms of Signora Landi.

Guarino seemed content to say nothing further. Finally, making no attempt to disguise his irritation, Brunetti asked, 'Perhaps you could stop wasting my time and explain why you're here?'

3

It was obvious that Guarino had been waiting for Brunetti's patience to expire, for his answer came without hesitation and quite calmly. 'The police treated his death as a robbery that went bad and turned into murder.' Before Brunetti could ask what the police made of the three shots, Guarino volunteered, 'We suggested that approach. I don't think they cared one way or the other. Doing it like that was probably easier for them.'

And, reflected Brunetti, probably ensured the murder's swift passage out of the news, but instead of remarking on that, he asked, 'What do you think happened?'

Again, that quick glance at the church, the flick at his knee, and then Guarino said, 'I think whoever it was, one or more of them were waiting when he went in. There were no other signs of violence on his body.'

Brunetti imagined the waiting men, their unsuspecting victim, and their interest in learning what he knew. 'Do you think he told them anything?'

Guarino's glance was sharp, and he answered, 'They could

get it out of him without having to hurt him, you know.' He paused, as if conjuring up the memory of the dead man, and added, with audible reluctance, 'I was his contact, the person he talked to.' This, Brunetti realized, explained Guarino's edginess. The Carabiniere glanced away, as if uncomfortable at the memory of how easy it had been for him to make the murdered man talk. 'He wouldn't have been hard to frighten. If they had threatened his family, he would have told them whatever they wanted.'

'And what would that have been?'

'That he had been talking to us,' Guarino said after only the faintest hesitation.

'How did he get mixed up in this to begin with?' Brunetti asked, fully aware that Guarino had not yet explained what it was the dead man had been involved with.

Guarino made a small grimace. 'That was what I asked him the first time I talked to him. He said that when the business started to go bad, he used up their savings, his and his wife's, then he went to the bank to try to take out a loan. Well, another loan: he already had a large one.

'They turned him down, of course,' Guarino went on. 'That's when he began not registering jobs or payments, even if he was paid by cheque or bank transfer.' He shook his head in silent criticism of such folly. 'As I told you, he was an amateur. Once he started to do that, it was only a question of time until he got caught.' With clear regret, as if reproaching the dead man for some minor offence, he said, 'He should have known.'

Absently, Guarino rubbed at his forehead and continued. 'He said that he was frightened at the beginning. Because he knew he was no good at accounting. But he was desperate, and . . .' Guarino left that unfinished, then resumed. 'A few weeks later – this is what he told me – a man came to see him at his office. He said he'd heard he might be interested in working privately, not bothering with receipts, and if so he

37

had some work to offer him.' Brunetti said nothing, so Guarino continued. 'The man he talked to,' he said, 'lives here.' He watched for Brunetti's reaction, then said, 'That's why I'm here.'

'Who is he?'

Guarino raised a hand, as if to push the question away. 'We don't know. He said the man never used a name and he never asked. There were bills of lading in case the trucks were stopped, but everything written on them was fake. He told me that. The destination, what was in the trucks.'

'And what *was* in the trucks?'

'That doesn't matter. I'm here because he was murdered.'

'Am I supposed to believe the two things aren't related?' Brunetti asked.

'No. But I'm asking you to help me find his killer. The other case doesn't concern you.'

'And neither does his murder,' Brunetti said mildly. 'My superior saw to that when it happened: he decided it was a territorial matter, and the case belonged to Mestre, which has administrative control over Tessera.' Brunetti filled his voice with deliberate punctiliousness.

Guarino got to his feet, but all he did was walk over to the window, as Brunetti did in moments of difficulty. He stared at the church, and Brunetti stared at the wall.

Guarino came back to his chair and sat down again. 'The only thing he ever said about this man was that he was young – about thirty – good looking, and dressed like he had money. I think "flashy" was the word he used.'

Brunetti stopped himself from saying that most Italian men of thirty were good looking and dressed like they had money. He asked, instead, 'How did he know he lives here?' He was finding it difficult to disguise his mounting displeasure at Guarino's reluctance to provide specific information.

'Trust me. He lives here.'

'I'm not sure they're the same thing,' Brunetti said.

'What aren't?'

'Trusting you and trusting the information you've got.'

The *Maggiore* considered this. 'One time when this man was out in Tessera, he got a call on his *telefonino* just as they were going into the office. He went back into the corridor to talk to whoever it was, but he didn't close the door. He was giving directions to someone, and he told them to take the Number One to San Marcuola and to call him when he got off, and he'd meet him there.'

'He was sure about San Marcuola?' Brunetti asked.

'Yes.'

Guarino glanced at Brunetti and smiled again. 'I think we should stop sparring with one another now,' he said. He sat up straighter and asked, 'Shall we begin all over again, Guido?' At Brunetti's nod, he said, 'My name is Filippo.' He offered the name as if it were a peace offering, and Brunetti decided to accept it as such.

'And the dead man's name?' asked a relentless Brunetti.

Guarino did not hesitate. 'Ranzato. Stefano Ranzato.'

It took Guarino some time to explain in greater detail Ranzato's descent from entrepreneur to tax evader to police spy. And from there to corpse. When he had finished, Brunetti asked, quite as though the *Maggiore* had not already refused to answer the question, 'And what was in the trucks?'

This, Brunetti realized, was the moment of truth. Either Guarino would tell him or he would not, and Brunetti was by now very curious which choice the other man would make.

'He never knew,' Guarino said, then seeing Brunetti's expression, he added, 'At least that's what he told me. He was never told, and the drivers never said anything. He'd get a call, and then he'd send his trucks where he was told to send them. Everything in order: bills of lading. He said very often things seemed legitimate to him, shipping from a factory to a train or from a warehouse to Trieste or Genova. And he said at the beginning it was a lifesaver' – Brunetti heard him stumble over that word – 'for him because it was all off the books.' Brunetti had the feeling that Guarino would be perfectly content to sit there for ever, talking about the dead man's business.

'None of this explains why you're here, though, does it?' Brunetti interrupted to ask.

Instead of answering, Guarino said, 'I think it's a wild goose chase.'

'Try to be a little more specific, and then perhaps we'll see about that,' Brunetti suggested.

Guarino, looking suddenly tired, said, 'I work for Patta.' Then he added, by way of explanation, 'Sometimes I think everyone works for Patta. I didn't know his name until today, when I met him, but I recognized him immediately. He's my boss, and he's most of the bosses I've ever had. Yours just happens to be called Patta.'

'I've had a few who don't have the same name,' Brunetti said, but added, 'just the same nature.' Guarino's answering smile helped both of them relax again.

Relieved to see that Brunetti understood, Guarino went on, 'Mine – my Patta, that is – sent me here to find the man who got the phone call at Ranzato's office.'

'So he expects you to go to San Marcuola and stand there and shout Ranzato's name and see who looks guilty?'

'No,' Guarino answered without a smile. He scratched at his ear, and said, 'None of the men in my squad is Venetian.' In response to Brunetti's startled look, he said, 'Some of us have been working here for years, but it's not the same as having been born here. You know that. We've checked the arrest records for anyone who lives near San Marcuola with a history of violence, but the only two men we've found are both in jail. So we need local help, the sort of information you have, or can get, and we can't.'

'You don't know where to look for what you want to

know,' Brunetti said, stretching out a palm in front of him. 'And I don't know what was in those trucks,' he continued, putting out the other. He moved them up and down in a balancing gesture.

Guarino gave him a level glance and then said, 'I'm not at liberty to discuss that.'

Encouraged by this frankness, Brunetti changed course. 'Did you speak to his family?'

'No. His wife's destroyed by this. The man who did speak to her said he was sure she wasn't pretending. She had no idea what he was doing, neither did the son, and the daughter goes home only two or three times a year.' He gave Brunetti a moment to assess this and then added, 'Ranzato told me they didn't know, and I believed him. I still do.'

'When did you speak to him?' Brunetti asked. 'The last time, I mean.'

Guarino looked at him directly. 'The day before he died. Was murdered, that is.'

'And?'

'And he said he wanted to stop, that he'd already given us enough information and didn't want to do it any more.'

Dispassionately, Brunetti observed, 'From what you've told me, it doesn't sound as if he gave you much information at all.' Guarino pretended not to have heard this, so Brunetti decided to give him a poke and said, 'Just as you're not giving me much.'

Once more, his words bounced off Guarino. Brunetti asked, 'Did he seem nervous?'

'No more than he had ever been,' Guarino answered calmly, adding, almost reluctantly, 'He wasn't a brave man.'

'Few of us are.'

Guarino glanced at him sharply and appeared to shrug the idea away. 'I don't know about that,' the *Maggiore* said, 'but Ranzato wasn't.'

'He had no reason to be, did he?' Brunetti asked, defending

the dead man as much as the principle. 'He was in over his head: first he cheated on his taxes, which forced him into doing something illegal, then he got caught by the Finanza, who turned him over to the Carabinieri, and they forced him into doing something dangerous. If he had reason to be anything, it wasn't brave.'

'You seem awfully sympathetic,' Guarino said, making it sound like a criticism.

This time it was Brunetti who shrugged and said nothing.

4

In the face of Brunetti's silence, Guarino chose to move away from the dead man's character. 'I told you. I'm not at liberty to provide you with full information about the cargoes,' he said with more than a touch of asperity.

Brunetti resisted the urge to observe that everything Guarino had said since they began to talk made that evident. He turned his gaze away from his visitor and stared out the window. For some time, Guarino allowed the joint silence to continue. Brunetti played the conversation back from the beginning, and liked very little of what he heard.

The silence expanded, but Guarino gave no sign of being made nervous by it. After what seemed, even to himself, an inordinately long time, Brunetti removed his feet from the drawer and set them on the floor. He leaned towards the man on the other side of his desk. 'Are you used to dealing with dull people, Filippo?'

'Dull?'

'Dull. Slow to understand.'

Guarino glanced, almost against his will, at Brunetti, who

smiled at him blandly and then turned his attention back to the contemplation of the view beyond the window.

Eventually Guarino said, 'I suppose I am.'

Brunetti said, quite amiably, though without bothering to smile, 'It must become a habit, after a while.'

'Believing that everyone is dull?'

'Something like that, yes, or at least behaving as if they were.'

Guarino considered this. At last he said, 'Yes, I see. And I've insulted you?'

Brunetti's eyebrows rose and fell as if by their own volition; his right hand sketched a short arc in the air.

'Indeed,' Guarino said and went silent.

The two men sat in companionable silence for a number of minutes until Guarino broke it by saying, 'I really *do* work for Patta.' In the face of Brunetti's failure to respond, Guarino added, 'Well, my own Patta. And he hasn't authorized me to tell anyone about what we're doing.'

Lack of authorization had never worked as a strong impediment to Brunetti's professional behaviour, and so he said, in an entirely friendly voice, 'Then you can leave.'

'What?'

'You can leave,' Brunetti repeated, with a wave towards the door just as pleasant as his voice had been. 'And I'll go back to doing my job. Which, for the administrative reasons I've already explained to you, does not include the investigation of Signor Ranzato's murder.' Guarino remained in his chair, and Brunetti said, 'It's been very interesting, listening to you, but I don't have any information to give you, and I don't see any reason to help you find whatever it is you might really be after.'

Had Brunetti slapped him, Guarino could have been no more astonished. And offended. He started to get to his feet, but then sank back on to the chair and stared at Brunetti. His face flushed a sudden red, either from embarrassment or

44

anger: Brunetti neither knew nor cared. Finally Guarino said, 'How about we think of someone we both know, and you call this person and I talk to him?'

'Animal, vegetable, or mineral?' Brunetti asked.

'Excuse me?'

'It's a game my children used to play. What type of person should we call: a priest, a doctor, a social worker?'

'A lawyer?'

'That I trust?' Brunetti asked, putting an end to that possibility.

'A journalist?'

After some consideration, Brunetti said, 'There are a few.'

'Good, then let's see if we can find one we know in common.'

'Who trusts us both?'

'Yes,' Guarino answered.

'And you think that would be enough for me?' Brunetti asked, injecting disbelief into his voice.

'That would depend on which journalist, I suppose,' Guarino said mildly.

After running through a few names that were unknown to one or the other, they discovered that they both knew and trusted Beppe Avisani, an investigative journalist in Rome.

'Let me call him,' Guarino said, coming around to stand beside Brunetti.

Brunetti got an outside line on his office phone and dialled Avisani's number. He pushed the button for the speaker phone.

The phone rang four times, and then the journalist answered with his name.

'Beppe, *ciao*, it's me, Filippo,' Guarino said.

'Good heavens. Is the Republic in peril and I have just one chance to save it by answering your questions?' the journalist asked in a falsely ponderous voice. Then, with real warmth,

'How are you, Filippo? I won't ask what you're doing, but how are you?'

'Fine. You?'

'As well as can be expected,' Avisani said, his voice veering towards the despair that Brunetti had so often heard over the years. Then, brightening, he went on, 'You never call without wanting something, so save us both time and tell me what it is.' The words were harsh, but the tone was not.

'I'm here with someone who knows you,' Guarino said, 'and I'd like you to tell him that I can be trusted.'

'You do me too much honour, Filippo,' Avisani said with arch humility. They heard the sound of paper rustling, and then the voice came through the speaker, saying, '*Ciao*, Guido. My phone told me the number was from Venice, and my notebook just told me it's the Questura, and God knows you're the only person there who would trust me.'

Brunetti said, 'Dare I hope you'll say I'm the only person here you'd trust?'

Avisani laughed. 'You might not believe this, either of you, but I've had stranger calls.'

'And so?' Brunetti asked, trying to save time.

'Trust him,' the journalist answered without hesitation and without explanation. 'I've known Filippo for a long time, and he's to be trusted.'

'That's all?' Brunetti asked.

'That's enough,' the journalist said and hung up. Guarino returned to his chair.

'You realize what was also proven by that call?' Brunetti asked.

'Yes, I know,' Guarino said: 'that I can trust you.' He nodded, seemed to digest this new information, and then went on in a more sober voice, 'My unit studies organized crime, specifically its penetration north.' Even though Guarino spoke earnestly and was perhaps finally telling the truth, Brunetti remained cautious. Guarino covered his face with his hands and made a washing gesture. Brunetti thought of racoons, always trying to clean things off. Elusive creatures, racoons.

'Because the problem is so multifaceted, it's been decided to try to approach it by applying new techniques.'

Brunetti held up a monitory hand and said, 'This isn't a meeting, Filippo: you can use real language.'

Guarino gave a short laugh, not a particularly pleasant sound. 'After seven years working where I do, I'm not sure I still know how to use it.'

'Try, Filippo, try. It might be good for your soul.'

As if in an attempt to remove the memory of everything he had said so far, Guarino sat up straighter and began for the third time. 'Some of us are trying to stop them coming north. There's not much hope of that, I suppose.' He shrugged, and went on. 'My unit is trying to keep them from doing certain things after they get here.'

The crux of this visit, Brunetti realized, lay in the nature of those still undisclosed 'certain things'. 'Like shipping things they should not?' he asked.

Brunetti watched the other man struggle with the habit of reticence, refusing to give him any encouragement. Then, as if he had suddenly tired of playing cat and mouse with Brunetti, Guarino added, 'Shipping, but not contraband. Garbage.'

Brunetti returned his feet to the top of the drawer and leaned back in his chair. He studied the doors to his *armadio* for some time and finally asked, 'The Camorra runs it all, don't they?'

'In the South, certainly.'

'And here?'

'Not yet, but there's more and more evidence of them. It's not as bad as Naples, though, not yet.'

Brunetti thought of the stories of that afflicted city that had filled the papers over the Christmas holidays and refused to go away, of the mountains of uncollected garbage, some of it rising to the first floor of the buildings. Who had not watched the desperate citizens burn not only the stinking heaps of uncollected rubbish but also their mayor in effigy? And who had not been appalled to see the Army sent in to restore order in time of peace?

'What's next?' Brunetti asked. 'UN peacekeepers?'

'They could have worse,' Guarino said. Then, angrily, 'They *do* have worse.'

Because the investigation of the Ecomafia was in the hands of the Carabinieri, Brunetti had always responded to the situation as a citizen, one of helpless millions who watched the news as trash smouldered on the streets and the Minister of Ecology reprimanded the citizens of Naples for not separating their rubbish, while the mayor improved the ecological situation by banning smoking in public parks.

'Is that how Ranzato was involved?' Brunetti asked.

'Yes,' Guarino answered. 'But not with the bags in the streets of Naples.'

'What, then?'

Guarino had grown still, as if his nervous motions had been a physical manifestation of his evasiveness with Brunetti and there was no longer any need for them. 'Some of Ranzato's trucks went to Germany and France to pick up cargo, took it south, and then came back here with fruit and vegetables.' A second later, the old Guarino said, 'I shouldn't have told you that.'

Unperturbed, Brunetti said, 'Presumably, they didn't go to pick up bags of garbage from the streets of Paris and Berlin.'

Guarino shook his head.

'Industrial, chemical, or . . .' Brunetti began.

Guarino finished the list for him. '. . . or medical, often radiological.'

'And took it where?' Brunetti asked.

'Some of it went to the ports, and from there to whatever Third World country would take it.'

'And the rest?'

Before answering, Guarino pushed himself upright in his chair. 'The garbage gets left on the streets in Naples. There's no more room for it in the landfills or the incinerators down there because they're busy burning what comes down from the North. Not only from Lombardia and the Veneto, but from any factory that's willing to pay to have it taken away and no questions asked.'

'How many shipments like this did Ranzato make?'

'I told you, he wasn't very good at keeping records.'

'And you couldn't . . .' Brunetti began. He shied away from using the word 'force' and settled for '. . . encourage him to tell you?'

'No.'

Brunetti remained silent. Guarino spoke again. 'One of the last times I spoke to him, he said he almost wished I could arrest him so he could stop doing what he was doing.'

'Stories were all over the papers by then, weren't they?'

'Yes.'

'I see.'

Guarino's voice softened. 'By then we'd become, well, not friends, not really, but something like friends, and he talked to me openly. In the beginning, he was afraid of me, but towards the end he was afraid of them and what they would do to him if they found out that he was talking to us.'

'It seems they did.'

Either his words or his tone stopped Guarino, who gave Brunetti a sharp look. 'Unless it was a robbery,' he said, dead level, signalling that the best measure of their friendship was in seeming trust.

'Of course.'

Brunetti, though by disposition a compassionate man, had little patience with retrospective protestations of remorse: most people – however much they might deny it – had an idea of what they were getting into when they got into it. 'He

49

must have known from the beginning who, or at least what, they were,' Brunetti said. 'And what they wanted him to do for them.' Despite all of Guarino's assurances, Brunetti judged that Ranzato had known perfectly well what was being carried on his trucks. Besides, all this talk of regret was exactly what people wanted to hear. Brunetti had always been bemused by people's willingness to be charmed by the penitent sinner.

'That might be true, but he didn't tell me that,' the *Maggiore* answered, reminding Brunetti how protective he had himself become of some of the people he used as – and had forced into becoming – informants.

Guarino continued. 'He said he wanted to stop working for them. He didn't tell me what made him decide, but whatever it was, it was clear – at least to me – that it disturbed him.' He added, 'That's when he spoke about wanting to be arrested. So it could stop.'

Brunetti forbore to suggest that it did stop. Nor did he bother to observe that the perception of personal danger very often set people on the path of virtue. Only an anchorite could have remained ignorant of the *'emergenza spazzatura'* that had captured the nation's attention in the last weeks of Ranzato's life.

Did Guarino look embarrassed? Or was he perhaps irritated at Brunetti's hard-heartedness? To keep the conversation going, Brunetti asked, 'What was the date when you last spoke to him?'

The Major shifted to one side, and took out a small black notebook. He opened it and licked his right forefinger, then flipped quickly through its pages. 'It was the seventh of December. I remember because he said his wife wanted him to go to Mass with her the next day.' Suddenly, Guarino's hand fell away and the notebook slapped against his thigh. *'Oddio,'* he whispered.

Guarino suddenly grew pale. He closed his eyes and

pressed his lips together. For an instant, Brunetti thought the man might faint. Or weep. 'What is it, Filippo?' he asked, pulling his feet back and putting them on the floor, leaning forward, one hand half-raised.

Guarino closed the notebook. He rested it on his knees and kept his eyes on it. 'I remember. He said his wife's name was Immacolata, and she always went to Mass on the eighth, her name-day.'

Brunetti had no idea why this information should prove so upsetting to Guarino until the other man said, 'He told me it was the one day of the year she asked him to come to Mass with her, and receive Communion. So he was going to go to Confession the next morning, before the Mass.' Guarino picked up the book and slipped it back into his pocket.

'I hope he went,' Brunetti said before he realized he had spoken.

5

Neither man knew what to say after that. Brunetti got up and went to stand by the window, as much to give himself a moment's calm as to provide the same to Guarino. He would have to tell Paola what he had said, how it had slipped out without a conscious thought.

He heard Guarino clear his throat and say, just as if he and Brunetti had come to some gentleman's agreement no longer to discuss Ranzato or what he might have known, 'I told you: because he was killed, and because the only link we have to the man he worked for is the link to San Marcuola, we need your help. You people here in Venice are the only ones who can tell us if there's someone who lives there who might be involved in . . . well, in something like this.' It did not sound like a finished statement, so Brunetti remained silent. After a moment, Guarino went on, 'We don't know who we're looking for.'

'Was it just the one man this Signor Ranzato worked for?' Brunetti asked, turning back to face him.

'He was the only one he told me about,' Guarino answered.

52

'That's not the same thing, is it?'

'I think it is, yes. Remember, I told you we'd become, if not friends, then at least close. We talked about things.'

'For instance?'

'I told him how lucky he was to be married to someone he loved so much,' Guarino said in a voice that was steady except for the word 'loved'.

'I see.'

'I meant it, too,' Guarino said with what Brunetti considered defensive self-revelation. 'It wasn't one of those things you tell them to get them to trust you.' He waited to be sure that Brunetti understood the distinction, then went on, 'Maybe that's how things were at the beginning, but as time passed, well, they changed between us.'

'Did you ever meet his wife? Or see her?'

'No. But her photo was on his desk,' Guarino said. 'I'd like to talk to her, but we can't contact her or give any sign that we were ever in touch with him.'

'If they killed him, then they already know that you were, wouldn't you say?' Brunetti asked, unwilling to be merciful.

'Perhaps,' Guarino agreed with some reluctance, then changed it to 'probably.' His voice grew a bit stronger. 'But those are the rules. We can't do anything that might put her at risk.'

'Of course,' Brunetti said and stopped himself from observing that that had already been amply taken care of. He returned to his desk. 'I don't know how much we'll be able to help you, but I'll ask around and have a look at the files. I have to tell you now that no one comes to mind.' It was implicit, in his use of the term 'ask around', that whatever was done beyond the usual search through the files would be done at the casual, private level: men talking to their informers, hinting, chatting in the bars. 'However,' Brunetti added, 'Venice isn't the best place to search for information about trucking.'

Guarino glanced at him, seeking sarcasm but finding none.

'I'll be grateful for whatever information you can give me,' he said. 'We're at a loss. It's always this way when we try to work someplace where we don't know . . .' Guarino's voice trailed off.

It occurred to Brunetti that the other man could as easily have stopped himself from saying 'who we can trust' as anything else. 'It's strange that he never set it up so that you could have a look at this man,' he said. 'After all, you knew about him for a long time.'

Guarino said nothing.

There were countless questions to be asked, Brunetti realized. Had a truck even been stopped and the driver asked for papers? What if there was an accident?

'You talked to the drivers?'

'Yes.'

'And?'

'And they weren't very helpful.'

'What does that mean?'

'It could mean that they drove where they were told to drive and didn't give it a thought.' Brunetti's expression showed how believable he found this, so Guarino added, 'Or that Ranzato's murder helped to wipe out their memories.'

'You think it's worth trying to find out which?'

'My guess is no. People up here don't have a lot of direct experience with the Camorra, but they've already learned not to cause them trouble.'

'If this is the way it is already, then there's no hope of trying to stop them, is there?' Brunetti asked.

Guarino got to his feet and leaned across Brunetti's desk to shake his hand, saying, 'You can reach me at the Marghera station.'

Brunetti shook his hand. 'I'll ask around.'

'I'd be grateful.' Guarino gave Brunetti a long look, nodded as if he believed him, and walked quickly to the door. He let himself out quietly.

54

'Oh my, oh my, oh my,' Brunetti muttered to himself. He sat at his desk for some time, thinking over what he had been told, then went down to Signorina Elettra's office. She looked up from her computer screen as he came in. The winter sun streamed through the window of her office, illuminating the roses he had seen earlier, and her shirt, which managed to make the roses look dingy.

'If you've got time, there's something I'd like to ask you to look into,' he said.

'For you or for *Maggior* Guarino?' she asked.

'For both of us, I think,' he answered, conscious of the warmth with which she pronounced the other man's name.

'In December, a man named Stefano Ranzato was killed in his office in Tessera,' he said. 'During a robbery.'

'Yes, I remember,' she said, then asked, 'And the *Maggiore* is in charge?'

'Yes.'

'How can I help you both?' she asked.

'He has reason to believe that his killer might live close to San Marcuola.' This was not exactly what Guarino had told him, but it was close enough to the truth. 'The *Maggiore*, as you noticed, is not Venetian, and it turns out no one else in his squad is.'

'Ah,' she exclaimed, 'the infinite wisdom of the Carabinieri.'

As if he had not heard her, Brunetti went on, 'They've already checked the arrest records for the area around San Marcuola.'

'For violent crime or assault?' she asked.

'Both, I imagine.'

'Did the *Maggiore* say anything else about the murderer?'

'That he was about thirty, good–looking, and dressed expensively.'

'Well, that cuts the number down to about a million.'

Brunetti did not bother to reply.

'San Marcuola, eh?' she asked. She sat silent for some time; as he waited, he saw her touch her cuff and button it closed. It was after eleven o'clock, yet there was no wrinkle to be seen in either of the stark cuffs of her blouse. Should he warn her to be careful about cutting her wrists on the edges?

She tilted her head and glanced at the space above Patta's door while one hand idly unbuttoned and rebuttoned the same cuff. 'The doctors are a possibility,' Brunetti said after some time.

She looked at him in open surprise, then smiled. 'Ah, of course,' she said appreciatively. 'I hadn't thought of that.'

'I don't know if Barbara . . .' Brunetti prompted, naming her sister, a doctor, who had in the past spoken to him but had always made a clear distinction between what she could and could not tell the police.

Signorina Elettra's answer was immediate. 'I don't think we'll have to ask her. I know two doctors who have offices near there. I'll ask them. People talk to them, so they might have heard something.' In response to Brunetti's look, she said, 'They're the ones Barbara would ask, anyway.'

He nodded and said, 'I'll ask down in the squad room.' The men there usually knew about the lives of the people living in the neighbourhoods they patrolled.

As he was turning away, Brunetti paused as if remembering something, and said, 'There's another thing, Signorina.'

'Yes, Commissario?'

'A part of another investigation, well, not really an investigation, but something I've been asked to look into: I'd like you to see what you can find about a businessman here in the city, Maurizio Cataldo.'

Her 'ah' could have meant anything.

'And his wife, as well, if there's anything about her.'

'Franca Marinello, sir?' she said, head lowered above the paper on which she had written Cataldo's name.

'Yes.'

'Anything specific?'

'No,' Brunetti said, then, offhandedly, 'The usual things: business, investments.'

'Are you interested in their personal life, sir?'

'Not particularly, no,' Brunetti said, then quickly added, 'But if you find anything that might be interesting, make a note of it, would you?'

'I'll have a look.'

He thanked her and left.

6

On the stairs back to his own office, Brunetti's thoughts moved away from the unknown dead man to the people he had met at the dinner party the night before. He decided that the business of asking Paola for gossip – perhaps best to be honest with himself and call it what it was – about Cataldo and his wife could be done after lunch.

January had declared itself unkind this year and had assailed the city with damp and cold. A grey cloud had taken up residence over northern Italy, a cloud that begrudged the mountains snow at the same time as it kept the temperature warm enough for fog but no rain.

The streets had thus not been washed clean for weeks, though a viscous layer of condensation covered them every night. The one *acqua alta*, four days before, had done nothing but shift the dirt and grime around without leaving the streets any cleaner. Undispersed by *bora* or *tramontana*, the air from the mainland had gradually oozed eastward and now spread across the city, nudging the levels of pollution higher each day, covering Venice in who knew what sort of chemical miasma.

58

Paola had responded to the situation by asking them to take their shoes off before coming into the house, and so the landing in front of their door was rich enough in clues to tell Brunetti that the others had all got home before him. 'Ah, superdetective,' he whispered aloud as he bent to untie his shoes; he set them side by side to the left of the door and let himself into the apartment.

He heard voices from the kitchen and turned towards them, moving silently. 'But it says in the paper,' Chiara's voice was filled with confusion and more than a touch of exasperation, 'that the levels are beyond the legally permitted limit. That's what it says here.' He heard what sounded like a hand slapping against a newspaper.

'What does that mean, "legally permitted"?' she continued. 'And if the levels are beyond the legal limit, then who's supposed to do something about it?'

Brunetti wanted to eat his lunch in peace and then gossip with his wife. He had little desire to be drawn into a conversation during which he feared he would be held responsible for the law or for what it permitted.

'And if they can't do anything about it, then what are we supposed to do, stop breathing?' Chiara concluded, and Brunetti's interest awoke at the sound of the same tone Paola used for her own most lyrical passages of denunciation and outrage.

Curious now to learn how the others would respond to her question, he moved closer to the door.

'I've got to meet Gerolamo at two-thirty,' Raffi interrupted in a voice that sounded frivolous in contrast to his sister's. 'So I'd really like to eat soon and get some of my calculus done before I leave.'

'The whole world's collapsing around us, and all you can think about is your stomach,' a female voice declaimed.

'Oh, come off it, Chiara,' Raffi said. 'This is just more of the same old stuff, like giving our pocket money to save Christian babies when we were in elementary school.'

'There will be no saving of Christian babies in *this* household,' a magisterial Paola declared.

Luckily, both of the children laughed at this, and so Brunetti timed his entrance to follow. 'Ah, peace and harmony at the table,' he said, taking his place and turning to look at the pots on the stove across the room. He took a sip of wine, liked it, and took another sip, set the glass down. 'It is a comfort and a joy to a man to return, after a hard day's work, to the peaceful bosom of his loving family.'

'It's only half a day, so far, *Papà*,' Chiara said in her deepest referee's voice, tapping at the crystal of her watch.

'And know that he will never be contradicted,' Brunetti forged on, 'and that his every word will be considered a gem of knowledge, his every utterance respected for its wisdom.'

Chiara moved her plate aside, laid her head on the table, and covered it with her hands. 'I was kidnapped as a baby and forced to live with lunatics.'

'Only one,' Paola said, approaching the table with a bowl of pasta. She spooned large helpings into Raffi's dish and Brunetti's, a smaller one into her own. By this time, Chiara was sitting upright, her dish back in place in front of her, and Paola filled it in turn with another large portion.

She set the bowl on the table in front of them, went to the stove and got the cover. The others waited for her. '*Mangia, mangia*,' she said, approaching the table with the cheese.

They all waited until she was seated, and no one started eating until the cheese had been passed around.

Ruote: Brunetti loved *ruote*. And with the *melanzane* and ricotta in tomato sauce, they seemed the perfect pasta. 'Why *ruote*?' he asked.

Paola seemed surprised. 'Why what?'

'Why do you use *ruote* with this sauce?' Brunetti clarified, spearing one of the wheel-like pastas and holding it up to examine it more closely.

She looked at her plate, as if surprised to find that particular shape of pasta there. 'Because . . .' Paola began, then prodded at the many-spoked pasta with the tip of her own fork. 'Because . . .'

She set her fork down and took a sip of wine. She glanced across at Brunetti and said, 'I've no idea, but it's what I've always used. It's just that *ruote* are right for this sort of sauce.' Then, with real concern, 'Don't you like them?'

'Quite the opposite,' he said. 'They seem entirely right to me, but I don't know why that is, and I wondered if you did.'

'I suppose the truth is that Luciana always used *ruote* with tomato sauces that had little pieces in them.' She speared a few and held them up. 'I can't think of a better explanation.'

'May I have some more?' Raffi asked, though the others at the table had eaten less than half of their portions. For him, the shape of any pasta was secondary to its quantity.

'Of course,' Paola said. 'There's plenty.'

As Raffi served himself, Brunetti asked, knowing he would probably regret doing so, 'What were you saying when I came in, Chiara? Something about legal limits?'

'The *micropolveri*,' Chiara said, continuing to eat. 'The Professoressa talked about it at school today, that there are all these tiny little particles of rubber and chemical and God knows what, and they're all trapped in the air, and we breathe them in.'

Brunetti nodded and served himself a bit more pasta.

'So I read the paper when I got home, and it said . . .' she set down her fork and reached to the floor to retrieve the newspaper. It was folded open at the article, and Chiara's eyes skimmed to the passage she meant. 'Here it is,' she said and read aloud: '. . . blah, blah, blah, "the *micropolveri* have risen to a point fifty times the legal limit".'

She dropped the paper back to the floor and looked across at her father. 'That's what I don't understand: if the limit is a legal limit, then what happens when it's fifty times as much?'

'Or, for that matter, twice as much,' Paola added.

Brunetti put his fork down and said, 'That's a problem for the Protezione Civile, I'd say.'

'Can they arrest anyone?' Chiara demanded.

'I don't think so, no,' Brunetti said.

'Make them pay a fine?'

'Not that either, I think.'

'Then what's the purpose of having a legal limit, if you can't do anything to people who break the law?' Chiara demanded in an angry voice.

Brunetti had loved this child from the instant he learned of her existence, since the moment Paola told him she was expecting their second child. All of that love stood between Brunetti and the temptation to tell her that they lived in a country where nothing much ever happened to anyone who broke the law.

Instead, he said, 'I suppose the Protezione Civile will file a formal *denuncia*, and someone will be asked to investigate.' The same impulse that had silenced his previous comment helped him refrain from observing that it would prove impossible to find a single offender, not when most factories did what they wanted, and the engines of docked cruise ships poured out whatever they pleased for as long as they stayed.

'But they've already investigated, or how else did they get those numbers?' Chiara demanded, as if she held him responsible, and then immediately repeated, 'And what are we supposed to do until they do investigate, stop breathing?'

Brunetti felt a surge of delight to hear his wife's rhetorical devices echoed in his daughter's voice, even that old warhorse of logic, the rhetorical question. Ah, she would cause a lot of trouble, this child, if only she could keep her passion and her sense of outrage.

Some time later, Paola came into the living room with coffee. She handed him a cup, saying, 'There's sugar in it', and sat down next to him. The second section of *Il Gazzettino* lay open on the table where Brunetti had set it down, and Paola inquired, with a nod in its direction, 'What revelations does it bring us today?'

'Two city administrators are under investigation for corruption,' Brunetti said and sipped at his coffee.

'They've chosen to ignore the rest of them, then?' she asked. 'I wonder why.'

'The prisons are full.'

'Ah.' Paola finished her coffee. She set her cup down and said, 'I'm glad you didn't toss oil on the fires of Chiara's enthusiasm.'

'It didn't sound to me,' Brunetti replied, setting his own empty cup on the face of the Prime Minister, 'as if she needed any encouragement.' He sat back, thought about his daughter for a while, and said, 'I'm glad she's so angry.'

'Me, too,' Paola said, 'though I suppose we'd better disguise our approval.'

'You really think that's necessary? After all, she probably got it from us.'

'I know,' Paola admitted, 'but it's still wiser not to let her know.' She studied his face for a moment, then added, 'Truth to tell, I'm surprised you approve; well, that you do so strongly.'

She laid her hand on his thigh, patted it twice. 'You let her rave on, and I could almost hear you ticking off the errors in logic she used.'

'Your very own favourite, *argumentum ad absurdum*,' Brunetti said with unconcealed pride.

Paola had a particularly idiotic smile on her face as she turned to him. 'It is my heart's delight, that one.'

'You think we're doing a good thing?' Brunetti asked.

'Doing what?'

'Raising them to be so clever in argument?'

Brunetti's tone, light as he tried to make it, failed to disguise his real concern. 'After all, if a person doesn't know the rules of logic, it will sound as if they're being sarcastic, and that's not something people like.'

'Especially when they hear it from a teenager,' Paola added. After a moment, as if trying to ease his fears, she offered, 'Very few people pay attention to what anyone else says during a discussion, anyway. So maybe we don't have to worry.'

They sat silent for some time until she said, 'I spoke to my father today, and he told me he has three days to decide about this thing with Cataldo. He asked me if you'd managed to find out anything about him.'

'No, I haven't,' Brunetti said, biting back the impulse to say it had been less than twenty-four hours since he had been asked to do it.

'Do you want me to tell him that?'

'No. I've already asked Signorina Elettra to see what she can find.' Then, vaguely, knowing how many times he had used this excuse, 'Something else came up. But she might have something by tomorrow.' It took some time before he asked, 'Does your mother say much about them?'

'Either of them?'

'Yes.'

'I know that he was very eager to divorce his first wife.' Her voice was a study in neutrality.

'How long ago was that?'

'More than ten years. He was over sixty.' Brunetti thought Paola had finished, but after a pause that might have been deliberate, she continued, 'and she was barely thirty.'

'Ah,' he contented himself with saying.

Before he devised a way to ask about Franca Marinello, Paola said, reverting to the original subject, 'My father doesn't tell me about his business involvements, but he's interested in China, and I think he sees this as a possibility.'

Brunetti decided to avoid a second round of discussion of

the ethics of investing in China. 'And Cataldo?' he asked. 'What does your father say about him?'

She patted his thigh in an entirely friendly way, as if Franca Marinello had disappeared from the room. 'Not much, at least not to me. They've known one another for a long time, but I don't think they've ever worked together on anything. I don't think there's much love lost between them, but this is business,' she said, sounding almost too much like her father's child.

'Thanks,' Brunetti said.

Paola leaned forward and picked up the cups. She got to her feet and looked down at him. 'Time for you to pick up your broom and get back to the Augean Stables.'

7

Back at the stables, things were reasonably quiet. Another of the commissari came in after four to complain about Lieutenant Scarpa, who was refusing to turn over some files relating to a two-year-old murder in San Leonardo. 'I can't figure out why he's doing this,' said Claudia Griffoni, who had been at the Questura only six months and thus was not yet fully acquainted with the Lieutenant and his ways.

Though she was Neapolitan, her appearance defied every racial stereotype: she was a tall, willowy blonde with blue eyes and skin so clear that she had to be careful of the sun. She could have posed on a poster for a Nordic cruise, though, had she actually worked on the ship, her doctorate in oceanography would have qualified her for a position more exacting than that of hostess. As would the uniform she was wearing in Brunetti's office, one of three she had had tailored to celebrate her promotion to commissario. She sat across from him, straight in her chair, long legs crossed. He studied the cut of the jacket, short and tight fitting, with hand-stitching along the lapels. The trousers, after a length that delighted Brunetti, were cut tight at the ankle.

'Is it because he wasn't given the case, so he wants to slow us all down and make it even harder to find the killer?' Griffoni asked. 'Or is it something personal between him and me that I don't know about? Or does he just not like women? Or women police?'

'Or women police who outrank him?' Brunetti tossed into the pot, curious to see how she would react but also convinced that this was the reason for Scarpa's constant attempts to undermine her authority.

'Oh, sweet Jesus,' she exclaimed, tilting her head back, as if to address the ceiling. 'It's not enough that I have to put up with this from killers and rapists. Now I've got to deal with it from the people I work with.'

Curious, Brunetti said, 'I doubt it's the first time.' He wondered how Signorina Elettra would respond to the quality of tailoring on the uniform.

She returned her attention to Brunetti and said, 'We all get a fair bit of it.'

'What do you do when it happens?' Brunetti asked.

'Some of us try to flirt our way out of it. You've seen it, I'm sure. You ask them to come along to help defuse a domestic argument, and they act like you've asked them for a date.'

Brunetti had indeed seen some of this.

'Or else we get tough and try to be more vulgar and violent than the men.'

Brunetti nodded in recognition. When she failed to provide a third category, Brunetti asked, 'Or?'

'Or we don't let it make us crazy and just try to do our jobs.'

'And if nothing works?' he asked.

'Well, I suppose we could shoot the bastards.'

Brunetti laughed out loud. In the time he had known her, he had never tried to suggest how she might deal with Scarpa: indeed, he was reluctant, ever, to give this kind of advice. He had learned over the years that most professional and social situations were pretty much like water on uneven ground: sooner or later, they would work themselves level. People, over time, generally decided who was the Alpha and who the Beta. Higher rank sometimes helped with the determination, but not always. In the end, he had little doubt that Commissario Griffoni would learn how to control Lieutenant Scarpa, but he was equally certain that the Lieutenant would find a way to make her pay for it.

'He's been here as long as the Vice-Questore, hasn't he?' she asked.

'Yes. They came together.'

'I suppose I shouldn't say this, but I've always been suspicious of Sicilians,' she said. Claudia Griffoni, like many upper-class Neapolitans, had been raised speaking Italian, rather than dialect, though she had picked it up from friends and at school and would occasionally use Neapolitan expressions. But they were always spoken within ironic quotation marks, set linguistically apart from the Italian that she spoke as elegantly as Brunetti had ever heard it spoken. Someone who did not know her would therefore believe that her suspicion of Southerners came from the mouth of a person from the North, certainly from someone who lived above Florence.

Brunetti was aware that she had offered him the remark as a test: if he agreed with her, she could place him in one category; if he disagreed, then she could put him in another. Because he belonged in neither – or in both – Brunetti chose to respond by asking, 'Does this mean you'll be joining the Lega next?'

This time it was she who laughed out loud. When she stopped, she asked, as if she had not noticed his refusal to take the bait, 'Does he have any friends here?'

'He was working for a time with Alvise on some sort of special European project, but the funds were cut before they did much of anything and before anyone could get an idea of what they were even supposed to be doing.' Brunetti thought for a while before adding, 'As to friends, I'm not sure. There's very little that seems to be known about him. I do know that he chooses not to socialize with anyone here.'

'It's not as if you Venetians were the most hospitable people in the world,' she said, smiling to defuse the remark.

Brunetti was surprised into saying, far more defensively than intended, 'Not everyone here is Venetian.'

'I know, I know,' she said, raising a hand in a placatory gesture. 'Everyone's very nice and very friendly, but it ends at the door, when we leave to go home.'

Had he not been a married man, Brunetti would have risen to the situation and invited her to dinner on the spot, but those days were gone, and Paola's response to his behaviour with Franca Marinello was sufficiently fresh in his memory to keep him from inviting this very attractive woman anywhere.

Brunetti's uncertainty was cut short by the arrival of Vianello. 'Ah, there you are,' he said, speaking to Brunetti but acknowledging the woman's presence with a nod and a gesture that, in some other lifetime, might have been a salute.

He came halfway to Brunetti's desk and stopped. 'I saw Signorina Elettra when I came in,' the Inspector said, 'and she asked me to tell you she's spoken to the doctors in San Marcuola and will be up soon to tell you about it.' When Brunetti nodded his thanks, the Inspector added, 'The men downstairs told me you'd spoken to them.' His message delivered, Vianello planted his feet and folded his arms, giving every indication that he had no plans to leave his superior's office until the meaning of his message had been revealed to him.

Griffoni's curiosity was just as easily read, and it forced Brunetti to wave Vianello to a seat. 'I had a Carabiniere here this morning,' he began, and told them about Guarino's visit, Ranzato's murder, and the man who lived near San Marcuola.

The other officers sat quietly for some time until finally Griffoni said fiercely, 'For God's sake, don't we have enough trouble with our own garbage? Now they're bringing it in from other countries, too?'

Both men were stunned by her outburst: Griffoni was usually calm in the face of talk of criminal behaviour. The silence lengthened until she said in an entirely different voice, 'Two cousins of mine died of cancer last year. One of them was three years younger than I am. Grazia lived less than a kilometre from the incinerator in Taranto.'

Brunetti said, voice careful, 'I'm sorry.'

She raised a hand, then said, 'I worked on it before I came up here. You can't work in Naples and not know about garbage. It piles up in the streets, or we go chasing after illegal dumps: everywhere you look in the countryside around Naples, there's garbage.'

Speaking directly to her, Vianello said, 'I've read about Taranto. I've seen photos of the sheep in the fields.'

'They die of cancer, too, it seems,' Griffoni said in her usual voice. As Brunetti watched, she shook her head, glanced towards him, and asked, 'Do we follow this, or does it belong to the Carabinieri?'

'Officially, it does,' Brunetti answered. 'But if we're looking for this man, then we're involved, too.'

'Does the Vice-Questore have to authorize it?' Griffoni asked in a neutral voice.

Before Brunetti could answer, Signorina Elettra came into the office. She greeted Brunetti, smiled at Vianello, and nodded to Griffoni. Brunetti was put in mind of one of Dickens's characters often mentioned by Paola who would assess a situation in terms of 'where the wind was coming from'. The north, Brunetti suspected.

'I've spoken to one of the doctors there, Commissario,' she said with exaggerated formality. 'But he can't think of anyone. He said he'd ask his colleague when he comes in.'

How fortunate, he thought, that in all these years they had never abandoned using the formal *Lei* with one another: it served perfectly for this very cool exchange.

'Thank you, Signorina. Let me know what he tells you, would you?' Brunetti said.

She looked at the three of them in turn, then added, 'Certainly, Commissario. I hope there's nothing I've overlooked.' She glanced at Commissario Griffoni, as if daring her to address herself to that possibility.

'Thank you, Signorina,' Brunetti said. He smiled, glanced down at the new calendar on his desk and listened for, and then to, the sound of her footsteps heading towards the door, and to the sound of its closing.

He looked up just late enough to avoid complicity in the glance that passed between Griffoni and Vianello. Griffoni got to her feet, saying, 'I think I'll go back to the airport.' Before either could ask, she said, 'The case, not the place.'

'The baggage handlers?' Brunetti, who had been in charge of the previous investigations, asked with a tired sigh.

'Questioning the baggage handlers is like hearing Elvis's Greatest Hits: you've listened to them all a thousand times, sung in different ways and sung by different people, and you never want to hear them again,' she said tiredly. She went to the door, where she turned back to them and added, 'But you know you will.'

When she was gone, Brunetti realized how the day, spent listening to people tell him things while he actually did very little, had tired him. He told Vianello that it was late and suggested they go home. Vianello, though he looked at his watch first, got to his feet and said it sounded like an excellent idea. When the Ispettore was gone, Brunetti decided to stop in the officers' squad room to use the computer before he went home, just to see how much he could find on his own about Cataldo. The men were accustomed to these visits and saw to it that one of the younger officers stayed in the room while the Commissario was there. This time, however, things proved easy enough, and he soon had a number of links to newspaper and magazine articles.

Few of them told him more than had the Conte. In an old issue of *Chi*, he found a photo of Cataldo arm in arm with Franca Marinello before their marriage. They appeared to be on a terrace or balcony, posed with their backs to the sea: Cataldo was broad and serious in a light grey linen suit. She wore white slacks and a short-sleeved black T-shirt and looked very happy. The definition of the screen was enough to show Brunetti how lovely she had been: perhaps in her late-twenties, blonde, taller than her future husband. Her face looked – Brunetti had to think a moment before the right word came to him – it looked uncomplicated. Her smile was modest, her features regular, her eyes blue as the sea behind them. 'Pretty girl,' he said under his breath. He touched a key to move the article down to read further, and the screen went blank.

That did it: he had to have his own computer. He got up, told the nearest man that something was wrong with the machine, and went home.

8

The next morning, Brunetti used his office phone to call the Carabinieri in Marghera, only to be told that *Maggior* Guarino was not there and was not expected until the end of the week. Brunetti pushed aside the thought of Guarino and returned to the idea of getting his own computer. If he did get it, could he continue to expect Signorina Elettra to find the unfindable? Would she then expect him to do basic things, like . . . like find telephone numbers and check vaporetto timetables? Once he could do that, she would probably assume he could easily find the health records of suspects or trace bank transfers into and out of numbered accounts. Still, once he had it, as well as begin to search for information, he would be able more easily to read newspapers on line: current issues, back issues, any issues he chose. But then what of the feel of the *Gazzettino* in his hand, that dry smell, the black streaks it left against the right-hand pocket of all of his jackets?

And what, his conscience forced him to confess, of that gentle surge of pride when he opened his copy on the vaporetto and thus declared his citizenship in this quiet city world? Who in their right mind but a Venetian would read the *Gazzettino*? *'Il Giornale delle Serve'*. All right, so it *was* the newspaper of the servant girls. So what? The national papers were often just as badly written, filled with inaccuracies and sentence fragments and wrongly captioned photos.

Signorina Elettra chose this moment to appear at the door of his office. He looked across at her and said, 'I love the *Gazzettino*.'

'There's always Palazzo Boldù, Dottore,' she said, naming the local psychiatric centre. 'And perhaps some rest, and certainly no reading.'

'Thank you, Signorina,' he said politely, and then to business, having had the night to think about it – 'I would like to have a computer here in the office.'

This time she made no attempt to disguise her reaction. 'You?' she asked. 'Sir,' she thought to add.

'Yes. One of those flat ones like the one you have.'

This explanation gave her some time to consider the request. 'I'm afraid they're terribly expensive, sir,' she protested.

'I'm sure they are,' he answered. 'But I'm sure there is some way it could be paid for out of the budget for office supplies.' The more he talked and thought about it, the more he wanted a computer, and one like hers, not that decrepit thing that the officers downstairs had to make do with.

'If you don't mind, Commissario, I'd like to have a few days to consider this. And see if I can find a way to arrange it.'

Brunetti sensed victory in her accommodating tone.

'Of course,' he said, smiling, expansive now. 'What was it you wanted?'

'It's about Signor Cataldo,' she said, holding up a blue manila folder.

'Ah, yes,' he said, waving her forward and half rising in his

74

chair. 'What have you found?' He said nothing about his own attempts at research.

'Well, sir,' she said, approaching the chair. With a practised gesture, she swept her skirt to one side as she sat. She placed the unopened file on his desk and said, 'He's very wealthy, but you must know that already.' Brunetti suspected everyone in the city knew it, but he nodded to encourage her to continue. 'He inherited a fortune from his father, who died before Cataldo was forty. That's more than thirty years ago, just in the middle of the boom. He used it to invest and expand.'

'In what?' he asked.

She slid the file back towards her and opened it. 'He has a factory up near Longarone that makes wooden panels. There are only two in Europe, apparently, that make these things. And a cement factory in the same area. They're gradually chipping away at a mountain and turning it into cement. In Trieste he's got a fleet of cargo ships; and a trucking line that does national and international shipping. An agency that sells bulldozers and heavy moving equipment, also dredges. Cranes.' When Brunetti said nothing, she added, 'All I've got, really, is a list of the companies he owns: I haven't begun to take a closer look at their finances.'

Brunetti held up his right hand. 'Only if its not too difficult, Signorina.' When she grinned at the unlikelyhood of this, he went on, 'And here in the city?'

She turned over a page, then said, 'He owns four shops in Calle dei Fabbri and two buildings on Strada Nuova. Those are rented to two restaurants, and there are four apartments above them.'

'Is everything rented?'

'Indeed. One of the shops changed hands a year ago, and the rumour is that the new owner had to pay a *buonuscita* of a quarter of a million Euros.'

'Just to get the keys?'

'Yes. And the rent is ten thousand.'

'A *month*?' Brunetti demanded.

'It's in the Calle dei Fabbri, sir, and it's on two floors,' she said, managing to sound faintly offended that he should question the price – or her accuracy. She closed the file and sat back in her chair.

If he read her expression correctly, she had something else to tell him, and so he asked, 'And?'

'There are voices, sir.'

'Voices?'

'About her.'

'His wife?'

'Yes.'

'What kind of voices?'

She crossed her legs. 'Perhaps I've exaggerated, sir, and it's more that there are certain suggestions or silences when her name is mentioned.'

'I dare say that's true for many people in the city,' Brunetti said, trying not to sound prim.

'I'm sure it is, sir,' she said.

Brunetti decided to rise above mere gossip, so he pulled the file towards him and hefted it, asking, 'Have you had enough time to get any idea of what his total worth is?'

Instead of answering, she sat back in her chair, studying his face as though he had just presented her with an interesting conundrum.

'Yes, Signorina?' Brunetti prodded. When she failed to answer, he asked, 'What is it?'

'The phrase, sir.'

'Which phrase?'

'"Total worth."'

Confused, Brunetti could say only, 'It's the total of his various assets, isn't it?'

'Yes, sir, in the fiscal sense, I suppose it is.'

'Is there some other sense?' Brunetti asked in honest confusion.

'Well, there's his "total worth" as a man, a husband, an employer, a friend.' Seeing Brunetti's expression, she said, 'Yes, I know it's not what you meant, but it's interesting, the way we all use that term to indicate only the monetary wealth of a person.' She gave Brunetti the chance to comment or question, and when he did not, she added, 'It's so reductive, as if the only thing about us that has value is how much money we have.'

In a person of lesser imagination than Signorina Elettra, this speculation might have been an elaborate admission of the failure to discover Cataldo's total assets. Brunetti, however, well familiar with the byways of her mind, said only, 'My wife spoke of someone who had the "ichor of capitalism" running in his veins. Perhaps we all do.' He set the file down and pushed it away from him.

'Yes,' she agreed, sounding as though she did not like to have to say it, 'we all do.'

'What else did you learn?' Brunetti asked, summoning her back to business.

'That he was married to Giulia Vasari for more than thirty years and then divorced her,' she said, bringing them back to the world of the personal.

Brunetti decided to wait to see what she had to tell him, thinking it unseemly to appear either too interested in Franca Marinello or already to have learned anything about her.

'She's much younger, as you know; more than thirty years. Rumour has it that they met when he took his wife to a fashion show, and Franca Marinello modelled the furs.' She glanced at him but Brunetti made no response.

'However they met, he appears to have lost his head over her,' she continued. 'Within a month, he had left his wife and moved into his own apartment.' She paused here and explained, 'My father knew him, and so I got some of this from him.'

'Knew or knows?' Brunetti asked.

'Knows, I think. But he's not really a friend: one of those people one is acquainted with.'

'What else did your father tell you?'

'That the divorce was not pleasant.'

'They seldom are.'

She nodded in agreement and said, 'He heard that Cataldo fired his lawyer because he had met with his wife's.'

'I thought that was the way these things were done,' Brunetti said. 'Lawyers talking to lawyers.'

'Usually, yes. All he said was that Cataldo behaved badly, but he didn't tell me what that means.'

'I see.'

He noticed that she was about to get to her feet and asked, 'Did you learn anything else about his wife?'

Did she study his face before she answered? 'Not much, sir, beyond what I've told you. She doesn't play much of a part in society, though he's certainly very well known.' Then, as in afterthought, she added, 'She was once thought to be very shy.'

Though curious about her phrasing, Brunetti said only, 'I see.' He glanced at the file again but did not open it. He heard Signorina Elettra get to her feet. He looked up and smiled. 'Thank you,' he said.

'I hope you enjoy reading it, sir,' she said, then added, 'however much it might lack the intellectual rigour of the *Il Gazzettino*.' And then she was gone.

9

He forced himself to read through the pages of financial information regarding Cataldo: the companies he had owned and managed, the boards on which he sat, the stocks and bonds that floated into and out of his various portfolios, all the while allowing the dreaming part of his mind to drift where it pleased, which decidedly was not anywhere inside this file. Addresses of properties bought and sold, official sale prices, mortgages given and paid off, bank and stock dividends: there were people, Brunetti knew, who found these details thrilling. That thought depressed him immeasurably.

He remembered playing tag when he was a kid, chasing after friends, keeping an eye on them as they turned into familiar and unfamiliar *calli*. No, it was more like trailing a suspect in the early days of his career: keep an eye on one person while appearing to be interested in everything else that passed by. So it was as he read more fiscal details: his counter's mind registered and would recall some of the sums as they mounted towards Cataldo's total worth, while his hunter's ear, against his will, kept returning to Guarino and the story he had told. And to the things he had failed to tell.

He put the file aside and used his office phone to call Avisani in Rome. This time, he kept the exchange of pleasantries to a minimum, and after enough of them had been made, Brunetti said, his voice rich in simulated affability, 'That friend of yours we spoke to yesterday, you think you could get in touch with him and ask him to give me a call?'

'Ah, do I detect the first faint cracks in the sincerity of your devotion to one another?' the journalist asked.

'No,' Brunetti answered, surprised into laughter, 'but he asked me to do him a favour, and they tell me he won't be in until the end of the week. I need to talk to him again before I can do what he asked me to do.'

'He's good at that,' Avisani conceded.

'At what?'

'Giving too little information.' When Brunetti did not rise to this, the journalist said, 'I can probably get in touch with him. I'll ask him to call you today.'

Brunetti said, 'I'm waiting for you to lower your voice and add, mysteriously, "If he can."'

'That goes without saying, doesn't it?' Avisani asked in quite a reasonable voice before hanging up.

Brunetti went down to the bar at Ponte dei Greci and had a coffee he did not much want; to ensure that he would not enjoy it, he put in too little sugar and drank it quickly. Then he asked for a glass of mineral water he did not want, either, because of the weather, and returned to his office disgruntled at not being able to contact Guarino.

The dead man – Ranzato – must have met this other man on more than one occasion, and yet Brunetti was supposed to believe that Guarino had never bothered to ask him to elaborate on the meaning of 'well dressed' and had never learned anything else about him? How did this man and

Ranzato communicate to organize shipments? Telepathy? And payments?

And, finally, a great deal of attention was being paid to this one crime. 'Any man's death', and all of that poetry that Paola was always talking about. Yes, that was true, at least in the abstract, poetic sense, but one man's death, no matter how much it diminished us all, no longer really mattered very much to the world, nor to the authorities, not unless it was related to some more important matter or unless the press got it between their teeth and ran with it. Brunetti did not have the latest national statistics – he left statistics to Patta – but he knew that less than half of the murders committed were ever solved, and the number diminished in almost direct proportion to how long they went unsolved.

It had been a month, and Guarino was only now following up on the reference to the man living near San Marcuola. Brunetti set his pen down and reflected upon this fact. Either they did not care or someone had . . .

The phone rang, and he chose to answer with 'Sì' rather than with his name.

'Guido,' Guarino said cheerfully. 'Glad to catch you still there. I was told you wanted to talk to me.'

Even though Brunetti knew that Guarino was speaking for anyone who might be listening to his phone or to Brunetti's, his chipper tone drove Brunetti past caring what he said. 'We need to talk about this again. You never told me that . . .'

'Look, Guido,' Guarino said, speaking very quickly and with no diminution of jollity, 'I've got someone waiting to talk to me, but it will only take a few minutes. How about we meet down at that bar you go to?'

'Down at the . . .' Brunetti began to say, but Guarino cut him off. 'You got it. I'll meet you there in about fifteen minutes.' The line went dead.

What was Guarino doing in Venice, and how did he know about the bar at the bridge? Brunetti did not want to return to the bar, he did not want another coffee, he did not want a sandwich, nor another glass of cold water, nor even a glass of wine. But then the idea of a glass of hot punch came to him, and he got his overcoat from the *armadio* and left.

Sergio was just sliding the glass of hot punch across the bar to Brunetti when the phone in the back room of the bar rang. Sergio excused himself, muttered something about his wife, and slipped through the door to the other room. He was back in less than a minute, as Brunetti was by then expecting, and said, 'It's for you, Commissario.'

Habit forced Brunetti to put on his brightest smile as the instinct of deceit prompted him to say, 'I hope you don't mind, Sergio. I was waiting for a call, but I needed something hot, so I asked them to tell him to call me here.'

'Sure, Commissario. No trouble. Any time,' the barman said and stepped behind the bar to let Brunetti pass into the small back room.

The receiver lay on its side, next to one of the heavy old SIP phones, the outmoded grey model with the round dial. He picked up the receiver, resisting the urge to fit his finger into the small hole and turn the dial.

'Guido?'

'Yes.'

'Sorry for the melodrama. What is it?'

'Your mystery man, the well-dressed one, the one who said he'd meet someone at that place you mentioned.'

'Yes?'

'How come all you told me was that he was well-dressed?'

'That's what I was told.'

'How many months did you talk to the man who died?'

'. . . A long time.'

'And all he told you was that the other guy was well-dressed?'

'Yes.'

'And you never thought to ask for anything more?'

82

'I didn't think it . . .'

'When you finish that sentence, I'm hanging up.'

'Excuse me?'

'I thought I should warn you. You say that, and I'm hanging up.'

'Why?'

'Because I don't like being lied to.'

'I'm not . . .'

'You finish that sentence, I'm hanging up, too.'

'Really?'

'Start again. What else did he tell you about the man he talked to?'

'Someone in your house got a private email address?'

'My kids. Why?'

'I want to send you a photo.'

'Not my kids. You can't do that.'

'Your wife, then?'

'All right. At the university.'

'Paola, dot, Falier, at Ca'Foscari, one word, dot, it?'

'Yes. How did you know that address?'

'I'll send it tomorrow morning.'

'Does anyone else know about this photo?'

'No.'

'Is there a reason for that?'

'I'd rather not go into it.'

'Is this the only lead you have?'

'No, it's not the only one. But we haven't been able to check it.'

'And the others?'

'Nothing worked out.'

'If I find anything, how do I get in touch with you?'

'That means you'll do it?'

'Yes.'

'I gave you my number.'

'They said you weren't there.'

'It's not easy to get me.'

'The email you'll be using tomorrow?'

'No.'

'Then what?'

'I can always call you there.'

'Yes, you can; but I can't move my office here to wait for your call. How do I get in touch with you?'

'Call that same number and leave a message, saying your name is Pollini and give a time when you'll call back. That's when I'll call you at this number.'

'Pollini?'

'Yes. But call from a public phone, all right?'

'The next time we talk, I want you to tell me what's going on. What's really going on.'

'But I've told . . .'

'Filippo, do I have to threaten to hang up again?'

'No. You don't. I have to think about it, though.'

'Think about it now.'

'I'll tell you what I can.'

'I've heard that before.'

'I don't like it that it's this way, believe me. But it's better for everyone involved.'

'Me, too?'

'Yes, you, too. I've got to go. Thanks.'

10

Brunetti studied his hand as he replaced the receiver to see if it trembled. Nope, steady as a rock. Besides, this cloak and dagger stuff from Guarino was more likely to cause him irritation than fear. What was next, leaving messages for one another in bottles and floating them down the Grand Canal? Guarino had seemed a sensible enough fellow, and he had accepted Brunetti's scepticism with good grace, so why persist with all this James Bond nonsense?

He went to the doorway and asked Sergio, 'You mind if I make a call?'

'Commissario,' he said with an open wave of his hands, 'call whoever you want.' Dark-complexioned, almost as wide as he was tall, Sergio always reminded Brunetti of the bear who was the hero of one of the first books he had ever read. Because the bear was in the habit of gorging himself on honey, Sergio's substantial paunch only added to the resemblance. And, like that bear, Sergio was affable and generous, though equally prone to giving a growl now and again.

He dialled the first five digits of his home number but replaced the phone. He came out from the back room and returned to his place at the bar. But his glass was gone. 'Someone drink my punch?' he inquired.

'No, Commissario. I thought it would be too cold to drink.'

'Could you make me another?'

'Nothing easier,' the barman said and pulled down the bottle.

Ten minutes later, considerably warmed, Brunetti went back to his office. From there, he dialled his home number.

'*Sì*,' Paola answered. When had she stopped answering with her name, he wondered?

'It's me. You going to your office tomorrow?'

'Yes.'

'Can you print a photo from your computer there?'

'Of course,' she said, and he heard the barely restrained sigh.

'Good. It should arrive for you by email. Could you print out a copy of it for me? And maybe enlarge it?'

'Guido, I could just as easily access my email from here,' she said, using the voice of studied patience she reserved for the explanation of the self-evident.

'I know,' he said, though he had not thought of that. 'But I'd like to keep this . . .'

'Out of the house?' she suggested.

'Yes.'

'Thank you,' she said and then laughed. 'I don't want to delve into what understanding you have of technology, Guido, but thank you at least for that.'

'I don't want the kids . . .' he began.

'You don't have to explain,' she cut him off. Her voice was softer still when she said, 'I'll see you later,' and then she was gone.

He heard a noise at his door and looked towards it, surprised to see Officer Alvise. 'Do you have a moment,

Commissario?' he asked, smiling, then serious, then smiling again. Short and weedy, Alvise was the least prepossessing man on the force: his intellect was in complete harmony with this lack of physical prowess. Affable and friendly, Alvise was usually eager to chat with anyone. Paola, the one time she met him, said he made her think of someone of whom an English poet had said, 'Eternal smiles his emptiness betray.'

'Of course, Alvise. Come in. Please.' Alvise had only recently reappeared in the squad room after half a year spent working in symbiosis with Lieutenant Scarpa on some sort of European-Union-sponsored crime squad the precise nature of which had never been defined.

'I'm back, sir,' Alvise said as he sat down.

'Yes,' Brunetti said. 'I know.' Lambent thought and concise explanation were not attributes usually associated with Alvise's name; thus, his declaration could refer to his return from his temporary assignment or, for all Brunetti knew, from the bar on the corner.

Alvise sat and looked around the room, as though seeing it for the first time. Brunetti wondered if the officer thought it necessary to reintroduce himself to his superior. The silence lengthened, but Brunetti decided to wait it out and see what Alvise had to say. The officer turned to look at the open door, then at Brunetti, then at the door again. After another minute's silence, he leaned forward and asked, 'Do you mind if I close the door, Commissario?'

'Of course not, Alvise,' Brunetti said, wondering if half a year spent closeted in a tiny office with the Lieutenant had perhaps rendered Alvise subject to draughts?

Alvise went to the door, stuck his head out and glanced both ways, closed the door quietly, and came back to his chair. The silence renewed itself, but Brunetti resisted the impulse to speak.

Finally Alvise said, 'As I said, sir, I'm back.'

'And as I said, Alvise, I know.'

Alvise stared at him, as if suddenly realizing that it fell to him to break free of the non-communication circle. He glanced at the door, turned to Brunetti, and said, 'But it's like I'm not, sir.'

Brunetti failed to prod at this, so the officer was forced to continue. 'The other men, sir, it's not like they're glad I'm back.' Perplexity was evident in his unlined face.

'Why do you say that, Alvise?'

'Well, no one said anything. About my being back.' He managed to sound both surprised and pained.

'What did you expect them to say, Alvise?'

Alvise tried on a smile, but it didn't work. 'You know, sir, something like, "Welcome back", or "Good to have you here again." Something like that.'

Where did Alvise think he had been, Patagonia? 'It's not as if you haven't been here, Alvise. Had you thought of that?'

'I know, sir. But I wasn't part of the squad. I wasn't a regular officer.'

'For a time.'

'Yes, I know sir, only for a time. But it was sort of a promotion, wasn't it?'

Brunetti folded his hands and pressed his teeth against his knuckles. When he could, he took his mouth away and said, 'I suppose you could see it that way, Alvise. But, as you say, you're back now.'

'Yes. But it would be good if they'd say hello or act like they're glad to see me.'

'Maybe they're waiting to see how easy it is for you to adjust to the working rhythms of the squad again,' Brunetti suggested, though he had no idea what that meant.

'I'd thought of that, sir,' Alvise said, and smiled.

'Good. Then I'm sure that's it,' Brunetti said with gruff forcefulness. 'Give them a little time to let them get used to you again. They're probably curious to see what new ideas you've brought back with you.' Ah, what the stage lost when I opted for the police, Brunetti thought.

Alvise's smile widened and, for the first time since he came in, seemed real. 'Oh, I wouldn't want to do that to them, sir. After all, this is sleepy old Venice, isn't it?'

Again, Brunetti's lips consulted with his knuckles. 'Yes. Good of you to keep that in mind, Alvise. Easy does it. Just try to go back to the old ways of doing things for now. It might take them a while to adjust, but I'm sure they'll come round. Maybe if you were to invite Riverre out for a drink this afternoon, ask him what's been going on, you could sort of reintroduce yourself. You were always good friends, weren't you?'

'Yes, sir. But that was before I was pro . . . before I was given the assignment.'

'Well, ask him out, anyway. Take him down to Sergio's and have a real talk. Take your time. Maybe if you went on patrol for a few days together, things would be easier for him,' Brunetti said, making a mental note to ask Vianello to see that the two were united again, and to hell with the idea of efficient policing of the city.

'Thank you, sir,' Alvise said, getting to his feet. 'I'll go down and ask him now.'

'Good,' Brunetti said, smiling broadly and happy to see that Alvise was already beginning to look more like his old self.

Alvise pulled his feet under the chair prior to standing, and Brunetti gave in to the impulse to say, 'Welcome back, Alvise.'

The officer stood to attention and snapped out a salute. 'Thank you, sir. It's good to be back.'

11

The Questura and the thought of the murdered man he had never met went home to dinner with Brunetti. Paola noticed their presence during the meal, when her husband failed to praise, and then to finish, the *coda di rospo* with scampi and tomatoes, and left a third of a bottle of Graminé undrunk when he went into the living room to read.

The dishes took a long time to wash, and when Paola joined him, he was standing at the windows, looking off towards the angel atop the campanile di San Marco, visible to the south-east. She set their coffee on the table in front of the sofa. 'Would you like grappa with this, Guido?' she asked.

He shook his head but said nothing. She went and stood beside him, and when he failed to put his arm around her, she nudged him gently with her hip. 'What's the matter?' she asked.

'It doesn't feel right to bring you into this,' he finally said.

She turned away from him and went to sit on the sofa. She sipped at her coffee. 'I could have refused, you know.'

'But you didn't,' he said before coming to sit beside her. 'What's it all about?'

'This man in Tessera who was murdered.'

'The newspapers told me that much, Guido.'

Brunetti picked up his coffee. 'You know,' he said after the first sip. 'Maybe I would like a grappa. There any of that Gaja left? The Barolo?'

'Yes,' she said, settling herself more comfortably on the sofa. 'Get me a glass, too, would you?'

He was quickly back, with the bottle and two glasses, and as they drank it, Brunetti repeated most of what Guarino had told him, ending up with the reason for the arrival of the photo in her email the next day. He also tried to explain his own contradictory feelings about having been drawn into Guarino's investigation. It was none of his business: the investigation belonged to the Carabinieri. Perhaps he was flattered by being asked to help, his vanity no different from Patta's at being considered 'the man in charge'. Or perhaps it was the desire to show that he could do something the Carabinieri could not.

'A photo's not going to make it any easier for Signorina Elettra to find him,' Brunetti admitted. 'But I wanted to make Guarino do something, even if it was only to make him admit that he'd been lying to me.'

'Well, withholding information, at any rate,' Paola corrected him.

'All right, if you insist,' Brunetti admitted with a smile.

'And he wants you to help him learn if anyone who lives near San Marcuola is capable of . . . of what?'

'I suppose he's interested in violent crime. After all, it's likely Guarino thinks the man in the photo is the killer. Or at any rate is mixed up in it.'

'Do you?'

'I don't know enough about it to think anything. All I know is that this man had Ranzato do some illegal shipping for him and that he dresses well and arranged to meet someone at the San Marcuola stop.'

'I thought you said that's where he lives.'

'Well, not exactly.'

Paola closed her eyes with a great display of much-put-upon patience and said, 'I never know whether that means yes or no.'

Brunetti smiled. 'In this case, it means I assumed so.'

'Why?'

'Because he said he'd meet someone there one evening, and that's what we do when people come to town: we meet them at the *imbarcadero* near where we live.'

'Yes,' Paola said, and then added, 'Professor.'

'Don't fool around, Paola. It's obvious.'

She leaned aside and took the point of his chin between the thumb and forefinger of her right hand. Gently, she turned his head to face her. 'It's also obvious that the judgement that someone is well-dressed can mean different things.'

'What?' Brunetti asked, his hand arrested on its way to the bottle of grappa. 'I don't know what you're talking about. Besides, he also said the way the man dressed was flashy, whatever that means.'

Paola studied his face as she would study that of a stranger. 'What we consider "flashy", even "well dressed", depends on how we dress ourselves, wouldn't you say?'

'I still don't understand,' Brunetti said, picking up the bottle.

Paola waved away his offer of more grappa and said, 'Do you remember that case – must be ten years ago – when you had to go out to Favaro every night for a week to question a witness?'

He thought for a while, remembered the case, the endless lies, the final failure. 'Yes.'

'Remember how the Carabinieri would bring you back and drop you at Piazzale Roma, and you'd take the Number One home?'

'Yes,' he answered, wondering where she was going with this. Would she suggest that this case, too, had the same feeling of failure about it, something he was beginning to feel himself?

'And do you remember the people you told me you saw on the vaporetto every night? Those shifty-looking types, with the cheap blondes? The men with the leather jackets and the women with the leather mini-skirts?'

'Oh, my God,' Brunetti said, giving himself a slap on the forehead so strong it literally knocked him back into the sofa beside her. 'Those who have eyes and see not,' he said.

'Please, Guido, don't *you* start quoting the Bible.'

'Sorry. The shock must have been too much for me,' he said with a broad smile. 'You're a genius. But I've known that for years. Of course, of course. The Casinò. They'd meet at San Marcuola and go together, wouldn't they? Of course. Genius, genius.'

Paola held up a hand in a patently false protestation of modesty. 'Guido: it's only a possibility.'

'Yes, it's only a possibility,' Brunetti agreed. 'But it makes sense and at least it lets me *do* something.'

'Do something?' Paola inquired.

'Yes.'

'As in letting us go to the Casinò?' she asked.

'Us?'

'Us.'

'Why us?'

She held up her glass to him, and he poured her another measure of grappa. She sipped it, nodded in appreciation as strong as his own had been, and then said, 'Because nothing is more likely to call attention to itself than a single man at the Casinò.'

Brunetti started to protest, but she cut off his opposition by holding up her glass between them. 'He can't just walk around, staring at the people at the tables and never gambling, can he? What better way to make himself visible? And if he does start to play, what's he going to do, spend the night losing our apartment?' When she saw that his expression had begun to lighten, she asked, 'After all, Signorina Elettra can't be expected to put *that* on the office equipment bill, can she?'

'I suppose not,' Brunetti admitted, as clear an admission of surrender as a man had ever given.

'I'm serious, Guido,' she said, setting her glass on the table. 'You need to look comfortable while you're there, and if you go alone, you're going to look like a policeman on the prowl, well, a man on the prowl, at any rate. If you go with me, we can at least talk and laugh and look like we're having a good time.'

'Does that mean we aren't going to have a good time?'

'Can you imagine having a good time watching people lose money gambling?'

'They don't all lose,' he said.

'And not everyone who jumps off a roof breaks a leg,' she shot back.

'What's that supposed to mean?'

'It means that the Casinò makes money, and it makes money because people lose it. Gambling. Maybe they don't lose every night, but they always lose in the end.'

Brunetti toyed with the idea of taking another small glass of grappa but put the idea behind him manfully and said, 'All right. But can we still have a good time?'

'Not until tomorrow night,' she answered.

Brunetti had decided to trust to luck that someone at the Casinò would recognize or recall the young man in the photo Paola brought home from the university, though Fortuna was perhaps the wrong deity to invoke in these circumstances, she no doubt having to endure other, and more urgent, solicitations. He was also aware that, even if he did discover the young man's identity, or even the man himself, the only thing he could do, after perhaps checking to see if the man had a criminal record, was to pass the information on to Guarino. Even with the Right returned to power in the government, it was still not a crime to have your photo taken.

However much Brunetti reminded himself that he was a private citizen, come to the Casinò in the company of his lady wife, he knew that as the person who had, in recent years, been in charge of two of the police investigations of the Casinò, he was unlikely to pass unremarked.

When they arrived, the man at reception recognized him immediately, but apparently the administration harboured no hard feelings towards him, and he was given VIP entrance, though he refused the complimentary *fiche* that were offered with it. He purchased fifty Euros in chips and gave half to Paola.

He had not been here in years, at least not since the last time he had arrested the Director. Not much had changed: he recognized some of the croupiers, two of whom had also been arrested the last time, charged with having organized the system by which the Casinò had been cheated out of an amount no one had ever been able to calculate, perhaps millions, certainly hundreds of thousands of Euros. Accused, convicted, sentenced, and now right back at their civil service jobs as croupiers. Regardless of Paola's company at his side, Brunetti began to suspect he was not going to have a good time.

They moved towards the roulette tables, this being the only game Brunetti felt capable of playing: it demanded no skill in counting cards or calculating the odds of anything. Put your money down. Win. Lose.

As they approached, he studied the people grouped around one of the tables, looking for the face he had seen only in three-quarters profile. It had not been a particularly good photo that had come through that morning, without explanation of when, where, or by whom it had been taken. Perhaps taken by a *telefonino*, it showed a clean-shaven man who looked to be in his early thirties. He was standing at a bar, a cup of coffee in one hand as he spoke to someone not visible in the photo. He had short dark hair, brown or black: there was not enough definition in the photo to tell. Only one cheekbone was visible and one full eyebrow, cut at an angle so sharp it looked like the sort one saw on cartoon characters. It was impossible to be sure about his height, though he was of medium build. Nor could the quality of his clothing be distinguished: tie, jacket, light-coloured shirt.

Brunetti and Paola stood for a few minutes on the outskirts of the oval of people drawn by the magic power of the wheel, listening to the click, click, click as the ball swirled round. Then the muted clack as it slipped into place, and then silence: defeat never caused a sigh, and victory passed unremarked. How devoid of enthusiasm they were, Brunetti thought, how tasteless they found joy.

Caught in the implacable tide of the game, a few losers were sucked away from the table and out of the oval; others swept in to fill their places, among them Brunetti and Paola. Without bothering to look where he put the chip, Brunetti set one down on the table. He waited, watching the faces on the opposite side, though they were all intent on the croupier and then, as soon as the ball left his hand, on the wheel.

Paola stood at his side, hugging his arm as the ball slipped into number seven and his chip followed many others into the narrow slit of oblivion, she as cast down as if it had been ten thousand Euros and not ten that he lost. They stood there for a few more spins, then were driven away by the bovine prodding of those behind them, eager with the anticipation of loss.

They drifted over to another table and stood on the outskirts for a quarter of an hour, watching the tides drift in and out. Brunetti's attention was caught by a very young man

– he could not have been much older than Raffi – standing directly across the table from them. Each time, just as the croupier called for last bets, he pushed a pile of chips on to number twelve, and each time they were swept away.

Brunetti studied his face, still soft with youth. His lips were full and gleaming, like the lips of one of Caravaggio's feral saints. His eyes, however, which should have glistened, if only with the pain of repeated loss, were as distant and opaque as those of a statue. Nor did the eyes deign to glance at his pile of chips, which he chose at random: red, yellow, blue. Thus no bet he placed was for the same amount, though the pile of chips was generally about the same height: ten chips, give or take.

He lost repeatedly, and when the chips in front of him were gone, he reached into the pocket of his jacket and pulled out another fistful, which he scattered randomly on the table in front of him, not looking at them and thus making no attempt to sort them by value.

It suddenly came to Brunetti to wonder if the boy were blind and could play only by touch and by sound. He watched him for a while with this possibility in mind, but then the boy glanced across at him, a look of such bleak dislike that Brunetti was forced to turn his eyes away as though he had caught someone engaged in an obscene act.

'Come away from here,' he heard Paola say, and he felt her grip on his elbow, not at all gentle, as she pulled him out into the empty space between the tables. 'I can't stand to look at that boy,' she said, voicing his thoughts.

'Come on,' he said. 'I'll buy you a drink.'

'Big spender,' she gushed, but she allowed herself to be led to the bar, where Brunetti talked her into having a whisky, something she seldom drank and never liked. He passed her the heavy square glass, touched hers with his own, and watched as she took her first sip. Her mouth screwed up, perhaps more than a bit melodramatically, and she said, gasping, 'I don't know why I always let you talk me into drinking this stuff.'

'You've been saying the same thing to me, if memory serves, for nineteen years, since we went to London for the first time.'

'But you're still trying to convert me,' she replied, taking another sip.

'You drink grappa now, don't you?' he asked mildly.

'Yes, but I *like* grappa. With this,' she said, flourishing the glass, 'I might as well be drinking paint thinner.'

Brunetti finished his whisky and set the glass on the bar; he ordered a *grappa di moscato* and took Paola's glass from her.

If he expected her to object, she surprised him by saying, 'Thanks' and taking the grappa from the barman. Turning back towards the room they had just left, she said, 'It's depressing, watching them in there. Dante writes about souls like this.' She sipped at the grappa and asked, 'Are brothels more fun?'

Brunetti choked, spitting the whisky back into the glass. He set the glass on the bar, took out his handkerchief, and wiped at his lips. 'I beg your pardon?'

'I mean it, Guido,' she said quite amiably. 'I've never been to one, and I wonder if there, at least, anyone manages to have any fun.'

'And you ask me?' he asked, not sure which tone to use and ending up with something between amusement and indignation.

Paola said nothing, sipped at her grappa, and Brunetti finally said, 'I've been in two, no, three.' He waved to the barman and when he came, shoved the glass towards him and signalled for a fresh drink.

When it arrived, Brunetti said, 'The first time was when I was working in Naples. I had to arrest the son of the madame: he lived there while studying at the university.'

'What was he studying?' she inquired, as he knew she would.

'Business management.'

'Of course,' she said and smiled. 'Was anyone having fun?'

'I didn't consider that at the time. I went in with three other men, and we arrested him.'

'For what?'

'Homicide.'

'And the other times?'

'Once in Udine. I had to question one of the women who worked there.'

'Did you go during working hours?' she asked, a phrase that conjured up an imaginary picture of the women coming in and punching their time cards, pulling their net stockings and high heels out of a locker, having regular coffee breaks, and sitting around a table, smoking, chatting, and eating.

'Yes,' he said, as if three in the morning were a regular working hour.

'Anyone having fun?'

'It was probably too late to tell,' he said. 'Almost everyone was asleep.'

'Even the woman you went to question.'

'She turned out to be the wrong woman.'

'And the third time?'

'That was a case in Pordenone,' he said in his most distant voice. 'But someone called them, and the place was empty when we got there.'

'Ah,' she said with winsome longing. 'I did want to know.'

'Sorry I can't help,' he said.

She set her empty glass on the bar and rose up on her toes to kiss his cheek. 'All things considered, I'm rather glad you can't,' she said, then, 'Shall we go back and lose the rest of our money?'

12

They went back inside, content to remain behind the groups crowding around tables, both of them paying more attention to the people playing than to what they won or lost. Like Santa Caterina di Alessandria, the young man was still bound to his wheel: Brunetti found him so immeasurably sad that he could no longer bear to watch him. He should be out chasing girls, cheering on some stupid soccer team or wild rock band, mountain climbing, doing something – anything – excessive and rash and foolish that would consume his youthful energy and leave joyful memories.

He grabbed Paola's elbow and all but pulled her into the next room, where people sat around an oval table, tipping up the corners of cards to take a furtive glance. Brunetti remembered the bars of his youth, where rough-looking workers congregated after work to play endless hands of *scopa*. He recalled the tiny flare-topped glasses of red wine, so dark it appeared black, that each man kept to his right and at which he sipped between hands. The level of liquid seemed never to decrease, and Brunetti could not remember that any of them ever ordered more than one glass a night. They played with exuberance, slapping winning cards down with a mighty thump that made the legs of the table tremble, sometimes leaning forward with a joyous hoot to pull towards them the evening's winnings. What had that been then, a hundred lire, enough to pay for the wine of the other players?

He remembered the shouts of encouragement from the men standing at the bar, the billiard players resting on their cues while they gazed at the men who were enjoying a different game, often commenting on its progress. Some of the men at the table had washed their faces and put on their good jackets before they came; others arrived straight from work still in their dark blue boiler suits and heavy boots. Where had those clothes and those boots gone? What, in fact, had happened to all the men who worked with their bodies and their hands? Had they been replaced by the smooth types who kept the exclusive shops and boutiques and who looked as though they would collapse under a heavy weight or before a heavy wind?

He felt the pressure of Paola's arm around his waist. 'How much more of this do we have to do?' she asked. He looked at his watch and saw that it was already after midnight. 'Maybe he came only that one night,' she suggested, then tried, unsuccessfully, to stifle a yawn.

Brunetti looked out over the heads of the people surrounding the tables. These people could be in bed, reading: they could be in bed, doing other things. But they were here, watching little balls and pieces of paper and little white cubes carry away what they had worked weeks, perhaps years, to earn. 'You're right,' he said, bending to kiss the top of her head. 'I promised you a good time, and here we are, doing this.'

He felt, rather than saw, her shrug.

'I want to find the Director, show him the picture, see if he recognizes the man. Want to come with me or do you want to wait here?'

Rather than answer, she turned and started towards the door that led to the stairs. He followed. Downstairs, she sat on a bench opposite the door of the Director's office, opened her bag, pulled out a book and her glasses, and began to read.

Brunetti knocked on the door, but no one responded. He went back to the reception desk and asked to speak to the man in charge of security, who arrived a minute later in response to a discreet phone call. Claudio Vasco was a tall man a few years younger than Brunetti who wore a dinner jacket so elegant he might well have shared a tailor with Commissaria Griffoni. Hired to replace one of the men who had been arrested, he shook hands and smiled when Brunetti gave his name.

Vasco led him down the hall, past Paola, who did not bother to look up from her book, and into the Director's office. Not bothering to sit down, he studied the photo, and Brunetti, watching him, could all but see his mental fingers flicking through a file of faces. Vasco let the hand holding the photo fall to his side and looked at Brunetti. 'Is it true you're the one who arrested those two up there?' he asked, raising his eyes towards the ceiling and the floor above, where the two croupiers were at work.

'Yes,' Brunetti answered.

Vasco smiled and handed the photo back to Brunetti. 'Then I owe you a favour. I just hope you frightened those two bastards enough to keep them honest for a while.'

'Not permanently?'

Vasco looked at Brunetti as though he had started speaking the language of the birds. 'Them? It's just a matter of time until they think of some new system, or one of them wants to go to the Seychelles for vacation. We spend more time watching them than we do the clients,' he said tiredly. He nodded at the photo and said, 'He's been here a few times, once with another guy. Your man's maybe thirty, a bit shorter than you, and thinner.'

'And the other?' Brunetti asked.

'I don't remember him well,' Vasco said. 'All my attention went to this one,' he said, giving the photo a backward flick with the fingers of his left hand.

Brunetti raised an eyebrow but Vasco said only, 'I'll tell you about it after I find the registration.' Brunetti knew records were kept of everyone who came to the Casinò, but he had no idea how long they had to be kept on file.

'As I said, I owe you a favour, Commissario.' He headed towards the door, turned and added, 'Even if I didn't, I'd be happy to help you find this bastard, especially if I knew it would get him into trouble.' Vasco gave a smile that made him ten years younger and was gone, leaving the office door open.

Through the opening Brunetti could see Paola, who had not looked up either at their approach or Vasco's departure. He went into the corridor and sat down next to her. 'What are you reading, sweetie?' he asked in a deep voice.

Ignoring him, she turned a page.

He moved closer and stuck his head between her and the page. 'What's that, Princess who?'

'Casamassima,' she said and slid away from him.

'Is it good?' he asked, sliding up against her.

'Riveting,' she answered, and, seeing that she had run out of bench, turned away from him.

'You read a lot of books, angel?' he persisted in the same intrusive, raspy voice, the voice of every crazy talker who comes to sit next to a person on the vaporetto.

'I read a lot of books, yes,' she said, then politely, 'My husband is a policeman, so maybe you better leave me alone.'

'You don't have to be unfriendly, angel,' he whined.

'I know. But I have his gun in my purse, and I'm going to shoot you with it if you don't leave me alone.'

'Oh,' Brunetti said and moved away from her. Sliding back to the other end of the bench, he crossed his legs and looked at the print of the Rialto Bridge on the wall opposite them. Paola turned a page and returned to London.

He shifted lower and rested his head against the wall. He considered whether Guarino might deliberately have misled him into thinking that the man lived near here. Perhaps Guarino feared that Brunetti's participation would compromise the Carabinieris' control of the investigation. Perhaps he was uncertain where his colleague's real allegiance lay. And who could fault him for that? Brunetti had but to think of Lieutenant Scarpa to recall that safety's best part was in seeming trust. And poor Alvise, six months working with Scarpa, learning to seek his praise. And so now Alvise was not to be trusted, not only because of his innate stupidity but because his silly little head had been turned by the attentions of the Lieutenant and he was now sure to rush to him with anything he learned.

He was dimly conscious of a hand being placed on his left shoulder; thinking it was Paola, coming back to him from Henry James, he placed his own on top of it and gave it a small squeeze. The hand was pulled roughly from under his, and he opened his eyes to see Vasco in front of him, face blank with shock.

'I thought you were my wife,' was all Brunetti could think to say, turning his head to where Paola sat, observing the two men without appearing to find them more interesting than her book.

'We were talking before he fell asleep,' she told Vasco, who blinked while he processed this and then smiled and leaned down to clap Brunetti on the shoulder.

'You wouldn't believe some of the things I've seen in this place,' he said. He held up some sheets of paper, saying, 'I've got copies of their passports.' He went into the Director's office.

Brunetti got to his feet and followed him.

Two papers lay on the desk, and two men looked up at him, the one in the photo and a younger man with hair that came to his collar and little evidence of a neck. 'They came in together,' Vasco said.

Brunetti picked up the first: 'Antonio Terrasini,' he read, 'born in Plati.' He looked at Vasco. 'Where's that?'

'I thought you might want to know,' he answered, smiling. 'I had the girls check. Aspromonte, just above the National Park.'

'What's a Calabrian doing here?'

'I'm Pugliese,' Vasco said neutrally. 'Might as well ask me the same question.'

'Sorry,' Brunetti said, setting the first paper down and picking up the other. 'Giuseppe Strega,' he read. 'Born in the same town, but eight years later.'

Vasco said, 'I noticed. The girls at the front desk share your curiosity about the first one, though I suspect for different reasons: they think he's handsome. Both of them, in fact.' Vasco took the papers back and studied the faces, Terrasini with the angled eyebrows over almond-shaped eyes and the other with wings of poet's hair sweeping in from both sides of his face. 'I don't see it, myself,' Vasco said and let the papers fall to the desk.

Neither did Brunetti, who said, 'Strange creatures, women.' Then he finally asked, 'Why's he a bastard?'

'Because he's a bad loser,' Vasco answered. 'None of them likes to lose. Though I think some of them don't really care one way or the other, only they can't let themselves know they think that.' He looked at Brunetti to see whether he was following, and at his nod continued.

'One night he lost, must have been close to fifty thousand Euros. I'm not sure exactly how much, but the other man on security called me and told me there was a heavy loser at one of the blackjack tables and he was afraid there was going to be trouble. That's where the ones who think they're smart always believe they're going to win: counting cards, this system, that system. They're all crazy: we always win.' He saw Brunetti's expression and said, 'Sorry, doesn't matter, does it? Anyway, when I got there I spotted him right away: guy looked like a ticking bomb. You could feel the energy coming from him, like from a furnace.

'I saw there weren't many chips in front of him, so I figured I'd stay around and be there when he finally lost it all. Took him two hands to do that, and as soon as the croupier raked them in, he started shouting, saying the deck was stacked, that he'd see the croupier never dealt another hand.'

Vasco gave a shrug that indicated irritation and resignation. 'Doesn't happen often, but when it does, they always say the same things. Make the same threats.'

'What did you do?'

'Giulio – the guy who called me – was on the other side of him by then, so we came up to him together and . . . well, we helped him from the table and to the stairs. And then downstairs. He quietened down some on the way, but we still thought we should get rid of him.'

'Did you?'

'Yes. We waited while he got his coat, and then we walked – escorted – him to the front door.'

'He say anything? Threaten you?'

'No, but you should have felt him,' Vasco began and then, as if he recalled the way Brunetti had touched his hand, said, 'I mean, you should have seen him. It's like electricity was going through him. So we took him to the door, calling him "*Signore*" and being extra-polite to him, the way we have to be, and then we waited until he walked away.'

'And then?'

'And then we went back and put him on the list.'

'The list?'

'The list of people who can't come back. If they behave like that, or if someone in their family calls up and gives their name and tells us not to let them in, then we bar them.' Again, that shrug. 'Not that it makes any difference. They can go to Campione, to Jesolo, or there's plenty of houses here in the city where they can gamble, especially since the Chinese got here. But at least we got rid of him.'

'How long ago did this happen?' Brunetti asked.

'I don't remember exactly: the date should be there,' he said, pointing to the paper on the desk: 'Yes, the twentieth of November.'

'What about the one who was with him?'

'I didn't know at the time that they had come in together. I was told, later, when I went down to bar him. I don't remember seeing the other guy.'

'Is he barred, too?' Brunetti asked.

'No reason to do it,' Vasco said.

'May I take these?' Brunetti asked, indicating the photocopies.

'Of course. I told you I owed you a favour.'

'Would you do me another one?' Brunetti asked.

'If I can.'

'Lift the ban on him and call me if he comes in.'

'If you give me your phone number, I will,' Vasco replied. 'I'll tell the girls at the desk to call you if I'm not here.'

'Yes,' Brunetti said and then thought to ask, 'You think they can be trusted? If they think the guy is so attractive?'

Vasco's smile bloomed. 'I told them it was you who arrested those two shits upstairs. You can trust them with anything now.'

'Thanks.'

'Besides,' Vasco said, picking up the papers and handing them to Brunetti, 'they're gamblers: none of the girls would touch either of them with a boathook.'

13

The next morning, Brunetti went into Signorina Elettra's office carrying the photocopies. As if in visual harmony with the papers, she was wearing black and white, a pair of what looked like black Levi's – though black Levi's that had spent some time in a tailor's hands – and a turtleneck so white it made him nervous that there might be some latent smudge on the documents. She studied the copies of the passport photos of the two men, looking back and forth from one to the other, and finally said, 'Handsome devils, aren't they?'

'Yes,' Brunetti answered, wondering why it seemed to be every woman's first reaction to these men. Perhaps they were good looking, but one of them was suspected of being involved in a murder, and the only thing women had to say about them was that they were good looking. It was enough to make a man question his belief in the basic good sense of women. His better self prevented him from adding to the list of charges the fact that they were from the South and one of them, at least, had the surname of a well-known Camorra family.

'I wondered if you had access, or could have access, to the files of the Ministry of the Interior,' Brunetti said with the calm of the habitual criminal. 'The passport files.'

Signorina Elettra held the photos to the light, glancing more closely at them. 'It's hard to tell from a copy if the passports are real or not,' she said with the calm of someone familiar with the work of habitual criminals.

'No hotline to the Minister's office?' he asked with false jocularity.

'Unfortunately, no,' she answered, straight faced. Absently, she picked up a pencil and put its point on the desk, ran her fingers down the sides, flipped it over, and repeated the motion a few times, then let it fall to her desk. 'I'll start with the Passport Office,' she said, just as if their files stood to her left, and all she had to do was leaf through them. Her hand reached out, as if by its own will, to the pencil, and this time she tapped the eraser against the photos and said, 'If they are real, I'll check our files to see what we have on them.' As an afterthought, she asked, 'When would you like to have this, Dottore?'

'Yesterday?' he asked.

'Unlikely.'

'Tomorrow?' he suggested, deciding to play fair and not ask for today.

'If these are their real names, I should have something by tomorrow. Or if they've used the names long enough for them to be in our system somewhere.' Her fingers slid up and down the pencil, and Brunetti had the sensation that he was watching her mind slide back and forth among possibilities.

'Is there anything more you can tell me about them?' she asked

'The man who was killed in Tessera was involved with that one,' Brunetti said, pointing to the man whose name was given as Antonio Terrasini. 'And the other one went to the Casinò with him, where Terrasini lost a great deal of money and had to be thrown out when he started threatening the croupier.'

'People always lose,' she said with little interest. 'Be intriguing, though, to know where he got a great deal of money, wouldn't it?'

'It's always intriguing to know where people get a great deal of money,' Brunetti offered. 'Even more so if they're willing to gamble it away.'

She stared at the photos for a moment, then said, 'I'll see what I can find.'

'I'd be grateful.'

'Of course.'

He left her office and started back to his own. As he reached the staircase, he glanced up and recognized Pucetti and, beside him, a woman in a long coat. He glanced at her ankles and was immediately reminded of his first sight of Franca Marinello and those elegant ankles walking up the bridge in front of him.

His eyes rose to the woman's head, but she was wearing a woollen hat that covered her hair except for some wisps at the back. Blonde wisps.

Brunetti quickened his pace, and when he was a few steps behind them, called, 'Pucetti.'

The young officer stopped, turned, and smiled awkwardly when he saw his superior. 'Ah, Commissario,' he began; then his companion turned, and Brunetti saw that it was indeed Franca Marinello.

The cold had mottled the sides of her face a strange dark purple while leaving the skin of her chin and forehead as pale as that of a person who never saw the sun. Her eyes softened, and Brunetti recognized what she used in place of a smile. 'Ah, Signora,' he said, not disguising his surprise. 'Whatever brings you here?'

'I thought I could take advantage of having met you the other night, Commissario,' she said in that deep voice.

'There's something I'd like to ask you, if I might,' she said. 'This young officer has been very kind.'

Put on the spot like this, Pucetti explained. 'The Signora said she was a friend of yours, Commissario, and asked to speak to you. I called your office a few times, but you weren't there, so I thought perhaps I could bring the Signora up to see you. Instead of keeping her waiting downstairs. I knew you were in the building.' He ran out of words.

'Thank you, Pucetti. You did the right thing.' Brunetti took the last few steps between them, extended his hand, and shook hers. 'Come along to my office, then,' he said and smiled, thanked Pucetti again, and continued past them to the top of the stairs.

Entering, he saw the office with her eyes: a desk covered with small landslides of papers, a telephone, a ceramic mug with a badger – given to him last Christmas by Chiara – filled with pencils and pens, an empty glass. The walls, he noticed for the first time, needed paint. A photo of the President of the Republic hung alone behind his desk, to its left a crucifix Brunetti had never cared enough about to take down. Last year's calendar had still not been removed from one wall, and the door to the wardrobe hung open, his scarf trailing on to the floor. Brunetti took her coat and hung it in the *armadio*, kicking the scarf inside while he was there. She placed her gloves inside her hat and handed them to him. He put them on the shelf, closed the door, and went across to his desk.

'I like to see where people work,' she said, glancing around as he pulled out a chair for her. When she was seated, he asked whether she would like a coffee and at her refusal he took the chair beside hers and turned to face her.

She continued to gaze around the room, then out of the window, and Brunetti took the opportunity to study her. She was dressed simply in a camel-coloured sweater and a dark skirt that came halfway down her calves. Her shoes were low-heeled and looked comfortably worn in. She held a leather purse on her lap; the only jewellery she wore was a wedding ring. He noticed that the warmth had caused the flood of colour to recede from her cheeks.

'Is that why you're here?' Brunetti finally asked: 'to see where I work?'

'No, not at all,' she answered and leaned aside to place her purse on the floor. When she looked up, he thought he saw a certain tension in her face, but then he abandoned the idea: her emotions registered only in her voice, rich and deep and as lovely as any he had ever heard.

Brunetti crossed his legs and put an interested half-smile on his face. He had outwaited masters, and he could out-wait her if he had to.

'It's really about my husband that I've come,' she said. 'His business.'

Brunetti nodded, saying nothing.

'Last night at dinner, he told me that someone has been trying to get into the records of some of his companies.'

'Do you mean a break-in?' Brunetti asked, though he knew she did not.

Her lips moved and her voice softened. 'No, no, not at all. I should have been clearer. He told me that one of his computer people – I know they have titles, these people, but I don't know what they are – told him yesterday that there was evidence that someone had broken into their computers.'

'And stolen something?' Brunetti asked. Then he said, meaning it, 'I have to confess that I'm probably not the right person to bring this to. I mean I don't have a very sophisticated understanding of what people can do with computers.' He smiled to show his good faith.

'But you know the law, don't you?' she asked.

'About things like this?' Brunetti asked, and at her nod, was forced to say, 'No, I'm afraid I don't. A magistrate would be a better person to ask, or a lawyer.' Then, as if the idea had

112

just come to him, he said, 'Surely, your husband must have a lawyer he could ask.'

She looked at her hands, neatly folded in her lap, and said, 'Yes, he does. But he told me he doesn't want to ask him. In fact, after he told me about this, he said in essence that he doesn't want to do anything about it.' She looked up at Brunetti.

'I'm not sure I understand,' Brunetti said, meeting her eyes.

'The man who told him, this computer person, said that all the person did was open some files that held his bank statements and property holdings, as if they were trying to find out what he owned and what it was worth.' Again, she looked at her hands, and when Brunetti followed her glance, he saw that they were the hands of a young woman. 'The man told him,' she went on, 'that it could have been an investigation by the Guardia di Finanza.'

'May I ask why you're here, then?' he asked, his curiosity not at all forced.

Her lips were full, red, and as he watched, her top teeth rubbed across the bottom one nervously in a kind of harmless chewing. The young hand brushed away a strand of pale hair that had strayed across her cheek, and he caught himself wondering if her skin still had normal sensitivity or if she had known it was there only because it had fallen across her eye.

After some time – and Brunetti had the feeling she had to find the right way to explain it even to herself – she said, 'I'm worried about why he doesn't want to do anything about it.' Before Brunetti could ask, she went on, 'What happened is illegal. Well, I assume it is. It's an invasion, in a way; a break-in. My husband told the computer man he would take care of it, but I know he's not going to do anything about it.'

'I'm still not sure I understand why you've come to talk to me,' Brunetti said. 'I can't do anything about it unless your husband makes a formal *denuncia*. And then a magistrate would have to examine the facts, the evidence, and see if a crime has taken place and, if so, what sort of crime, or how serious a crime.' He leaned forward and said, speaking as to a friend, 'And all of that would take some time, I'm afraid.'

'No, no,' she said, 'I don't want that to happen. If my husband doesn't want to pursue it, that's his decision. What I'm afraid of is why he doesn't want to.' Her glance was level when she said, 'And I thought I could ask you.' She did not explain further.

'If it's the Guardia di Finanza,' Brunetti began after some time, seeing no reason not to speak honestly, at least about this, 'then it would be about taxes, and that's another area where I have no competence.' At her nod, he went on, 'Only your husband and his accountants know about that.'

'Yes, I know,' she quickly agreed. 'I don't think there's anything to worry about there.'

That, Brunetti understood, could mean a number of things. Either her husband did not cheat on his taxes, which Brunetti was not prepared to believe, or his accountants were experts at making it appear that he did not, an altogether more likely explanation. Or, just as easily, given Cataldo's wealth and position, he knew someone in the Guardia di Finanza who could make any irregularities disappear. 'Can you think of another possibility?' he asked.

'It might be any number of things,' she said with a seriousness that Brunetti found troubling.

'Such as?' he inquired.

She waved his question away then reunited her hands, latching her fingers, and said, looking across at him. 'My husband is an honest man, Commissario.' She waited for him to comment, and when he did not, she repeated, 'Honest.' She gave Brunetti more time to comment, and still he did not. 'I know that sounds an unlikely thing to say about a man as successful as he is.' Suddenly, just as if Brunetti had voiced opposition, she said, 'It sounds like I'm talking about his business dealings, but I'm not. I don't know much about them, and I don't want to. That's his son's concern – his right – and I don't want to be involved. I can't speak of what he does in business. But I know him as a man, and I know he's honest.'

Brunetti listened, part of him making a list of men he himself knew to be honest men, all of them driven to dishonesty by the various depredations of the state. In a country where false bankruptcy was no longer a serious crime, it took little for a man to be considered honest.

'. . . he were a Roman, he would be considered an honourable man,' she concluded, and Brunetti had little difficulty in reconstructing the parts that his own thoughts had distracted him from hearing.

'Signora,' he began, deciding to try to establish a more formal tone, 'I'm still not sure I can be of any help to you here.' He smiled to show his good will, adding, 'It would help me immeasurably if you told me, specifically, what it is you're afraid of.'

She began, in a gesture he thought entirely unconscious, to rub the skin of her forehead with her right hand. She turned and looked out the window as she did it, and Brunetti, not without a twinge of discomfort, watched the trail of whitened skin that was left behind by each stroke. She surprised him by getting suddenly to her feet and going over to the window, then surprised him again by asking, without glancing back, 'That's San Lorenzo, isn't it?'

'Yes.'

She continued to gaze across the canal at the eternally unrestored church. Finally she said, 'He was put on the grill and roasted to death, wasn't he? They wanted him to renounce his faith, I believe.'

'So the story has it,' Brunetti answered.

She turned then and came back towards him, saying, 'So much suffering, these Christians. They really loved it,

115

couldn't have enough of it.' She sat and looked at him. 'I think that's one of the reasons I admire the Romans so much. They didn't like to suffer. They seem not to have minded dying, were really quite noble about it. But they didn't enjoy pain – at least if they had to suffer it themselves – not the way the Christians did.'

'Have you finished with Cicero and moved on to the Christian era, then?' he asked ironically, hoping to lighten her mood.

'No,' she said, 'the Christians really don't interest me. As I said, they like suffering too much.' She stopped talking and gave him a long, level look, and then said, 'At the moment, I'm reading Ovid's *Fasti*. I never did before, never saw the need.' Then, with special emphasis, as if the words were being forced from her and as if to suggest she thought Brunetti might want to go home and begin reading it, she added, 'Book Two. Everything's there.'

Brunetti smiled and said, 'It's been so long that I don't even remember if I've ever read it. You must forgive me.' It was the best he could think of to say.

'Oh, there's nothing to forgive, Commissario, in not having read it,' she said, her mouth hinting at a smile. Then, her voice suddenly different and her face returned to immobility, she added, 'Nothing to forgive in what's there, either.' Again, that long look. 'You might want to read it some time.'

Then, with no transition, as if this incursion into Roman culture had not taken place or she had seen his growing restlessness, she said, 'It's kidnapping that I'm afraid of.' She nodded a few times as if to confirm it as the truth. 'I know it's foolish, and I know Venice is a place where it never happens, but it's the only explanation I can come up with. Someone might have done it because they wanted to know how much Maurizio might be able to pay.'

'If you were kidnapped?'

116

Her surprise was completely unfeigned, 'Who'd want to kidnap me?' As if hearing herself, she hastened to add, 'I thought of his son, Matteo. He's the heir.' Then, with a shrug that Brunetti could describe only as self-effacing, she added, 'Even his ex-wife. She's very rich, and she has a villa out in the countryside near Treviso.'

Speaking lightly, Brunetti said, 'It sounds as if you've been thinking about this a great deal, Signora.'

'Of course I have. But I don't know what to think. I don't know anything about all of this: that's why I came to you, Commissario.'

'Because it's my line of work?' he asked, smiling.

If nothing else, his tone broke her mounting tension: she relaxed visibly. 'You could say that, I suppose,' she said with a small laugh. 'I suppose I needed someone I trust who can tell me I'm worrying about nothing.'

The plea was there: Brunetti could not have ignored it had he wanted to. Luckily, though, he had an answer to give her. 'Signora, as I told you, I'm not an expert on these things, certainly not on the way the Guardia di Finanza chooses to conduct its business. But I think in this case the correct answer to who's been trying to break in could also be the most obvious one, and the Finanza seems to be it.' Unable to bring himself to the lie direct, Brunetti could do no more than tell himself that it *could* be the Finanza.

'*La Finanza*?' she asked in the voice of every patient who has ever received the less-bad diagnosis.

'I think so. Yes. I don't know anything about your husband's businesses, but I'm sure they must be protected against anything except the most expert invasion.'

She shook her head and raised her shoulders in an admission of ignorance. Brunetti chose his words carefully. 'It's been my experience that kidnappers are not sophisticated people; much of what they do is impulsive.' He saw how attentively she was following what he said. 'The only people,' he continued, 'who could do something like this would have to have the technical skills to get past whatever barriers are in place at your husband's companies.' He smiled, then permitted himself a small ironic snort. 'I must confess this is the only time in my career I've ever been happy to suggest to someone they've been the target of an exam by the Finanza.'

'And the first time in the history of this country when someone's been relieved to hear it,' she finished, and this time she laughed. Her face took on the same mottled pattern Brunetti had seen when she first came in from the cold, and he realized she was blushing.

Signora Marinello got to her feet quickly, bent to retrieve her purse, then put out her hand. 'I don't know how to thank you, Commissario,' she said, keeping his hand in hers while she spoke.

'He's a lucky man, your husband,' Brunetti said.

'Why?' she asked, and he thought she meant it.

'To have someone so concerned about him.'

Most women would smile at a compliment like this, or feign false modesty. Instead she pulled back from him and gave him a level gaze that was almost fierce in its intensity. 'He's my *only* concern, Commissario.' She thanked him again, waited while he retrieved her things from the *armadio*, and left the room before Brunetti could move to the door to open it for her.

Brunetti took his normal seat behind his desk, resisting the temptation to phone Signorina Elettra and ask if her foray into the computers of Signor Cataldo's businesses could have been detected. To do so would require that he explain his curiosity, and that was something he preferred not to do. He had not lied: a search by the Finanza was far more likely than an attempt by some putative kidnapper to gain information about Cataldo's wealth. A search by the Finanza, however, was far less likely than the one he had asked Signorina Elettra to perform, but that was hardly information that would have comforted Signora Marinello. He had to find a way to warn Signorina Elettra that her deft hand had faltered while inside Cataldo's computer systems.

Though it made sense that a wife should be worried to learn that her husband's business interests were being tampered with, Brunetti thought her reaction had been excessive. Everything she had said to Brunetti that evening at dinner had revealed a sensible, intelligent woman: her response to her husband's information suggested a different person entirely.

After a while, Brunetti decided he was spending too much time and energy on something that was not related to any of his current cases. In order to make a clean break with it before getting back to work, he would go and have a coffee or perhaps *un'ombra* to clear his mind.

Sergio saw him come in and, instead of his usual smile, narrowed his eyes and moved his chin minimally to the right, in the direction of the booths near the window. In the last one, Brunetti made out the back of a man's head; narrow skull, short hair. The angle was such that he could see, opposite the first man and facing him, the halo of another man's head; wider, with longer hair. He recognized those ears, pressed down and out by years spent under a policeman's cap. Alvise: and that identified the back of Lieutenant Scarpa's head. Ah, so much for the idea that Alvise would return to the flock and mingle again as an equal with his fellow officers.

Approaching the bar, Brunetti gave Sergio an equally minimal nod and asked quietly for a coffee. Something in Alvise's expression must have alerted Scarpa, who turned and saw Brunetti. Scarpa's face remained impassive, but Brunetti saw that Alvise's face was crossed by something stronger than surprise – guilt, perhaps? The machine hissed, then a cup and saucer rattled and slid across the zinc bar.

None of them spoke; Brunetti nodded at the two men,

turned back to the bar and ripped open a packet of sugar. He poured it into his coffee and stirred it around slowly, asked Sergio for the newspaper, and spread the *Il Gazzettino* on the counter beside him. He decided to wait them out and settled in to read.

He glanced at the first page, where the world outside Venice was referred to, then skipped over to page seven, lacking the mental energy – and the stomach – to endure the five pages of political chatter; one could hardly call it news. The same faces had been appearing and the same things happening, the same promises made – with a few minimal variations in cast and title – for the last forty years. The lapels of their jackets expanded and narrowed as fashion dictated, but those same front trotters remained in the trough. They opposed this, and they opposed that, and by their selfless efforts they vowed to bring the current government crashing down. So that what? So that, next year, he could stand at the bar and drink a coffee and read the same words, now in the mouths of the new opposition?

It was almost with relief that he turned the page. The woman convicted of infanticide, still at home, still crying out her innocence through the mouths of yet another legal team. And who now responsible in her mind for the murder of her son – extraterrestrials? More flowers placed at the curve in the road where four more teenagers had died a week before. Yet more uncollected garbage filling the streets in the suburbs of Naples. Another worker crushed to death by heavy equipment at his workplace. Another judge transferred away from the city where he had begun an investigation of a cabinet minister.

Brunetti slid the Venezia section out from under the first. A fisherman from Chioggia, arrested for assault after coming home drunk and attacking a neighbour with a knife. Yet more protests against the damage done by the cruise ships using the Giudecca Canal. Two more vendors going out of business at the fish market. Another five-star hotel to open next week. The mayor denounces the increased number of tourists.

Brunetti pointed down to the last two articles. 'Lovely: the city administration can't give out licences for hotels fast enough, and when they're not busy with that, they're denouncing the number of tourists,' he said to Sergio.

'*Vottá á petrella, e tirá á manella*,' Sergio said, looking up from the glass he was drying.

'What's that, Neapolitan?' asked a surprised Brunetti.

'Yes,' Sergio answered, and translated: 'Throw the stone, then hide the hand.'

Brunetti laughed out loud, then said, 'I don't know why one of these new political parties doesn't take that as its motto. It's perfect: you do it, then you hide the evidence that you did it. Wonderful.' He continued to laugh, something in the honesty of the phrase having touched him with delight.

He sensed motion on his left, then heard the men's feet as they pushed themselves out of the benches. He turned the page, allowing his attention to be caught by the news of the farewell party given at Giacinto Gallina for a third-grade teacher who was leaving after teaching forty years in the same school.

'Good morning, Commissario,' Alvise said in a small voice from behind him.

'Morning, Alvise,' Brunetti said, tearing his eyes away from the photo of the party and turning to greet the officer.

Scarpa, as if to emphasize the equality resulting from their superior rank, limited himself to a curt nod, which Brunetti returned before turning his attention back to the party. The children had brought flowers and home-baked cookies.

When the two were gone, Brunetti folded closed the paper and asked, 'They come in here often?'

'Couple of times a week, I'd say.'

'Always like that?' Brunetti asked, gesturing towards the two men walking side by side back towards the Questura.

121

'Like it's their first date, you mean?' Sergio asked, turning to place the glass carefully upside down on the counter behind him.

'Something like that.'

'Been that way for about six months. In the beginning, the Lieutenant was sort of stand-offish and made poor Alvise work hard to please him.' Sergio picked up another glass, held it up to the light to check for spots, and began to wipe it dry. 'Poor fool, couldn't see what Scarpa was doing.' Then he interjected, conversationally, 'Real bastard, that one is.'

Brunetti pushed his cup closer to the barman, who took it and placed it in the sink.

'You have any idea what they talk about?' Brunetti asked.

'I don't think it matters. Not really.'

'Why?'

'All Scarpa wants is power. He wants poor Alvise to jump when he says "frog" and smile whenever he says something he thinks is funny.'

'Why?'

Sergio's shrug was eloquent. 'As I said, because he's a bastard. And because he needs someone to push around and someone who will treat him like a big shot important Lieutenant, not like the rest of you, who have the sense to treat him like the nasty little shit he is.'

At no time in this conversation did it occur to Brunetti that he was inciting a civilian to speak badly of a member of the forces of order. If truth be told, he thought Scarpa a nasty little shit, too, so the civilian was merely reinforcing the received wisdom of the forces of order themselves.

Changing the subject, Brunetti asked, 'Anyone call me yesterday?'

Sergio shook his head. 'Only person who called here yesterday was my wife, telling me that if I didn't get home by ten, there'd be trouble, and my accountant, telling me I was already in trouble.'

122

'With?'

'With the health inspector.'

'Why?'

'Because I don't have a bathroom for handicapped people. I mean people with different abilities.' He rinsed the cup and saucer and slipped them into the dishwasher behind him.

'I've never seen a handicapped person in here,' Brunetti said.

'Neither have I. Neither has the health inspector. Doesn't change the rule that says I've got to have a toilet for them.'

'Which means?'

'Handrail. Different seat, button on the wall to make it flush.'

'Why don't you?'

'Because it will cost me eight thousand Euros to get it changed, that's why.'

'That sounds like an awful lot of money.'

'It includes permissions,' Sergio said elliptically.

Brunetti chose not to follow that up and said only, 'I hope you can stay out of trouble.' He put a Euro on the counter, thanked Sergio, and went back to his office.

14

Griffoni was just coming out of the Questura as Brunetti approached. Seeing her, he gave a friendly wave and quickened his pace. But by the time he reached her, he had seen that something was wrong. 'What is it?'

'Patta's looking for you. He called down and asked where you were. He said he couldn't find Vianello, so he told me to find you.'

'What's the matter?'

'He won't tell me.'

'How is he?'

'Worse than I've ever heard him.'

'Angry?'

'No, not angry, not really,' she answered, as if surprised at the realization. 'Well, sort of, but it's as if he knows he's not allowed to be angry. It's more like he's frightened.'

Brunetti started towards the door of the Questura, Griffoni falling into step beside him. There was nothing he could think of to ask her. Patta was far more dangerous frightened than angry, and they both knew it. Anger usually rose from other people's incompetence, while it was only the thought that he might himself be at risk that brought Patta close to fear, and that heightened the risk for anyone else who might be involved.

Inside, they went up the first ramp of steps together, and Brunetti asked, 'Does he want to see you, too?'

Griffoni shook her head and, with a look of undisguised relief, went to her office, leaving Brunetti to turn towards Patta's.

There was no sign of Signorina Elettra, probably already at lunch, so Brunetti knocked on the door and went in.

A sober-faced Patta sat at his desk, hands clenched into fists on the desk in front of him. 'Where were you?' he demanded.

'Questioning a witness, sir,' Brunetti lied. 'Commissario Griffoni told me you wanted to see me. What is it?' He balanced concern and urgency in his voice.

'Sit down, sit down. Don't stand there gaping at me,' Patta said.

Brunetti took his place directly in front of the Vice-Questore but said nothing.

'I've had a call,' Patta began. He glanced at Brunetti, who did his best to produce a look of eager attention, then went on, 'About that man who was here the other day.'

'Do you mean *Maggior* Guarino, sir?'

'Yes. Guarino. Whatever he called himself.' Patta's voice had grown more strident after he said the name, Guarino the source of his anger. 'Stupid bastard,' Patta muttered, surprising Brunetti by his unaccustomed use of bad language, but not making it clear whether he was referring to Guarino or the person who had called about him.

Guarino had perhaps not been telling the complete truth, but he was by no means stupid, nor did Brunetti think he was a bastard. But Brunetti made no mention of these judgements and asked, voice level, 'What's happened, sir?'

'He's got himself killed: that's what's happened. Shot in the back of the head,' Patta said with no diminution of his anger, though it seemed now to be aimed at Guarino for having been killed. Murdered.

Possibilities clamoured for attention, but Brunetti pushed them away, waiting for Patta to explain. He kept the same intent expression on his face and his eyes on Patta. The Vice-Questore raised a fist and slammed it on the surface of his desk. 'Some captain from the Carabinieri called this morning. He wanted to know if I'd had a visitor last week. He was very cagey, didn't name the visitor, just asked if I'd had a visit from an official from out of town.' Petulance replaced anger in his face and voice as Patta said, 'I told him I have lots of visitors. How did he expect me to remember them all?'

Brunetti had no answer and Patta continued. 'At first I didn't know what he was talking about. But I had a suspicion he meant Guarino. It's not like I have a lot of visitors, is it?' Seeing Brunetti's confusion at this contradiction, Patta deigned to clarify. 'He was the only person who came last week that I didn't know. Had to be him.'

The Vice-Questore pushed himself suddenly to his feet, took a step away from his desk, then turned and sat down again. 'He asked if he could send me a photo.' Brunetti had no need to feign confusion. 'Imagine that,' Patta went on. 'They'd taken it with a *telefonino* and he sent it to me. As if he expected me to recognize him from what was left of his face.'

This last phrase stunned Brunetti; it was not until some moments had passed that he was able to ask, 'And did you?'

'Yes. Of course. The bullet went in at an angle, so only the chin was damaged. I could still recognize him.'

'How was he killed?' Brunetti asked.

'I just told you,' Patta said in a loud voice. 'Weren't you paying attention? He was shot. In the back of the head. That's enough to kill most people, wouldn't you think?'

Brunetti raised a hand. 'Perhaps I didn't express myself

clearly, sir. Did this man who called tell you anything about the circumstances?'

'Nothing. All he wanted was for me to say whether I recognized him or not.'

'What did you say?'

'That I wasn't sure,' Patta answered and gave Brunetti a sharp look.

Brunetti bridled the impulse to ask his superior why he had done that.

Patta followed on by saying, 'I didn't want to give them anything until I knew more.' It took Brunetti very little time to translate this from Patta-speak into Italian: it meant that Patta wanted to pass the responsibility on to someone else. Hence this conversation.

'Did he tell you why he called you?' Brunetti asked.

'It seems they knew he had an appointment at the Questura in Venice, so they called and asked to talk to the person in charge to see if he had come here.' Indeed, Brunetti reflected, even a bullet through a man's skull could not prevent Patta from that little burst of pride: 'the person in charge'.

'When did he call, sir?' Brunetti asked.

'Half an hour ago.' With no attempt to disguise his irritation, Patta added, 'I've been trying to locate you since then. But you weren't in your office.' As if to himself, Patta muttered, 'Questioning a witness.'

Ignoring this, Brunetti asked, 'When did it happen?'

'He didn't say,' Patta answered vaguely, as if he saw no reason why the question mattered.

By force of will, Brunetti removed all trace of interest from his expression while he allowed his mind to lunge ahead. 'Did he say where he was calling from?'

'From there,' Patta answered in the voice he used for addressing the weak of mind and character. 'Where they found him.'

'Ah,' Brunetti said, 'so that's when he sent you the photo.'

'Very clever, Brunetti,' Patta snapped. 'Of course that's when he sent me the photo.'

'I see, I see,' Brunetti said, stalling for time.

'I've called the Lieutenant,' Patta said, and again Brunetti washed all expression from his face. 'But he's in Chioggia and can't get there until the afternoon.'

Brunetti felt his heart tighten at the thought that Patta wanted to involve Scarpa in this. 'Excellent idea,' he said, then allowed a bit of enthusiasm to drain from his voice as he added, 'I just hope the . . .' He dragged his voice to a stop, then repeated, 'Excellent idea.'

'What don't you like about it, Brunetti?' Patta demanded.

Brunetti this time plastered confusion across his face and did not answer.

'Tell me, Brunetti,' Patta said, his voice slipping towards menace.

'It's really a question of rank, sir,' Brunetti said hesitantly, speaking only to keep the bamboo shoots from being stuck under his fingernails. Before Patta could inquire, he explained. 'You said the man who called was a captain. My only concern is how it's going to look if we're represented by a person of lower rank.' He studied Patta's body and saw the first tightening of the muscles.

'It's not that I have doubts about the Lieutenant,' he said. 'But we've had jurisdictional trouble with the Carabinieri before, and sending a person of superior rank would eliminate the possibility of that.'

Patta's eyes were suddenly hooded with mistrust. 'Who are you talking about, Brunetti?'

Looking as surprised as he could manage, Brunetti said, 'Why, you, sir. Of course. You should be the person to represent us, sir. After all, as you said yourself, Vice-Questore, you're the person in charge here.' Though this

128

rendered the Questore irrelevant, Brunetti doubted that Patta would notice.

Patta's glance was fierce, filled with unvoiced suspicions, probably ones that Patta did not realize he felt. 'I hadn't thought of that,' he said.

Brunetti shrugged, as if to suggest it would have been only a matter of time before he had done so. Patta bestowed his most serious look on Brunetti, then asked, 'You think it's important, then?'

'That you go, sir?' asked an alert Brunetti.

'That someone who outranks a captain should go.'

'You certainly do, sir, and by a great degree.'

'I wasn't thinking about me, Brunetti,' Patta snapped.

Brunetti made no attempt to disguise his inability to understand and said, fresh-faced, 'But you have to go, Dottore.' Brunetti suspected that a case of this nature was bound to gather national attention, but this was not something he wanted Patta to realize.

'You think this investigation will drag on?' Patta asked.

Brunetti allowed himself to measure out the tiniest of shrugs. 'I have no way of knowing that, sir, but these cases sometimes tend to.' Brunetti, as he spoke, had no idea what he meant by 'these cases', but the prospect of sustained effort would suffice to discourage Patta.

Patta leaned forward and put a smile on his face. 'I think, Brunetti, since you were the person who liaised with him, that you should be the one to represent us.'

Brunetti was trying to find the proper tone of moderate resistance when Patta said, 'He was killed in Marghera, Brunetti. That's in our territory, so it's our jurisdiction. It's the sort of call a commissario would answer, so it makes complete sense for you to go out there and have a look.'

Brunetti started to protest, but Patta cut him short: 'Take that Griffoni woman along with you. That way there will be two commissari.' Patta smiled with grim satisfaction, as though he had just come up with a clever move in chess. Or draughts. 'I want the two of you to go there and see what you can find out.'

Brunetti got to his feet, doing his best to appear disgruntled and unwilling. 'All right, Vice-Questore, but I don't think . . .'

'What you think isn't important, Commissario. I told you I want the two of you out there. And while you're there, it's your duty to show this captain who's in charge.'

Good sense intervened and prevented Brunetti from overplaying the role of bumbling reluctance: at times even Patta was capable of noticing the obvious. 'All right,' he limited himself to saying. All business now, he asked, 'Where exactly was this man calling from, sir?'

'He said he was at the petrochemical complex in Marghera. I'll give you his number, and you can call him and ask where exactly,' Patta said. He picked up his *telefonino*, which Brunetti had failed to notice resting just beside his desk calendar. He flipped it open with negligent ease. Patta, of course, had the most recent slim-line model. The Vice-Questore refused to use the BlackBerry he had been issued by the Ministry of the Interior, saying he did not want to become a techno-slave, though Brunetti suspected he rather feared its effect on the line of his jackets.

Patta pressed buttons then suddenly held the phone out to Brunetti, saying nothing. Guarino's face filled the tiny screen. His deep-set eyes were open, though he was glancing off to the side as if embarrassed that someone would see him lying like this, so inattentive to life. As Patta had said, the chin was damaged, though destroyed might have been a better word. There was no mistaking the thin face and the greying temples. His hair would never grow grey now, Brunetti found himself thinking, and he would never get to call Signorina Elettra, if that had been his intention.

'Well?' Patta asked, and Brunetti almost shouted at him, so

unnecessary was the question, so easily recognizable the dead man.

'I'd say it's he,' Brunetti limited himself to saying, flipped the phone closed, and handed it back to Patta. Long moments passed, during which time Brunetti watched Patta wash everything save affability and the selfless desire for co-operation from his face. As soon as Patta began to speak, Brunetti realized that the same transformation had taken place in Patta's voice. 'I've decided it might be wiser to tell them he was here.'

Like an Olympic relay racer, Brunetti did his best to sprint up to the man in front of him, reach his hand forward while they were both running full tilt, and pluck the stick from him, allowing the other runner to slow down and eventually drop out of the race.

For a moment, Brunetti feared that Patta was going to press the call-back number and pass the phone to him: he would not trust himself if Patta did. Perhaps Patta saw this. Whatever did happen, Patta opened the phone again. He pulled a sheet of paper towards him, wrote down the caller's number and slid the paper across the desk to Brunetti. 'I don't remember his name, but he's a captain.'

Brunetti took the paper and read it a few times. When it was obvious that the Vice-Questore had nothing further to contribute, Brunetti got up and moved towards the door, saying, 'I'll call him.'

'Good. Keep me posted,' Patta said, his voice filled with the relief that came from so artfully having passed it all to Brunetti.

Upstairs, he dialled the number. After only two rings, a man's voice answered, '*Sì?*'

'I'm returning your call to Vice-Questore Patta,' Brunetti said neutrally, having decided to use the weight of Patta's rank for whatever it was worth. 'Someone called from this number and spoke to the Vice-Questore, then sent a photo.' He paused but there was no expression of acknowledgement or curiosity from the other end. 'Vice-Questore Patta has shown me the photo of what appears to be a dead man, and from what the Vice-Questore has told me, he was killed in our territory,' Brunetti went on in his most officious voice. 'The Vice-Questore has tasked me to go out there and then report to him.'

'There's no need for that,' the other man said coolly.

'I disagree,' Brunetti answered with matching coolness, 'that's why I'm coming.'

Doing his best to sound like someone who was trying only to do his job, the other man said, 'We've got a positive identification. We recognize the man as a colleague involved in one of our ongoing cases.'

As if the other man had not spoken, Brunetti said, 'If you tell me where you are, we'll come out.'

'That's not necessary. I told you, the body's already been identified.' He waited a moment then added, 'I'm afraid the case is ours.'

'And who are we?' Brunetti asked.

'The Carabinieri, Commissario. Guarino was with Nas, which I think doubles our authority to investigate.'

Brunetti said only, 'I can certainly discuss it with a magistrate here.'

Stalemate.

Brunetti waited, sure that the other was doing the same thing. He reflected that waiting was what he had done with Guarino, what he had done with Patta, what he spent too much time doing.

Still no sound from the other end of the line. Brunetti broke the connection. Of course, Guarino would have to have been with the Nas, and how could anyone keep all of these acronyms straight? The Nuclei Anti-Sofisticazione section of the Carabinieri was supposed to see that environmental laws were enforced. Brunetti's thoughts turned to the images of the garbage-filled streets of Naples, but they were pushed aside by the memory of the photo of Guarino.

He dialled Vianello's number, but the officer who answered said the Inspector had gone out. Brunetti tried his *telefonino*, but it was turned off and not receiving messages. He called Griffoni and told her they were to go out to the scene of a murder in Marghera and that he would explain on the way. Downstairs, he went into Signorina Elettra's office.

'Yes, Commissario?' she asked.

It didn't seem the right time to tell her about Guarino, but then there was never a right time to tell people that someone had died.

'I've just had some bad news, Signorina,' he said.

Her smile grew more tentative.

'Vice-Questore Patta had a phone call this morning,' he began. Brunetti watched her response to his use of Patta's title: it was enough to warn her that whatever she was going to hear might be something she would not like. 'A captain from the Carabinieri told him that the man who came here earlier this week, *Maggior* Guarino, has been killed. Shot.'

She closed her eyes for a moment, long enough to hide whatever emotion this caused her but not long enough to hide the fact that she felt something.

Before she could ask anything, he went on. 'They sent a photo, and they wanted to know if he had been here to talk to us.'

'It really is?' she asked.

'Yes.' Truth was mercy.

'I'm very sorry,' was all she could find to say.

'So am I. He seemed like a decent man, and Avisani vouched for him.'

'You needed someone to vouch for him?' she asked in a voice that seemed to be seeking an outlet for anger.

'If I was going to trust him, yes. I had no idea what he was involved in or what he wanted.' Perhaps irritated by her manner, he added, 'I still don't.'

'What does that mean?'

'It means that I don't know whether the story he told me is true or not, and that means I don't know why the man who called is interested in knowing why the *Maggiore* came here in the first place.'

'But he's dead?'

'Yes.'

'Thank you for telling me.'

Brunetti went to meet Griffoni.

15

The shipbuilding works and the petrochemical and other factories littering the landscape of Marghera had exercised a fascination over Brunetti's imagination ever since he was a boy. For a period of about two years, from when he was six until a bit after his eighth birthday, his father had worked as a warehouseman for a factory producing paint and solvents. Brunetti recalled it as one of the quietest and happiest times of his childhood, with his father steadily employed and proud to maintain his family with what he earned.

But then had come the strikes, after which his father had not been taken back. Things changed then and peace fled from their home, but for some years his father kept in contact with some of his fellow workers from the factory. Brunetti could still remember these men and their stories of work and each other, their rough good humour, their jokes, and their endless patience with his volatile father. Cancer had taken them all, as it had, over the years, taken so many of the people who worked in the other factories that sprang up on the edge of the *laguna*, with its welcoming and oh-so-unprotected waters.

Brunetti had not been to the industrial area for years, though the plumes from its smokestacks formed an eternal backdrop for anyone arriving in the city by boat, and the highest plumes of smoke could sometimes be seen from Brunetti's terrace. He was always struck by their whiteness, especially at night, when the smoke swirled so beautifully against the velvet sky. It looked so very harmless, so pure, and never failed to make Brunetti think of snow, first communion dresses, brides. Bones.

Over the years, all efforts to shut down the factories had met with failure, often with the violent protests of the men whose lives might have been saved, or at least prolonged, by their closure. If a man cannot provide for his family, is he any longer a man? Brunetti's father had thought not; Brunetti could understand only now why he thought that way.

As they climbed into the car waiting for them at Piazzale Roma, Brunetti began to explain to Griffoni his phone call from Guarino and the call that was taking them out to Marghera. They crossed the causeway in a series of manoeuvres that made sense only to the driver, then doubled back towards the factories; by the time they pulled up at the main gates, Brunetti had filled her in on almost everything.

A uniformed man stepped out of a small guardhouse to the left of the gate and raised a hand to wave them through, as if familiar with the sight of police cars. Brunetti had the driver stop and ask where the others were. The guard pointed off to his left, told him to go straight ahead, over three bridges, then turn to the right after a red building. From there, they would see the other cars.

Their driver followed the directions, and as they turned at the red building, which stood isolated at a crossroads, they did indeed see a number of vehicles, including an ambulance with flashing lights; beyond the vehicles was a group of people facing the other way. The paving on the road ahead of them was broken and uneven; beyond the parked vehicles Brunetti saw four enormous metal oil-storage tanks, two on each side of the road. Their walls were gnawed through in places by rust; a square had been cut out near the top of one of them and the metal peeled back, creating a window or door. The land around them was desolate and littered with papers and plastic bags. Nothing grew.

The driver pulled up not far from the ambulance; Brunetti and Griffoni got out. Those heads that had not turned at the sound of the engine turned when the doors slammed shut.

Brunetti recognized one of them as a Carabiniere he had worked with some years before, though he had been a lieutenant then. Rubini? Rosato? Finally it came – Ribasso, and then he realized that his must have been the voice he had failed to recognize on the phone.

Beside Ribasso stood another man in the same uniform and two men and a woman whose white paper suits defined them as the crime squad. Two attendants stood beside the ambulance, a rolled-up stretcher propped beside them. Both were smoking. All of them had by now turned to watch Brunetti and Griffoni approach.

Ribasso stepped forward and extended his hand to Brunetti, saying, 'I thought it was you on the phone, but I wasn't sure.' He smiled but said nothing further about the call.

'Maybe I'm watching too many programmes about tough cops on television,' Brunetti, who was not, said by way of explanation or apology. Ribasso patted him on the shoulder and turned to say hello to Griffoni, addressing her by name. The others took their cue from Ribasso's manner and nodded at the newcomers, then shifted around and opened up a space large enough for Brunetti and Griffoni to join them.

About three metres away, the body of a man lay on his back at the centre of a space marked off by red and white plastic tape attached to a series of thin metal poles. Without the photo he had already seen, Brunetti might not have recognized Guarino from this distance. Part of his jaw was missing, and what remained of his face was turned away. His coat was dark, so no blood could be seen on it or on the lapels of his jacket. His shirt, however, was a different matter.

Small patches of mud had dried on the knees of his trousers and the right shoulder of his coat, and some strands of what looked like plastic fibre were stuck to the sole of his right shoe. Footsteps had churned up whorls in the frosty mud around the body, cancelling one another out.

'He's on his back,' was the first thing Brunetti said.

'Exactly,' Ribasso answered.

'So where was he moved from?' Brunetti asked.

'I don't know,' Ribasso said, then, failing to disguise his anger, 'The idiots were all over the place before they called us.'

'Which idiots?' Griffoni asked.

'The ones who found him,' Ribasso said, giving in to his anger. 'Two men in a truck who were making a delivery of copper tubing. They got lost, turned into the road up there,' he said, waving back the way Brunetti and Griffoni had come. 'They were about to turn around, but they saw him on the ground and came down to have a look.'

Brunetti could read some of what must have followed from the mass of footprints in the mud around the body and the two breast-like impressions left when one of them knelt beside the dead man.

'Is it possible they turned him over?' Griffoni asked, though it sounded as if she hardly believed it.

'They said they didn't,' was the best answer Ribasso could give. 'And it doesn't look as though they did, though they certainly walked around enough to destroy any evidence.'

'Did they touch him?' Brunetti asked.

138

'They said they couldn't remember.' Ribasso's disgust was audible. 'But when they called, they said there was a dead Carabiniere, so they must have taken out his wallet.'

In the face of this, nothing could be said.

'Did you know him?' Brunetti asked.

'Yes,' Ribasso said. 'In fact, I'm the one who told him to go and talk to you.'

'About that man he wanted to find?'

'Yes.' Then, after a pause, 'I thought you'd help him.'

'I tried to.' Brunetti turned away from the dead man.

The woman, who seemed to be in charge of the scene of crime team, called to Ribasso, who went over and had a word with her. He then signalled to the attendants and told them they could take the body to the morgue at the hospital.

The two men tossed their cigarettes to the ground, adding them to the ones lying there. As Brunetti watched, they took the stretcher over to the dead man and lifted him on to it. Everyone stepped aside to allow them to carry him to the ambulance, where they slid the stretcher into the back. The sound of the slamming doors broke the spell that had rendered them all silent.

Ribasso stepped aside and spoke to the other Carabiniere, who went over to the car, propped himself up against the side, and pulled out a packet of cigarettes. The three technicians stripped off their paper suits, rolled them up and put them in a plastic bag, which they tossed into the back of their van. They collapsed their tripod and stashed the cameras in a padded metal case. There was a great slamming of doors and sound of engines, and then the ambulance drove off, followed by the technicians.

Into the expanding silence, Brunetti asked, 'Why did you call Patta?'

Ribasso's answer was preceded by an exasperated grunt. 'I've dealt with him before.' He looked back at the place where Guarino had been, then at Brunetti. 'It was best to do it officially from the beginning. Besides, I knew he'd pass it on, maybe to someone we could work with.'

Brunetti nodded. 'What did Guarino tell you?'

'That you'd try to identify the man in the photo.'

'Is this your case, too?'

'More or less,' Ribasso said.

'Pietro,' Brunetti said, taking advantage of the familiarity that had been formed between them the last time. 'Guarino – may he rest in peace – tried that with me.'

'And you threatened to throw him out of your office,' Ribasso said. 'He told me.'

'So don't start,' said a relentless Brunetti.

Griffoni's head turned back and forth as the two men spoke.

'All right,' Ribasso said. 'I said more or less because he talked with me as a friend about it.'

This seemed all Ribasso was prepared to say, so Brunetti prodded him by asking, 'You said he was working for Nas?' So that explained Guarino's interest in the transport of garbage: Nas handled everything that had to do with pollution or the destruction of the physical heritage of the country. Brunetti had long considered the location of their office in Marghera, source of generations of pollution, an ironic, not an accidental, choice.

Ribasso nodded. 'Filippo studied biochemistry: I think he joined that branch because he wanted to do something useful. Maybe important. They were glad to get him.'

'How long ago was that?'

'Eight, nine years. Maybe. I've known him only for the last five or six.' Then, before Brunetti could ask, Ribasso added, 'We never worked on a case together.'

'Not this one?' Griffoni asked.

Ribasso shifted his weight from one foot to another. 'I told you, he would talk to me.'

'What else did he tell you?' Brunetti asked. Quickly,

Griffoni broke in to add, 'It can't make any difference to him now.'

Ribasso took a few steps towards his car. He turned back to face them. 'He told me the whole thing stank of Camorra. The man who got killed – Ranzato – he was only one of the people mixed up in it. Filippo was trying to find out how all this stuff got moved around.'

'How much are we talking about?' Griffoni broke in to ask. 'Tons?'

'Hundreds of tons, I'd say,' Brunetti added.

'Hundreds of thousands of tons is closer to the truth,' Ribasso said, silencing them both.

Brunetti attempted to do the numbers, but he had no idea what weight a truck could carry and so could not do even the most basic calculation. His mind flashed to his children, for it was they and their children who would inherit the contents of those trucks.

Ribasso, as if chastened by his own words, prodded at the frosted mud with the tip of his boot, then looked at them and said, 'Someone tried to drive him off the road a week ago.'

'He didn't tell me that,' Brunetti said. 'What happened?'

'He avoided them. They pulled up level with him – this was out on the autostrada coming down from Treviso – and when they started to move towards him, he slammed on his brakes and pulled over and stopped. They kept going.'

'Did you believe him?'

Ribasso shrugged and turned back to the place where Guarino's body had been. 'Someone got him.'

Brunetti and Griffoni rode back to Piazzale Roma in relative silence, both of them burdened by the sight of death and chilled by their long exposure to the cold and waste of Marghera. Griffoni asked Brunetti why he had failed to tell Ribasso he had identified the man in the photo Guarino had sent him, and Brunetti explained that the Captain, who must

141

surely have known about it, had not considered it necessary to tell him anything. No stranger to the rivalry that existed between the different branches of the forces of order, she said no more.

Brunetti had called ahead, and there was a launch waiting to take them to the Questura. But even inside the warm cabin of the boat, and with the heater turned on high, they did not grow warm.

Inside his office, he stood by the radiator, reluctant to call Avisani and justifying the delay until he felt warm again. Finally he went to his desk, found the number, and dialled it.

'It's me,' he said, striving to sound natural.

'What's wrong?'

'The worst,' Brunetti said, immediately embarrassed by the melodrama.

'Filippo?' Avisani asked.

'I'm just back from seeing his body,' Brunetti said. No questions came. Into the silence, he said, 'He was shot. They found him this morning at the petrochemical complex in Marghera.'

After a long pause, Avisani said, 'He always said it was a possibility. But I didn't believe him. I mean, who could? But . . . it's different. When it happens. Like this.'

'Did he tell you anything else?'

'I'm a journalist, remember,' came the immediate reply, just short of anger.

'I thought you were his friend.'

'Yes. Yes.' Then, in a more sober voice, Avisani said, 'It was the usual thing, Guido: the more he found out, the more obstacles he encountered. The magistrate in charge of the case was transferred, and the new one didn't seem very interested. Then two of his best assistants were transferred. You know what it's like.'

Yes, Brunetti thought, he did know what it was like. 'Anything else?' he asked.

142

'No, just that. It was nothing I could use: I've heard it too many times.' The line went dead.

Like many people involved in police work, Brunetti had long ago realized that the tentacles of the various mafias penetrated deep into every aspect of life, including most public institutions and many businesses. It would be impossible to count the number of policemen and magistrates who had found themselves transferred to some provincial dead end just at the point when their investigations began to uncover embarrassing links to the government. No matter how people tried to ignore it, the evidence of the depth and breadth of penetration was overwhelming. Had the newspapers not recently proclaimed the mafias, with 93 billion Euros in yearly earnings, the third largest enterprise in the country?

Brunetti had observed the Mafia and its close relatives, the N'Dragheta and the Camorra, grow ever more powerful, moving from the dark corners of his investigations until they were now the Prime Mover in the universe of crime. Like that French nobleman in the book he had read as a boy – *The Scarlet Pimpernel*. He tried to recall the poem describing those who tried to find and destroy him: 'They seek him here, They seek him there, Those Frenchies seek him everywhere.'

Or was the Lernean Hydra a better image, impossible to destroy because of its many heads? He remembered the joyous feeding frenzy of the press after the arrests of Riina, Provenzano, Lo Piccolo, the suggestion endlessly repeated that finally the government had been triumphant in its long battle against organized crime. As if the death of the president of General Motors or British Petroleum would bring those monoliths to their knees. Had no one ever heard of vice-presidents?

If anything, the arrests of those dinosaurs would give opportunities for younger men, university-trained men, better able to direct their organizations like the multinational

143

corporations they had become. And, he could never forget, the arrests of two of those men had taken place at about the same time as the *indulto*, that beneficent wave of the legal wand that had set free more than 24,000 criminals, many of them the foot soldiers of the Mafia. Ah, how accommodating the law could be, when it was in the hands of those who best knew how to use it.

16

Brunetti decided it would be better to talk to Patta about Guarino, but when he arrived at the Questura, the guard at the entrance told him the Vice-Questore had left an hour before. Relieved, he went up to his office and called Vianello to ask him to come up. When the Inspector arrived, Brunetti told him about going out to Marghera and seeing Guarino, lying dead on his back in the field.

'Where had they moved him from?' Vianello asked immediately.

'There's no way of knowing. The men who found him walked around him as if they were at a picnic.'

'Convenient,' Vianello observed.

'Before you begin with conspiracy theories,' Brunetti – who had already begun to do so – said, but Vianello cut him short.

'You trust this Ribasso?'

'I think so, yes.'

'Then not telling him you put a name to the man in the photo Guarino sent you doesn't make any sense.'

'Habit.'

'Habit?'

'Or territoriality,' Brunetti compromised.

'Lot of that around,' Vianello observed, then added, 'Nadia says it's because of the goats.'

'What goats? What are you talking about?'

'Well, inheritance, really, who we leave the goats to or who gets them after we die.' Had Vianello suddenly taken leave of his senses, or was Nadia using the garden behind their apartment for something other than flowers?

'I think you better tell me in a way I can understand, Lorenzo,' he said, welcoming the diversion.

'You know Nadia reads, don't you?'

'Yes,' he said, and the verb forced his thoughts to another woman who read.

'Well, she's been reading an introduction to anthropology, or something like that. Sociology, maybe. She talks about it at dinner.'

'Talks about what?'

'Lately she's been reading about inheritance rules and behaviour, as I said. Anyway, there's this theory about why men are so aggressive and competitive – about why so many of us are bastards. She says it's because we want to have access to the most fertile females.'

Brunetti propped his elbows on his desk and sank his head in his hands, moaning. He had wanted diversion, but not this.

'All right, all right. But you needed the introduction,' Vianello protested. 'Once they get the most fertile females, they impregnate them, and that way they're sure that the children who inherit the goats are really their own.' Vianello looked across the desk to see if Brunetti was following, but he still had his head buried in his hands. 'It made sense to me when she explained it, Guido. We all want our stuff to go to our kids, not to some cuckoo.'

Brunetti's continuing silence – at least he had stopped

146

moaning – forced Vianello to add, 'So that's why men compete. Evolution's programmed it into us.'

'Because of the goats?' Brunetti raised his head to ask.

'Yes.'

'Do you mind if we talk about this some other time?'

'As you will.'

Their light-heartedness seemed suddenly out of tune to Brunetti, who looked at the papers on his desk, at a loss what to say. Vianello got to his feet, said something about having to talk to Pucetti, and left. Brunetti continued to look at the papers.

His phone rang. It was Paola, reminding him that she had to attend the farewell dinner for a retiring colleague that evening and that the kids were attending a horror film festival and would not be there for dinner, either. Before he could ask, she told him she'd leave him something in the oven.

He thanked her, then asked, remembering the Conte's request and his failure to pursue it, 'Did your father say anything about Cataldo?'

'The last time I spoke to my mother, she said she thought he was going to turn him down, but she didn't know why.' Then she added, 'You know my father enjoys talking to you, so pretend you're his concerned son-in-law and call him and ask. Please, Guido.'

'I *am* his concerned son-in-law,' Brunetti found himself protesting.

'Guido,' she said, with a long pause after his name. 'You know you never take any interest – or at least you never voice any interest – in his business dealings. I'm sure he'd be glad to hear you finally doing so.'

Brunetti's position vis-à-vis his father-in-law's business dealings was an uneasy one. Because Brunetti's own children would some day inherit the Falier fortune, any display of curiosity on Brunetti's part, no matter how innocent, was open to the interpretation of self-interest: even the idea caused Brunetti a certain embarrassment.

Asking about Cataldo, he realized, as Paola waited for his response, was complicated, for the man was married to a woman who had so interested Brunetti that he had not managed to disguise that fact. 'All right,' he forced himself to say, 'I'll call him.'

'Good,' she said and was gone.

Left with the phone still in his hand, Brunetti dialled the number of his father-in-law's office, gave his name, and asked to speak to Conte Falier. This time there were none of the usual clicks, hums, or delays, and within seconds he heard the Conte's voice, 'Guido, how good of you to call. You're fine? The kids?' Someone unfamiliar with their family, and with the fact that Paola spoke to her parents every day, would no doubt believe a significant time had passed since the Conte had last had news of the family.

'Everyone's fine, thank you,' Brunetti answered. Then, with no preamble, 'I wondered if you'd decided what to do about that investment. I'm sorry I never got back to you, but I haven't heard anything, certainly nothing you didn't already know.' The habit of discretion while speaking on the phone had so seeped into Brunetti's bones that, even in what was no more than an expression of interest in the doings of a member of his family, he followed the drill of using no names and giving as little information as possible.

'That's all right, Guido,' his father-in-law's voice broke into his reflections. 'I've decided what to do.' After a pause, he added, 'If you like, I can tell you more about it. Are you free for an hour or so?'

With the prospect of an empty house before him, Brunetti said he was, and the Conte went on, 'I'd like to go and have another look at a painting I saw last night. If you're interested, you could come along. Tell me what you think of it.'

'Gladly. Where should we meet?'

'Why not San Bortolo? We can go together from there.'

They agreed on seven-thirty, the Conte certain that the dealer would stay open if he called and asked. Brunetti glanced at his watch and saw that there was time to attend to some of the papers that had rained on to his desk that day. He collared his wandering attention and read on. In less than an hour, one entire pile had moved from right to left, though Brunetti, however proud of his industry, remembered little of what he had read. He got up and walked to his window and stared at the church across the canal without really seeing it. He retied his shoes, opened the door to the *armadio* to look for the wool-lined boots that had lain there, abandoned, for years: he'd last worn them during a particularly high *acqua alta*. He had noticed, months ago, that one of them was covered in mould, and he now took the opportunity to put them both in the wastebasket, hoping he would not be trapped at the Questura by another flood and find himself without boots. He hoped even more that Signorina Elettra would not discover that he had put rubber in the paper garbage.

Back at his desk, he had a look at the staffing plan and saw that Alvise was scheduled to be at the front desk all of next week. He switched this around and sent him out on patrol with Riverre.

Finally it was time to go. He decided to walk, something he regretted as soon as he turned into Borgoloco S. Lorenzo and the temperature skidded down, leaving him wishing he had taken the scarf from the *armadio*. The wind abated as he entered Campo Santa Maria Formosa, but when he saw the ice splashed on the pavement around the fountain, he felt still colder.

He cut around the church, down to San Lio, through the underpass and out into the *campo*, where the wind awaited him. As did Conte Orazio Falier, his throat comfortably nestled in a pink woollen scarf few men his age would dare to wear.

The two men kissed, as had become their habit with the passing of the years, and the Conte latched his arm into Brunetti's, turning him away from the statue of Goldoni and down towards Ponte del'ovo.

'Tell me about the painting,' Brunetti said.

The Conte nodded to a man passing by and stopped to shake hands with an elderly woman who looked familiar to Brunetti. 'It's nothing special, but there's something about his face I like.'

'Where did you see it?'

'Franco's. We can talk there,' the Conte answered as he nodded to an elderly couple.

They neared Campo San Luca, walked past the bar that had replaced Rosa Salva, then over the bridges and down towards what had been done to La Fenice. In front of the theatre they turned to the left, past Antico Martini, both disappointed that the time was not right to slip in for a meal, and into the gallery at the bottom of the bridge. Franco, long known to both of them, waved at the pictures on the wall, inviting them to look, and returned to his book.

His father-in-law took him to stand in front of a portrait Brunetti guessed to be sixteenth-century Veneto. The painting, no more than sixty by fifty centimetres, showed a bearded young man with his right hand placed rather artfully on his heart. His left hand pressed open the pages of a book while he assessed the viewer with intelligent eyes. Behind his right shoulder a window gave on to a view of mountains that made Brunetti think the painter might have been from Conegliano, perhaps from Vittorio Veneto. The subject's handsome face was painted against a dark brown curtain, contrast provided by the high white collar of his shirt. Beneath it, he wore a red over-garment of some sort, and on top of that a black doublet. Two more flashes of white appeared at his cuffs, fluffy and frilly and very well painted, as were his face and hands.

'Do you like it?' the Conte asked.

'Very much. Do you know anything about it?'

Before answering, the Conte stepped closer to the painting and drew Brunetti's attention to the coat of arms just beside the subject's right shoulder. The Conte held his finger in the air above it and turned to Brunetti to ask, 'Do you think this could have been painted later?'

Brunetti stepped back to allow a longer perspective. He held up a hand to cover the coat of arms and saw that the proportions improved. He studied the portrait for a few moments more, then said, 'I think so. Yes. But I don't think I'd notice it unless someone pointed it out to me.'

The Conte gave a murmur of agreement.

'What do you think happened?' Brunetti asked.

'I'm not sure,' the Conte answered. 'There's really no way to know. But my guess is that this man somehow gained a title after the portrait was finished, so he took it back to the painter and asked him to add the coat of arms.'

'Like backdating a cheque or a contract, isn't it?' Brunetti asked, interested that the impulse towards deceit should have remained so constant over the centuries. Then he said, 'No new fashions in crime, I suppose.'

'Is that your way of leading me to a discussion of Cataldo?' the Conte asked, then quickly added, 'And I mean that quite seriously, Guido.'

'No,' Brunetti said levelly. 'All I've learned is that he's rich. There's no suggestion of crime.' He looked at his father-in-law. 'Do you know something I don't?'

The Conte moved aside to look at another painting, a life-sized portrait of a fat-faced woman bedecked in jewels and brocade. 'If only she weren't so vulgar,' he said, glancing back at Brunetti. 'It's so beautifully painted, I'd buy it in a minute. But I couldn't stand to live with her in the house.' He reached out his hand and literally dragged Brunetti to stand in front of the painting. 'Could you?'

Fashions in beauty and body size changed over the centuries, Brunetti knew, and so her girth might have been appealing to some seventeenth-century lover or husband. But her look of swinish gluttony would be offensive through the ages. Her skin glistened with grease, not with health; her teeth, however white and even, were those of an eager carnivore; the creases in the fat of her wrists spoke of embedded dirt. The gown from which her bosom spilled did not so much cover her flesh as restrain it from bursting out.

But, as the Conte had observed, she was gloriously well painted, with brush strokes that captured the glint of her eyes, the rich abundance of her golden hair, even the plush red brocade of the gown that exposed too much of her bosom.

'It's a remarkably modern painting,' the Conte said and took Brunetti aside to a pair of velvet-covered armchairs that might originally have been made to seat members of the senior clergy.

'I don't see it,' Brunetti said, surprised at how comfortable the formidable chair was. 'Not modern.'

'She represents consumption,' the Conte said, waving back at the painting. 'Just have a look at the size of her and think of the amount she's had to eat in her lifetime to create that mass of flesh, to make no mention of what she'd have to eat to maintain it. And look at the colour of those cheeks: that's a woman much given to drink. Again, just imagine the quantities. And the brocade: how many silkworms perished to produce her dress and mantle, or the silk on her chair? Look at her jewellery. How many men died in the gold mines to produce it? Who died digging out the ruby in the ring? And the bowl of fruit on the table next to her? Who cultivated those peaches? Who made the glass next to the fruit bowl?'

Brunetti looked at the painting with this new optic, seeing it as a manifestation of the wealth that feeds consumption and is in turn fed by it. The Conte was right: it could easily be read this way, but just as easily it could be seen as an example of the skill of the painter and the tastes of his age.

'And are you going to make some connection in all of this to Cataldo?' Brunetti asked in a light voice.

'Consumption, Guido,' the Conte went on as if Brunetti had not spoken. 'Consumption. We're obsessed by it. Our desire is to have not one, but six, televisions. To have a new *telefonino* every year, perhaps every six months, as new models are produced. And advertised. To upgrade our computers every time there is a new operating system, or every time the screens become bigger, or smaller, or flatter or, for all I know, rounder.' Brunetti thought of his request for his own computer and wondered where this speech was going.

'If you're wondering where all of this is leading,' the Conte astonished him by saying, 'it's leading into the garbage.' The Conte turned to him as though he had just delivered the final proof of the validity of a syllogism or an algebraic formula, and Brunetti stared at him.

The Conte, no mean showman, allowed time to pass. From the other room of the gallery, they heard the owner turn a page of his book.

At last the Conte said, 'Garbage, Guido. Garbage. That's what Cataldo wanted to propose to me.'

Brunetti remembered the list of Cataldo's businesses and began to study them in a new light. 'Aha,' he permitted himself to say.

'You at least did some research on him, didn't you?' the Conte asked.

'Yes.'

'And you know what businesses he's involved in?'

'Yes,' Brunetti said, 'at least some of them. Shipping: cargo ships and trucks.'

'Shipping,' the Conte repeated. 'And heavy equipment for excavation,' he added.' He has a shipping line, and trucks.

153

And earth-moving equipment. He also – and I found out about this only through my own people, who are sometimes as good as yours – has a waste disposal business that gets rid of all of those things I was just talking about that we don't want any more: *telefonini*, computers, fax machines, answering machines.' The Conte glanced back at the portrait of the woman and said, 'Most desirable model one year; the next year, useless junk.'

Brunetti, who knew where this was leading, decided to remain silent.

'That's the secret, Guido: new model one year, junk the next. Because there are so many of us and because we consume so much junk and throw away so much junk, someone has to be around to pick it up and dispose of it for us. It used to be that people were happy to be handed old junk: our kids took our old computers or our old televisions. But now everyone has to have new junk, their own junk. So now we not only have to pay to buy it; we also have to pay to get rid of it.' The Conte's tone was calm, descriptive. Brunetti had heard his daughter and granddaughter give much the same speech, but the Conte's descendants delivered it with anger, not with his cool dispassion.

'And this is what Cataldo does?'

'Yes. Cataldo is the garbage man. Other people amass it, and when they get tired of it, or it breaks, he sees that it is taken out of their way.'

When Brunetti did not reply, the Conte went on more quietly. 'That's what his interest in China is all about, Guido. China, the garbage heap of the world. But he waited too long.'

'Too long for what?' Brunetti asked.

'He overestimated the Africans,' the Conte said. In response to the inquisitive noise with which Brunetti greeted this, the Conte continued. 'Three ships he chartered left Trieste a month ago.' Before Brunetti could ask, he said, 'Yes, garbage ships. Filled with material it would be very expensive to dispose of here. He's been working with the Somalians for years. If what my people have told me is to be believed, he's sent them hundreds of thousands of tons. If he paid them enough, they'd take anything he wanted to send them: no questions asked about where it came from or what it was. But times change, and there's been so much bad press – especially after the tsunami – that the UN is trying to blockade the traffic, so it's almost impossible to send things there any more.' From the Conte's tone, it was impossible to judge his opinion of this.

'Besides, it doesn't make sense now. You have to pay the Africans to take it,' he added, shaking his head at the thought of these old-fashioned business practices. 'The Chinese will pay you to bring most things to them. Then they pick through it and save what they can and, I suspect, send the really dangerous stuff out to be dumped in Tibet.' He shrugged, 'There's very little they won't take.'

He gave Brunetti a long look, as if weighing whether he could be trusted with information. He must have liked what he saw, for he expanded, 'Have you ever asked yourself why the Chinese went to the trouble and expense of building a railway line from Beijing to Tibet, Guido? You think there are enough tourists to justify an expense like that? For a *passenger* train?'

All Brunetti could do was shake his head.

'But I was talking about Cataldo,' the Conte resumed. 'And his ships. He miscalculated. There are some things even the Chinese balk at taking now, and he's got three ships full of it. They've got nowhere to go, and they can't come back here until they get rid of their cargo because no European port would let them in.'

As the Conte paused to order his thoughts, Brunetti wondered how it was that some European port let the ships sail in the first place, a question he thought it best not to propose to the Conte. Instead, he asked, 'What will happen to the cargo?'

'He has no choice but to contact the Chinese and make a deal with them. They're sure to know all about it by now. They learn everything, sooner or later. So they'll hold him up and he'll have to pay a fortune to get rid of it.' Seeing Brunetti's response, he tried to explain. 'Cataldo has chartered these ships, mind you: they're not his,' the Conte continued. 'And they're sailing around in the Indian Ocean, waiting for him to find a place for them to unload. So every day is costing him a significant amount. And the longer they stay there, the more people will know what's on them and the more the price for taking it will rise.'

'What is it?'

'My guess is that it's nuclear waste and highly toxic chemicals,' the Conte said in as cool a voice as Brunetti had ever heard him use. After he said this, the Conte turned his attention back to the portrait of the woman, studying her anew. Then, as if he could read Brunetti's mind, he continued, eyes still on the portrait, 'I know you, Guido, and I know how you think. So I suspect what I've just said has you hoping, even if only half hoping, that I've had some sort of epiphany.'

Brunetti kept his face motionless, neither acknowledging nor denying what the Conte had just said.

'I did have an illumination, Guido, but I'm afraid it's not the kind you'd like me to have.' Before Brunetti could ask himself what sort of father-in-law that would make him, the Conte said, 'I haven't begun to repent my ways, Guido, and I haven't been converted to seeing the world the way you do – or Paola does.'

'Then what's happened?' Brunetti asked, keeping his voice level.

'I've spoken to Cataldo's lawyer: that's my illumination. Well, to tell the truth, one of my lawyers spoke to one of his lawyers, and he's learned that Cataldo is stretched too far and too thin – he's already beginning to sell his real estate here – and his banker has told him it's better if he doesn't ask for another loan.' The Conte turned from the portrait and looked at his son-in-law, reached out to put a hand on his arm. 'I think this might be privileged information, Guido, and so I'd like you to keep it to yourself.'

Brunetti nodded, understanding now why Signorina Elettra had not been able to see the full extent of Cataldo's financial difficulties.

'Greed, Guido, greed,' the Conte surprised him by saying. He was being descriptive, not judgmental.

'And so what will happen to him?'

'I have no idea. The news about him isn't public yet, but when that happens – and it's only a matter of time – he won't be able to find a partner for his Chinese venture. He waited too long.'

'What will happen to him?'

'He'll take an enormous loss.'

'Could you help him?' Brunetti asked.

'If I wanted to, I suppose I could,' the Conte said, turning to meet his glance.

'But?'

'But it would be a mistake.'

'I see,' Brunetti said, realizing this was something he did not need to know about. 'What will you do?' he asked.

'Oh, I'll make the deal in China, but not with Cataldo.'

'Alone?'

The Conte's smile was minimal. 'No. In partnership with someone else.' Brunetti could not prevent himself from wondering if the someone else was Cataldo's lawyer. 'Everything Cataldo told me was wrong. He painted a rosy picture of his contacts in China, but none of it was true. He offered me a chance to get in on the ground floor.' The Conte closed his eyes, as if he could not imagine someone's being so foolish as to make him an offer like this and not expect him to investigate.

'What did you tell him?' Brunetti asked.

'I said I was over-extended at the moment and don't have the capital it would take to form the partnership he suggested.'

'Why didn't you just say no and leave it at that?' Brunetti said, feeling not a little bit foolish with the question.

'Because, to tell the truth, I've always been slightly afraid of Cataldo, but this time I was sorry for him.'

'And for what was going to happen to him.'

'Exactly.'

'But not enough to help him?'

'Guido. Please.'

17

Even though Brunetti had had a generation to accustom himself to the Conte's business ethics, he was still surprised. He glanced away from him, as if suddenly interested in the portrait of the woman, then back at the Conte. 'And if he's ruined?' Brunetti asked.

'Ah, Guido,' the Conte said, 'people like Cataldo are never ruined. I said he'd take a loss, but it won't ruin him. He's been in business a long time, and he's always been politically well connected: his friends will take care of him.' Conte Falier smiled. 'Don't waste your time feeling sorry for him. If you want to feel sorry for anyone, feel sorry for his wife.'

'I do,' Brunetti confessed.

'I know,' the Conte said coolly. 'But why? Because of the sympathy you feel for a person who reads?' he asked, but without any hint of sarcasm. The Conte was also a reader, and so it was a normal question. He went on, 'When Cataldo was courting me – and that's what it was – I went to dinner at their home. I told you, I was placed next to her, not him, and she talked to me about what she was reading. Just as she did with you the other night. All the time she was talking to me about the *Metamorphoses*, I had the sense that she was very lonely. Or very unhappy.'

'Why?' Brunetti asked, struck by how her choice of reading brought his attention back to her face and the changes it must have undergone.

'Well, there's the fact that she reads what she does, but there's also her face. People immediately think what they want about her because of all the lifting.'

'And what do you think they think?' Brunetti asked.

The Conte turned to the portrait of the woman and studied it for some time. 'We find that face strange,' he observed, waving a negligent hand at the painting. 'But in her epoch she was probably perfectly acceptable, perhaps even attractive. Whereas to us, she's just a fat barrel of a woman with greasy skin.' Then, unable to resist the temptation, he added, 'Not unlike the wives of many of my business associates.'

Brunetti saw the similarities but said nothing.

'In our times,' the Conte went on, 'Franca Marinello is not acceptable because of the way she looks. What she has done to her face is too unusual for most people to observe without comment.' He paused; Brunetti waited. The Conte closed his eyes and sighed. 'God knows how many of the wives of my friends have done it: the eyes, the chin, then the whole face.' He opened his eyes and looked at the portrait, not at Brunetti. 'So she's doing what they're doing, only she's doing it to a degree that makes the whole thing grotesque.' He looked at Brunetti and said, 'I wonder, when women talk about her, whether they're thinking about themselves and whether, by talking about her as though she were some sort of freak, they're trying to assure themselves that they'd never do anything like that, that they'd stop themselves from going so far.'

'That still doesn't explain why she did it, though, does it?' Brunetti asked, recalling that strange, otherworldly face.

'God knows,' the Conte said, then, after a moment, 'Perhaps she told Donatella.'

'Told her?' Brunetti asked, wondering why Marinello should tell such a thing to anyone, let alone the Contessa.

'Why she did it, of course. They've been friends since she was a girl at the university. Donatella has a cousin who's a priest up there where she comes from, and Franca's related to him somehow. He gave Donatella her name when she came to Venice and didn't know anyone. And they became great friends.' Then, before Brunetti could speak, the Conte said, holding up one hand, 'Don't ask me. I don't know how, only that Donatella thinks very highly of her.' With a grin that was both boyish and mischievous, he asked, 'Didn't you wonder why she ended up opposite you?'

Of course he had. Brunetti said, 'No, not really.'

'Because Donatella knows how much Franca misses being able to talk about what she reads. You, too. So she agreed when I suggested that you would enjoy talking to her.'

'I did.'

'Good. Donatella will be pleased.'

'Did *she*?'

'Who?'

'Signora Marinello,' Brunetti answered. 'Enjoy herself, that is.'

The Conte gave him a strange look, as though surprised by both his formality of address and his question, but said only, 'I've no idea.' Then, as if tired of this talk of a living woman, the Conte waved toward the painting, saying, 'But we were talking of beauty. Someone thought this woman beautiful enough to paint her or commission a portrait of her, didn't they?'

Brunetti considered the suggestion, then the painting, and reluctantly said 'Yes.'

'So someone, perhaps Franca herself, is likely to find what she has had done to her face beautiful,' the Conte said. More

161

soberly, he added, 'I've heard talk that there's someone else who does. You know what this town is like, Guido: there's always talk.'

'You mean there's talk about another man?'

The Conte nodded. 'Donatella let drop something the other evening, but when I tried to ask her what she meant, she realized she had said too much and went clam-like.' He could not resist adding, 'I imagine you are familiar with this behaviour in Paola.'

'Am I not,' Brunetti observed. After a moment's reflection, he asked, 'What else have you heard?'

'Nothing. It isn't exactly the sort of thing people tell me.'

Suddenly reluctant to prolong talk of Franca Marinello, Brunetti asked abruptly, 'What was it you wanted to talk to me about?'

Disappointment – and could it be offence? – flashed across the Conte's face. Brunetti watched him prepare an answer, and eventually the Conte said, 'There was no precise reason, Guido. I enjoy conversation with you: nothing more than that. And we seldom get to talk, what with one thing and another.' He flicked a speck from his sleeve, then looked back at Brunetti and said, 'I hope you don't mind.'

Brunetti leaned across and placed his hand on the Conte's forearm. 'I'm delighted, Orazio,' he said, unable to explain fully how touched he was by the Conte's remark. Then he turned his attention back to the portrait of the woman. 'Paola would probably say it's the portrait of a woman, not a lady.'

The Conte laughed and said, 'No, she won't do, not at all, will she?' He got to his feet and went over to the portrait of the young man, saying, 'That, however, is something I'd like to have.' He went to the back of the gallery to talk to the dealer, leaving Brunetti to contemplate the two paintings, the two faces, the two visions of what was beautiful.

*

By the time they had walked back to Palazzo Falier, Brunetti carrying the carefully wrapped portrait under one arm, and then discussed where to hang it, it was after nine.

The Contessa was not at home, Brunetti was disappointed to learn. In recent years, he had come to appreciate both her decency and her good sense, and he had half a mind to ask her if she would talk to him about Franca Marinello. Instead, he took his farewell of an unusually silent Conte, still warmed by their conversation and pleased that the older man took such pleasure in something as simple as a new painting.

He walked home slowly, vaguely discomfited, as he was every winter, by the early arrival of the darkness and oppressed by the dampness and cold that had been increasing since the morning. At the bottom of the bridge where he had first seen Franca Marinello and her husband, he paused to lean against the parapet, struck by how much he had learned in the last – how long had it been? – less than a week, he was surprised to realize.

Suddenly Brunetti recalled the Conte's expression when he had asked why his father-in-law had wanted to speak to him, with its implication that he could be motivated only by self-interest. Brunetti had been concerned at first that his question had offended the Conte, but what he had failed to admit then was the other man's pain. It was the pain of an old man who feared the rejection of his family, the expression he had seen on the faces of elderly people when they feared they were no longer loved, or had never been. The image of that bleak field in Marghera seeped back into his memory.

'Sta bene, Signore?' a young man asked, pausing beside him.

Brunetti looked at him, tried to smile, and nodded. 'Yes, thank you,' he said. 'I was just thinking of something.'

The boy was wearing a bright red ski parka, his face surrounded by the fur that lined the hood. As Brunetti met his gaze, the boy's face drifted slightly out of focus, and Brunetti wondered if this was what happened before people fainted. He turned to look out over the waters, seeking the other side of the Grand Canal, and saw the same cloudiness there. He placed his other hand on the parapet. He blinked, hoping to clear his sight, blinked again.

'Snow,' he said, turning back to the boy with a smile.

The boy gave him another long look, then continued over the bridge and past the gates of the university.

Just at the top of the bridge ahead of him, preserved by the cooler surface, the snow was sticking to the pavement. Keeping his hand on the railing, Brunetti crossed the bridge and walked carefully down the other side. The pavement here was wet, and there was not enough snow to make it slippery. He remembered all those stories he had read as a boy about Arctic explorers trudging off to their deaths in the endless wasteland of snow. He thought of the descriptions he had read of the way they walked, head down into the oncoming wind, their only thought to place one resolute foot ahead of the other and keep going. So too did Brunetti place his feet ahead of him, intent only on getting back to warmth and to a place where he could rest and stop, if only for a time, this ceaseless struggle toward some eternally retreating goal.

The spirit of Captain Scott carried him up the stairs and into his apartment. He was so caught up in the image of his trek that he almost bent down to remove his sealskin boots, toss his fur-lined parka on the ground. Instead, he removed his shoes and hung his coat from one of the hooks beside the door.

He measured his strength, found that he still had enough, and went into the kitchen to open a cabinet, take a glass, and uncork the grappa. He poured out a generous helping and took it into the living room, where darkness awaited him. He snapped on the light, which prevented him from seeing the snow banging against the windows to the terrace. He switched it off again.

He lowered himself on to the sofa, lay back and pulled up

164

his feet. He stretched out, pounded two pillows into submission, and took a sip of the grappa, then another. He watched the snow fall, thinking of how tired Guarino had seemed at the realization that everyone worked for Patta.

In moments of great necessity, his late mother was known to call upon a few saints she kept in reserve. There was Saint Gennaro for the protection of orphans; Saint Mauro, who kept a watchful eye on cripples, in which task he was aided by Sant'Egidio; and there was Santa Rosalia, generally invoked for protection against pestilence, and thus invoked by his mother against measles, mumps, and influenza.

Brunetti lay on the sofa, sipping at his grappa, waiting for Paola to come home, and thought about Saint Rita di Cascia, who protected against loneliness. 'Santa Rita,' he prayed, '*aiutaci.*' But whom, he wondered, was he asking her to help? He set his empty glass on the table and closed his eyes.

18

He heard a voice, and for a moment he thought it was his mother's, praying. He lay still, happy at the thought of listening to her voice, even though he knew that she was gone, and he would never hear her or see her again. He wanted the illusion, knew it would do him good.

The voice continued for another moment, then he felt a kiss on his forehead, where his mother used to kiss him when she put him to bed. But the scent was different.

'Grappa before dinner?' she asked. 'Does this mean you're going to start beating us and end up in the gutter?'

'Aren't you supposed to be at some dinner?' he replied.

'At the last minute,' she said, 'I couldn't stand the idea. I went as far as the restaurant with them and then said I felt sick – which is certainly true – and came home.'

A warm flush of contentment at her mere physical presence flooded Brunetti. He felt the weight of her body on the edge of the sofa. He opened his eyes and said, 'I think your father is lonely and afraid of being old.'

In a calm voice, she said, 'At his age, that's normal.'

'But he shouldn't,' Brunetti protested.

She laughed out loud. 'Emotions don't respond to "should" and "shouldn't", Guido. There are enough impulsive murders in the world every year to prove that.' She saw his response and said, 'I'm sorry. I should have found a better comparison. Enough impulsive marriages, then?'

'But do you agree?' Brunetti asked. 'You know him better than I do, so you should know what he's thinking. Or feeling.'

'Do you really think that?' she asked, sliding down the sofa to sit at the end, beside his feet, which she patted and tucked behind her hip.

'Of course. You're his daughter.'

'Do you think Chiara understands you better than anyone else?' she countered.

'That's different. She's still a teenager.'

'So it's age that makes the difference?'

'Oh, stop pretending you're Socrates,' he shot back and asked, 'Do you think it's true?'

'That he feels old and lonely?'

'Yes.'

Paola placed a hand on his shin, flicked away a piece of mud that clung to the cuff of his trousers, and allowed some time to pass before she said, 'Yes, I think he does.' She rubbed his leg. 'But if it's any consolation to you, I've believed he's felt lonely most of my adult life.'

'Why?'

'Because he's intelligent and cultured and spends most of his working life in the company of people who aren't. No,' she said with two gentle taps on his leg to stop him from protesting, 'before you contradict me, let me admit that many of them are intelligent, but not in the way he is. He functions at the abstract level, and the people he works with are usually concerned with profit and loss.'

'And he's not?' Brunetti asked, voice clear of any hint of scepticism.

'Of course he wants to make money. I told you, it runs in the family. But he's always found it too easy. What he really wants to do is think things out, see big patterns and understand them.'

'The failed philosopher?' Brunetti asked.

She gave him a sharp look. 'Don't be mean-spirited, Guido. I'm not saying this well, I know. I think what troubles him, now that he can't deny how old he's become, is that he thinks his life has been a failure.'

'But . . .' Brunetti could think of no way to begin the list of his objections: A happy marriage, a wonderful child, two decent grandchildren, wealth, financial success, social position. He wiggled his toes to call her attention. 'I really don't understand.'

'Respect. He wants people to respect him. I think it's as simple as that.'

'But everyone does.'

'You don't,' she shot back with such force that Brunetti suddenly suspected she had been waiting years, perhaps decades, to say this.

He pulled his feet out from under her and sat up. 'I realized today that I love him,' he offered.

'That's not the same thing,' she said fiercely.

Something in Brunetti snapped. He had stood that day over the body of a man younger than himself who had been shot in the head. And he suspected the man's murder would be, or was in the process of being, covered up by men like her father: rich, powerful, politically connected. And he had to have respect, too?

In a cool voice, Brunetti said, 'He told me today, your father, that he is planning to invest in China. I did not ask what sort of investment it was going to be, but during our conversation he mentioned, completely as an aside, that he thinks the Chinese are sending toxic garbage to Tibet and have built that railway in order to do so.'

He stopped and waited, and finally Paola asked, 'And your point?'

'That he is going to invest there; that none of that seems to bother him in the least.'

She turned and stared at him as if puzzled to find this strange man sitting next to her. 'And who, pray tell, employs you, Commissario Brunetti?'

'The Polizia di Stato.'

'And who employs them?'

'The Ministry of the Interior.'

'And who employs *them*?'

'Are we going to go up the food chain until we get to the head of government?' Brunetti inquired.

'We are already there, I suspect,' she answered.

Neither of them said anything for some time: silence percolated towards recrimination. Paola took a step closer to it by saying, 'You work for *this* government, and you dare to criticize my father for investing in China?'

Brunetti took a short breath and started to speak, but at that moment Chiara and Raffi burst into the apartment. There was a great deal of noise and enough stomping and banging to force Paola to her feet and out into the corridor, where the children were stamping snow from their shoes and shaking more of it from their coats.

'The horror movie festival?' Paola asked.

'Terr – i – ble,' Chiara said. 'They begin with *Godzilla*, which is about a hundred years old and has the most awful special effects you ever saw in your life.'

Raffi broke in to say, 'Did we miss dinner?'

'No,' Paola said with patent relief, 'I was just going to start making something. Twenty minutes?' she asked.

The children nodded, stamped about a bit more, remembered to put their shoes outside the door, and went to their rooms. Paola went down to the kitchen.

It was purely by chance that Paola prepared *insalata di*

polipi for antipasto that evening, but Brunetti could not help seeing the elusive, self-defensive habits of those timid sea creatures reflected in the caution with which his children treated their silent mother once they sat at the table and read the expression on her face. Like the tentative manner in which an octopus stretched out a tendril to touch and examine what it saw, the better to assess its possible menace, the children, significantly more verbal than the *octopi*, used language to sense peril. Thus Brunetti was compelled to listen to the patently false enthusiasm of their joint request to be allowed to do the dishes that evening and to the general docility of their response to Paola's pro forma questions about school.

After her outburst before dinner, Paola remained calm throughout the meal, limiting her conversation to asking who would like more of the lasagne that had indeed been waiting for Brunetti in the oven. Brunetti noticed that the children's caution extended to their eating: both of them had to be asked twice before they would accept another helping, and Chiara refrained from setting her uneaten peas to the side of her plate, a habit that always annoyed her mother. Luckily, the baked apples with *crème* managed to elevate everyone's mood, and by the time Brunetti drank his coffee, some semblance of tranquillity had been restored.

Having no interest in grappa, Brunetti went into their bedroom to get his copy of Cicero's legal cases, which his original conversation with Franca Marinello had encouraged him to begin rereading. He hunted for, and found, his copy of Ovid's minor works, unopened for decades: if he finished with Cicero, he could begin her other recommendation.

When he came back to the living room, Paola was just sitting down in the easy chair she preferred. He stopped at her side long enough to tilt her still-closed book so that he could see the title on the cover. 'Still faithful to the Master, I see?' he asked.

'I shall never abandon Mr James,' she vowed and opened the book. Brunetti's breathing grew easier. Luckily, they were a family where no one held grudges, and so it seemed that there was to be no resumption of hostilities.

He sat, then lay, on the sofa. After some time enmeshed in the defence of Sextus Roscius, he allowed the book to fall to his stomach and, turning his head at an awkward angle to see Paola, said, 'You know, it's strange that the Romans were so reluctant to put people in prison.'

'Even if they were guilty?'

'Especially if they were guilty.'

She looked up from her own book, interested, 'What did they do instead?'

'They let them run away if they were convicted. There was a grace period before they were sentenced, and most of them took the opportunity to go into exile.'

'Like Craxi?'

'Exactly.'

'Do other countries have as many convicted men in their governments as we do?' Paola inquired.

'The Indians are said to have a fair number,' Brunetti answered and returned to his reading.

After some time, when Paola heard him chuckle, then laugh out loud, she looked up and said, 'I admit that the Master has made me smile upon occasion, but he has never made me laugh outright.'

'Then listen to this,' Brunetti said, turning his eyes back to the passage he had just been reading. '"The philosophers declare, very aptly, that even a mere facial expression can be a breach of filial duty."'

'Should we copy that out and put it on the refrigerator?' she asked.

'One moment,' Brunetti said, flipping back towards the front of the book. 'I've got a better one here, somewhere,' he said, turning pages quickly.

171

'For the refrigerator?' she asked.

'No,' Brunetti said, pausing in his search for the passage. 'I think we should put this one above all public buildings in the country; carved into stone, perhaps.'

Paola made a turning gesture with her hand, encouraging him to hurry up.

A few moments passed as he riffled back and forth, and then he found it. He lay back and held the book out at arm's length. He turned his head to her and said, 'Cicero says this is the duty of the good consul, but I think we can extend that to all politicians.' She nodded and Brunetti turned back to the book. In a declamatory voice he read out, '"He must protect the lives and interests of the people, appeal to his fellow citizens' patriotic interests, and, in general, set the welfare of the community above his own."'

Paola remained silent, considering what he had just read to her. Then she closed her book and tossed it on the table in front of her. 'And I thought *my* book was a work of fiction.'

19

They woke to snow. A certain slant of light told Brunetti what had happened even before his eyes were fully opened or he was really awake. He looked towards the windows and saw a thin ridge of snow balanced on the railing of the terrace and, beyond it, white-roofed houses and a sky so blue it hurt his eyes. Not even the merest whisper of a cloud could be seen, as if all of them had been ironed in the night and thrown out flat over the city. He lay and looked and tried to remember the last time it had snowed like this, snowed and stayed and not been washed away immediately by the rain.

He had to know how deep it was. In his enthusiasm, he turned to tell Paola, but the sight of that thin ridge of white lying motionless beside him gave him pause, and he contented himself with getting out of bed and going over to the window. The bell tower of San Polo was covered, and, beyond it, that of the Frari. He went down the hall to Paola's study, and from there he could see the bell tower of San Marco, its golden angel glistening in the reflected light. From some distant place, he heard the tolling of a bell, but the reverberation was transformed by the snow covering everything, and he had no idea which church it was or from what direction it was coming.

He went back into the bedroom and over to the window again. Already there were tiny trails of a triple-toed bird's prints in the snow on the terrace. One of them went right to the edge and disappeared, as if the bird had been unable to resist the temptation to hurl himself into the midst of all of that whiteness. Without thinking, he opened the tall door and bent down to touch it, to feel whether it was the solid wet kind that was good for making snowballs or the dryer kind that fluffed up if you kicked your feet ahead of you when you walked.

'Are you out of your mind?' a voice behind him asked, no less indignant for being muffled by a pillow. A younger Brunetti would perhaps have brought a handful of snow back to the bed, but this one contented himself with pressing his hand into the snow and leaving the print there. It was the dry kind of snow, he noticed.

He closed the door and came back to sit on the bed. 'It snowed,' he said.

He raised the hand that had left the print in the show and moved it closer to her shoulder. Though her head was turned away from him and mostly covered by a pillow, he had no trouble hearing her say, 'If you put that hand anywhere near me, I will divorce you and take the children.'

'They're old enough to decide themselves,' he answered with what he thought was Olympian calm.

'I cook,' she said.

'Indeed,' he said in acknowledgement of defeat.

She lapsed again into coma and Brunetti went to take a shower.

When he left the apartment more than half an hour later, he had had his first coffee and remembered to wear his scarf. He had also put on a pair of rubber-soled boots. It was indeed the fluffy kind of snow, stretching ahead of him undisturbed all the way to the first cross-street. Brunetti stuffed his hands in the pockets of his overcoat and slid one foot forward, telling himself that it was to test how slippery the pavement was. Not at all, he was glad to discover: it was like walking through feathers. He kicked out, first one foot and then the other, and great plumes of snow rose in front of him.

When he got to the crossing, he turned and looked proudly back at his work. Many people had passed towards the *campo*, and the snow had been kicked and brushed aside, leaving balding spots of pavement where the snow was already beginning to melt around the edges. The people walking by moved with stiff caution, like sailors just put to sea and not yet sure of their sea legs. But it was delight, not caution, that he read on most of their faces, as if school had just closed and they had all been let out to play. People smiled at one another, and strangers all had something to say about the snow.

He stopped at his usual news-stand and bought *Il Gazzettino*. 'Recidivist,' he said to himself as he took the paper. There was a small article on the front page about the murder in Marghera: only two sentences and an instruction to turn to the first page of the second section. He did so and read that the body of an unidentified man had been found in the Marghera industrial complex. The man had been shot and left in the open, where his body had been found by a night watchman. The Carabinieri said that they were following leads and hoped soon to be able to identify the dead man.

Brunetti was amazed at how cursory the story was, almost as if the fictitious watchman were in the daily habit of stumbling across bodies. There was no description of the dead man, no indication of the precise location where he had been found, and no mention of the fact that he was a member of the Carabinieri. Brunetti was curious about the source, and the motive, of this reporting of near and non-facts.

Brunetti folded the paper closed when he got to the bottom of the Rialto and stuck it under his arm. On the other side of the bridge, he was torn between continuing to walk or taking the vaporetto. He opted for the latter, drawn by the thought of being able to pass in front of a snow-covered Piazza San Marco.

He took the number 2 because it would be faster, standing on deck as they moved up the Grand Canal, enchanted by the transformation that had taken place during the night. The docks running out into the canal were white, the tarpaulins that covered the sleeping gondolas were white; so were the smaller, still unwalked *calli* that led back from the canal to the various hearts of the city. He noticed, as they passed the Comune, how grimy the snow made so many of the buildings look; only the ochre and red ones could remain respectable under the contrast. They passed the Mocenigo *palazzi*, and he remembered going to one of them with his uncle once; he could no longer remember why. Then ahead on the right, Palazzo Foscari, snow filigree dusting all of the windowsills. On the left he saw Palazzo Grassi, that now-charmless storehouse of second-rate art; then they slipped under the Accademia Bridge, where he saw people clinging to the railing as they went down the steps. He glanced back after they passed under the bridge and saw the same on the other side: a wooden surface would be far more treacherous than stone, especially one that gave the sense of tilting the walker forward.

Then they were abreast of the Piazzetta, and the reflection from the expanse of snow between the library and the palace was so strong that Brunetti was forced to put his hand above his eyes to reduce the glare. Good old San Teodoro was still up there on his pillar, driving his spear into the head of his mini-dragon. What struggle to escape! All to no purpose, though, even if San Teodoro was slowed down by the snow.

Patches of the domes poked through the snow, which

Brunetti could see was beginning to melt in the morning sun. Saints popped up from everywhere, a lion flew by, boats hooted at one another, and Brunetti closed his eyes from the joy of it.

When he opened them, they were opposite the bridge, jammed even at this hour under its weight of milling tourists, all trying to have a photo taken at the place where so many people had paused for the last time before being taken off to imprisonment, torture, or death.

Farther along here, the snow was almost gone, and by the time he got off at San Zaccaria, there was so little left as to make his boots an encumbrance as well as an affectation.

The guard at the front door greeted him with a lazy salute. He asked for Vianello, but the Ispettore was not yet in. Nor had the Vice-Questore arrived – no surprise to Brunetti, who imagined Patta at home, still in his pyjamas, hoping someone would write him a note explaining that he was late for work because of the snow.

He went to Signorina Elettra's office.

When he came in, she said with no introduction, 'You didn't tell me you saw a photo of him.' She wore a black dress and an orange silk jacket the colour a Buddhist monk would wear: it stood in sharp contrast to the soberness of her voice.

'Yes,' he answered soberly. 'I did.'

'Was it very bad? For him?' she asked, a question which filled Brunetti with relief because of its admission that she had only learned of the photo and not seen it.

Brunetti resisted the impulse to make things sound better than they were. Instead, he said, 'It was instant. He must have been taken completely by surprise.'

'How can you say that?' she asked.

He remembered Guarino, lying on the ground: his jaw. 'You don't have to know. Believe me and leave it at that.'

'What was he?' she asked.

The question troubled Brunetti because of the answers that

came tumbling into his head. He was a Carabiniere. He was a man Avisani trusted implicitly. He was investigating the illegal transport of garbage, though Brunetti knew little more about the investigation than that. He was interested in a man of short temper who gambled and did not like to lose and whose name might be Antonio Terrasini. He was separated from his wife.

As he listed these things in his mind, Brunetti was forced to realize that he did not doubt anything Guarino had told him. He had evaded and avoided answering certain questions, but Brunetti found himself believing that what he had said was true.

'I think he was an honest man,' Brunetti said.

She made no reply to that but then said, 'It doesn't change anything – having the photo – does it?' Brunetti made a noise of negation. She went on, 'But it does, somehow. Makes it more real.'

Signorina Elettra was seldom at a loss for words: Brunetti failed to find the right thing to say to her. Perhaps there was none.

'That's not what I wanted to tell you, though,' she began, but before she could explain, they heard footsteps approaching and turned to see Patta, but a Patta dressed as might have been Captain Scott had he had time and opportunity to outfit himself in the shops of the Mercerie. Patta's beige parka had a fur-lined hood and was carelessly left open to show the lining. Under it he wore a Harris tweed jacket and a burgundy turtleneck that looked like cashmere. His boots were rubber gumboots like the ones Raffi had called Brunetti's attention to in the window of Duca d'Aosta just the week before.

The snow, which had enhanced the mood of almost everyone Brunetti had met on the way to work, appeared to have had the opposite effect on Patta. The Vice-Questore nodded to Signorina Elettra – he never nodded curtly to her, but this was not a friendly nod – and said to Brunetti, 'Come into my office.'

Brunetti followed him and waited while his superior disburdened himself of his parka. Patta laid it, lining out – the better to display the distinctive Burberry plaid – on one of the chairs in front of his desk and pointed to the other one for Brunetti.

'Is this going to be trouble?' Patta said with no preamble.

'You mean the murder, sir?'

'Of course I mean the murder. A Carabiniere – a *maggiore*, for God's sake – gets himself murdered in our territory. What's going on here? Are they going to try to pass it on to us?'

Brunetti waited to see if these were rhetorical questions, but Patta's confusion and indignation seemed sufficiently real for him to venture, 'No, I don't know what's going on, sir. But I doubt they want us to get involved. The captain I spoke to there yesterday – I think he was the one who called you – he made it clear that they're claiming jurisdiction.'

Patta's relief was visible. 'Good. Let them have it. I don't understand how this could happen to a Carabinieri officer. He seemed like a sensible person. How could he let himself get killed like that?'

Like the Furies circling the head of a guilt-crazed Orestes, sarcastic responses crowded on to Brunetti's tongue, but he drove them off and said, instead, 'There's no telling how it happened, sir. There could have been more than one of them.'

'But still . . .' Patta said and let his voice drift away from this unspoken reproach for carelessness.

'If you think it's best for us, sir . . .' Brunetti began, his voice a symphony of uncertainty, '. . . but perhaps . . . no, better let them have it.'

Patta was on him like a ferret. 'What is it, Brunetti?'

'When I spoke to him, sir,' Brunetti began with affected reticence, 'Guarino told me he had a suspect for that murder in Tessera.' Then, before Patta could ask, he added, 'The man with the trucking company. Before Christmas.'

'I'm not an idiot, Brunetti. I read the reports, you know.'

'Of course, sir.'

'Well, what did he say? This Carabiniere?'

'He told me he didn't give the name of his suspect to his colleagues, sir,' Brunetti said.

'That's impossible,' Patta said. 'Of course he'd give it to them.'

'I'm not sure he trusted them entirely.' This could well be true, though Guarino had never said it.

Brunetti watched as Patta decided to pretend to be surprised at such a thing. Before he could express his disbelief, Brunetti went on. 'He as much as told me that.' This was a lie.

'He didn't give you the name, did he?' Patta asked sharply.

'Yes,' Brunetti offered, with no explanation.

'Why?' It was almost a shout.

Patta, Brunetti knew, would not understand it if Brunetti were to suggest Guarino had trusted him because he recognized in him another honest man. Instead, he answered, 'He suspected his investigation was being interfered with: he said it had happened in the past. Perhaps he thought we'd be more likely to run a careful investigation. And perhaps find the killer.' Brunetti was tempted to suggest more, but caution prevailed and he left it to Patta to consider the advantages. When Patta did not respond, Brunetti went for broke, saying, 'I have no choice but to give them the name, then, do I, sir?'

Patta studied the surface of his desk, a priest reading the runes. 'Did you believe him about the suspect?' he finally asked.

'I did, yes.' There was no need to tell Patta about the photo, about the trip to the Casinò: Patta was not a detail man.

'Do you think we can continue this without their knowing

what we're doing?' Patta's use of the plural was enough to tell Brunetti that his superior had already decided to pursue the investigation: now what Brunetti had to do was ensure that it be left to him to do so.

'Guarino thought we'd have the advantage because of our local knowledge, sir.' Brunetti spoke as though neither Patta nor Scarpa was Sicilian.

In a contemplative voice, Patta said, 'I'd like to be able to do that.'

'What, sir?'

'Take this right out of the mouths of the Carabinieri. First, Mestre took that murder investigation away from us, and now the Carabinieri want to take this, too.' The speculative man had been replaced by the man of action, one who had buried the memory of his original delight when he believed the investigation was not to be theirs. 'They'll see they can't do that, not while I'm Vice-Questore in this city.'

Brunetti was glad Patta managed to restrain the impulse to slam his fist down on his desk: it would have been a gesture too far. What a pity Patta had not worked in the historical archive of some Stalinist state: how he would have loved altering the photos, airbrushing out the old and replacing them with the new. Or writing, and then rewriting, the history books: the man had a call.

'. . . and Vianello, I suppose,' Brunetti heard Patta conclude and dragged himself away from the delights of speculation.

'Of course, sir. If that's what you think is best,' Brunetti said and got to his feet, a motion prompted by Patta's tone, not whatever it was he had been saying that Brunetti had not heard.

He stood, waiting for Patta's final remark, but he failed to make it and Brunetti went out to Signorina Elettra's office. In a voice that might well have carried into Patta's office,

Brunetti said, 'If you have a moment, Signorina, I have a few things I'd like to ask you to take care of.'

'Of course, Commissario,' she said formally, turning her head in the direction of Patta's office. 'I have some things to finish for the Vice-Questore. I'll come up when I'm free.'

20

The first thing Brunetti noticed when he entered his own office was the light streaming in through the window. Beyond it he saw the glistening roof of the church, tiny patches of snow still clinging to it and, beyond that, the burnished sky. Now that the snow had drawn the pollution from the atmosphere, the mountains would be visible from the kitchen, should he get home while there was still light enough to see them.

He went over to the window and studied the play of light on the roof while he waited for Signorina Elettra to arrive. She had caught Guarino's interest, and he felt himself blush at the thought of how he had resented her response to it. There was no better word to describe it: resented. Each had tried to learn about the other, and Brunetti had stifled their attempts. He placed both hands flat on the windowsill and contemplated his fingers, but that did not help him feel any better about the way he had behaved. He distracted himself with the memory of Guarino's wry acceptance of his own secretary's resemblance to Signorina Elettra. Her name had been an exotic one, as well, something operatic: Leonora, Norma, Alcina? No, it had been one of those droopy, suffering ones: Lord, there were so many of those.

Gilda, that was it. Gilda Landi. Or had she been one of those false trails people were always laying in spy novels? No, Guarino had been caught entirely off guard and had spoken quite impulsively of the – what was the word – indomitable? No, formidable, Signora Landi. A civilian, then.

Brunetti heard Signorina Elettra come in and turned to see her sit down in one of the chairs in front of his desk. She glanced in his direction but, in truth, she was looking beyond him and at the roof and the patch of clear sky beyond.

He took his place behind his desk and asked, 'What was it you wanted to tell me, Signorina?'

'This Terrasini,' she said. 'Antonio. It seems to be his real name.' She had a manila file with her but made no attempt to open it.

Brunetti nodded.

'He's a member of a branch of the Terrasini family in Aspromonte, a cousin of one of the bosses.'

The news set Brunetti's imagination running, but however much he managed to make possible connections with Guarino's death, he always ran into the blank fact that he had no reason to question the man, let alone to arrest him. Guarino had never explained the photograph to Brunetti, and now never would.

'How did you find this out?' he asked her.

'He's in the files, sir. He was arrested the first few times using that name, but he's also been arrested using an assortment of aliases.' She glanced at Brunetti and said, 'What I don't understand is why he'd use his real name to go to the Casinò.'

'It might be that they take more care in examining documents than we do,' he suggested. He had spoken ironically, but as soon as he heard himself, he realized he was probably telling the truth.

'What sort of things has he been arrested for?' he asked.

'The usual,' she answered. 'Assault, extortion, selling drugs, rape – this in the early stages of his career.' Then, almost as an afterthought, 'Since then he's moved on to association with the Camorra. And twice for murder. But neither of those cases made it to trial.'

'Why?'

'In one case, the chief witness disappeared, and in the other the chief witness retracted his testimony.'

Comment being superfluous, Brunetti asked, 'Where is he now, in jail?'

'He was, but he was released with the *indulto*, though he'd been inside only a few months.'

'For what?'

'Assault.'

'When was he let out?'

'Fifteen months ago.'

'Any idea where he's been since then?'

'In Mestre.'

'Doing what?'

'Living with his uncle.'

'And what does his uncle do?'

'Among other things, he owns a few pizzerias: one in Treviso, one in Mestre, and one here, up near the train station.'

'Among what other things?'

'He has a shipping line – trucks that bring fruit and vegetables up from the South.'

'And take back?'

'I haven't been able to find that out, sir.'

'I see. Anything else?'

'He has, in the past, rented trucks to Signor Cataldo.' Her face was motionless when she said this, almost as though she had never heard the name before.

'I see,' Brunetti remarked, then asked, 'and what else?'

'The nephew, sir: Antonio. It would seem, but this is only at the level of rumour, that he is involved with Signora Cataldo.' Her voice could not have been more level or dispassionate.

There were times when Signorina Elettra annoyed Brunetti almost past bearing, but he thought of the way he had behaved when caught in the crossfire of flirtation between her and Guarino and so said only, 'The first wife or the second?'

'The second.' She paused, then added, 'People couldn't wait to tell me.'

'What, exactly?'

'That he's taken her to dinner at least once; when the husband was away.'

'That could be easily explained,' Brunetti said.

'I'm sure it could be, sir, especially if her husband and his uncle have common business interests.'

He knew she had more, and he knew it would be more damning, but he would not ask.

After it became apparent that Brunetti was not going to speak, she said, 'He was also seen leaving their apartment – well, to be fair, the building in which they have an apartment, at two in the morning.'

'Seen by whom?'

'By people who live there.'

'How did they know who he was?' Brunetti asked.

'At the time, they didn't, but they paid attention to him, as would anyone meeting an unfamiliar man on the steps of their building at that time of night. Some weeks later, they met her in a restaurant, having dinner with the same man, and when they went over to say hello to her she had no choice but to introduce them. Antonio Terrasini.'

'And how did you come to learn all of this?' Brunetti inquired with false lightness.

'When I asked about Cataldo, I got told this as an extra. Twice.'

'Why is everyone so eager to repeat gossip about her?' Brunetti asked in a neutral tone that allowed her to include herself in the category or not.

She looked away from him and out the window again before she answered. 'It probably has nothing to do with her specifically, sir. There's the trope of the older man who marries a much younger wife: folk wisdom says it's only a matter of time before she betrays him. And there's the fact that people just like to gossip, especially when it's someone who keeps aloof from them.'

'And she does?'

'It would seem so, sir.'

Brunetti said only, 'I see.' The snow was entirely gone from the roof of the church by now; he thought he could see steam rising from the tiles.

'Thank you, Signorina.'

Franca Marinello and Antonio Terrasini. A woman about whom he thought he knew something and a man about whom he wanted to know a great deal more. Who was it who said that she had been working to impress Brunetti? Paola?

Was it that easy, he wondered? Just talk to him about books and sound like you know what you're talking about, and Brunetti falls into your hands like a ripe fig? Tell him you're in love with Cicero and then go out to dinner with . . . with whom and to do what, Brunetti wondered? What was that expression the Americans were always using to describe men like Terrasini? Rough something. Rough time? Rough taste? Rough traffic? The expression would not come, no matter how many times he tried to summon it. Rough something. In the photo, Terrasini did not look rough: he looked slick.

Thinking back over the evening he had spent with Franca

Marinello, Brunetti was forced to admit that her face, even after the hours opposite her, would still occasionally shock him. If she found something he said amusing, he could read it only in her eyes or in the tone of her response. Occasionally he had succeeded in making her laugh, but even then her face had remained as immobile as when she spoke of her loathing of Marc Antonio.

She was still in her thirties, and her husband was twice her age. Did she not want, at times, the company of a younger man, the feel of a stronger body? Had he been so concerned with her face that he had forgotten about the rest of her?

But still, why this thug? Brunetti kept coming back to this question. He and Paola knew enough about the workings of the city to have a good idea which of the wives of the powerful and wealthy sought the solace of arms other than their husbands'. But all of that was usually carried out among acquaintances and friends: discretion was thus assured.

Then what of all of her talk of being worried about kidnapping? Perhaps Brunetti had been too eager to dismiss her story of the computer intruder; and perhaps the signs of tampering had not been left by Signorina Elettra but by some other person curious to learn the extent of Cataldo's wealth. Terrasini's past certainly suggested that he would not mind having a try at kidnapping, but computer exploration hardly seemed the way he would begin things.

Years ago, Conte Falier had observed that he had never met anyone who could resist flattery. Brunetti had been younger then and had taken this as a comment on a technique of which the Conte approved, but as the years passed and he knew the man better, Brunetti realized that it was nothing more than another of the Conte's merciless observations about the nature of human activity. 'And Cataldo's wife was working to impress you,' he heard

Paola's voice again. If he eliminated all sympathy for the woman, how much of what she told him would he still believe? Was he to be seduced by the fact that she had read Ovid's *Fasti* and he had not?

21

Brunetti called down to the squad room and asked for Vianello. The Ispettore was out of the office, but someone passed the phone to Pucetti. By now everyone knew that when Vianello was not present, Brunetti would want Pucetti. 'Come up for a moment, would you?' Brunetti asked.

It seemed only seconds after Brunetti replaced the phone that Pucetti was there, swinging around the door and into his office, fresh-cheeked, as though he had run, or flown, up the steps. 'Yes, Commissario?' he said, eager, all but straining at the leash that might get him out of the office or at least out of whatever it was he had been doing downstairs.

'Gilda Landi,' Brunetti said.

'Yes, sir?' Pucetti asked with no sign of surprise, only curiosity.

'She is a civilian employee of the Carabinieri. Well, I assume she's a civilian and I assume it's the Carabinieri, but maybe not. Perhaps the Ministry of the Interior. I'd like you to see if you can find out where she works and, if possible, what she does.' Pucetti raised a hand in a vestigial salute, and left.

Though there was no reason to do it, aside from the fact that he had spent so much of the morning thinking about another woman, Brunetti called Paola and said he could not come home for lunch. She asked no questions, a reaction which bothered Brunetti more than if she had complained. Alone, he left the Questura and walked down into Castello, where he had a bad meal in the worst sort of tourist trap and left feeling both cheated and somehow justified, as if he had paid for having been dishonest with Paola.

When he got back, he stopped in the officers' squad room, but there was no sign of Pucetti. He went to Signorina Elettra's office, where he found her at her computer, Pucetti standing behind her, eyes intent on the screen.

When Pucetti saw Brunetti come in, he said, 'I had to ask her, sir. There was no way I could do that alone. There was one place where if I had . . .'

Brunetti stopped him by holding up a hand. 'Good. I should have told you to ask.' Then, to Signorina Elettra, who had glanced at him, 'I didn't want to burden you with anything else. I had no idea it would be so . . .' He allowed his voice to trail off.

He smiled at them, and the idea came to him that they were, in a sense, his surrogate children at the Questura, Vianello their uncle. And what did that make Patta? The dotty grandfather and Scarpa the wicked stepbrother? He pulled himself back from these thoughts and asked, 'Did you find her?'

Pucetti moved back, leaving the stage to Signorina Elettra. 'I started with the Ministry of the Interior,' she said. 'It's easy to get into a certain level of their system.' She was being calmly descriptive and made no attempt to show off by criticizing the laxity with which some agencies guarded their information. 'After a time, I began to find some places were blocked off to me, and so I had to go back and find other means of access.' Reading Brunetti's expression, she said, 'But the details of how I did it don't matter, do they?'

Brunetti glanced at Pucetti and saw the look the younger man gave her when she said this. He had last seen that expression on the face of a drug addict when he had smacked a needle out of his hand and crushed it under his heel.

'. . . special squadron set up to examine the Camorra's control of the garbage industry, and it turns out that Signorina Landi works for the Ministry of the Interior and has done so for some time.'

Suspecting that this was the least of what she had to say, he asked, 'What else did you learn about her?'

'She *is* a civilian, and she is also an industrial chemist with a degree from Bologna.'

'And her job?' Brunetti asked.

'From the little I could see before the . . . she does the chemical analysis of what the Carabinieri find or manage to sequester.'

'What were you about to say?' Brunetti asked.

She gave Brunetti a long look, then glanced aside at Pucetti before answering, 'I found it before the connection was interrupted.'

With a start, Brunetti turned towards the door to Patta's office; Signorina Elettra, seeing this, said, 'Dottor Patta has a meeting in Padova this afternoon.'

Recalling her hesitation, Brunetti asked, 'What does that mean to an ignorant person, that the connection was interrupted?'

She considered this briefly before answering him. 'It means that they've got a warning system that shuts everything down the instant it detects an unauthorized access.'

'Can they trace it?'

'I doubt it,' she said in a more confident voice. 'And if they did, it would lead to a computer at the offices of a company owned by a member of parliament.'

'Are you telling me the truth?' he asked.

'I try always to tell you the truth, Commissario,' she said, not indignantly, but close.

'Only try?' he asked.

'Only try,' she answered.

Brunetti chose to let this lie, but he could not pass up the opportunity to take a bit of wind out of her sails. 'Cataldo's computer people reported an attempt to break into their system.'

That stopped her, but after a moment's reflection she said, 'That trail leads back to the same company.'

'You seem remarkably nonchalant about this, Signorina,' Brunetti observed.

'No, I'm not, not really. I'm glad you told me about it, though: I won't make the same mistakes again.' And that, her tone signalled, was that.

'Does this Signorina Landi work in the same unit as Guarino did?' Brunetti asked.

'Yes. From what I managed to see, there are four men and two women, plus Dottoressa Landi and another chemist. The unit's based in Trieste, with another group working in Bologna. I don't know the names of the others and found her only because I had a specific name to look for.'

Silence fell. Pucetti looked back and forth between them but said nothing.

'Pucetti?' Brunetti asked.

'Do you know where he was killed, sir?'

'Marghera,' Signorina Elettra answered for him.

'That's where he was found, Signorina,' Pucetti corrected in a deferential voice.

'Other questions, Pucetti?' Brunetti asked.

'Who moved the body, and when will the autopsy be done, why was there so little in the newspaper, and what was he doing wherever it was he was killed?' Pucetti said, not managing to keep his voice calm as he recited this list.

Brunetti saw the look, and then the smile, that Signorina Elettra gave the young officer when he finished. However interesting it would be to have the answers to that list of questions, Brunetti realized that the first one was, at least for the present, the most important: where had Guarino been killed?

He left these thoughts and turned to Signorina Elettra. 'Would it be possible to contact this Dottoressa Landi?'

She did not respond immediately, leaving Brunetti to wonder if those same alarms would sound were she now to try to find something as simple as a phone number. She glanced at him and her eyes moved to distant focus as she planned some cyber manoeuvre he could never hope to understand.

'It's all right,' she finally said.

'Which means?' Brunetti asked, sparing Pucetti the need to ask.

'I'll get you her number.' She rose to her feet, Pucetti quick to pull back her chair. 'I'll call you when I have it, sir,' she said, then added, 'There's no risk.' Pucetti and Brunetti left the office.

Twenty minutes later, good as her word, she called with Signorina Landi's *telefonino* number, but when he dialled it, the client was unavailable. There was no invitation to leave a message.

To distract himself, Brunetti pulled towards him the oldest pile of papers that had accumulated on his desk and began to read through them, forcing himself to concentrate. One of Vianello's informers had recently told the Ispettore that he should pay attention to some of the shops in Calle della Mandola that had recently changed hands. If this was money laundering, as the informer suggested, then it was not his concern: let the Guardia di Finanza worry about money.

Besides, it was a street he seldom used, so it was difficult for him to cast his visual memory along it and register the changes of merchandise in the windows. The antique book store was still there, as were the pharmacy, and the optician. The other side of the street was more difficult, for it was there that changes had taken place. There were shops selling trendy olive oil and bottled sauces, glass, then the fruit vendor and the flower shop that was the first to put out lilacs in the spring. They could ask around, he supposed, but it was all rather like the question about Ranzato: were they meant to walk up and down the street, calling on the Camorra to come out of hiding?

He thought of an article he had read months before in one of Chiara's animal magazines about some sort of toad that had been imported into Australia. Taken there to combat a pest or insect that was endangering the sugar cane crop, this toad – was it the cane toad? – had no natural predators and thus increased relentlessly as it spread north and south. Its poison, it was discovered only after its numbers had shot past control, was strong enough to kill dogs and cats. Cane toads could be stabbed, pierced, run over by cars and still not be killed. Only the crows, it seemed, had learned how to kill them by flipping them over and devouring their viscera.

Did he need a more perfect comparison with the Mafia? Brought back to life by the Americans after the war to control the perceived Communist menace, it had got out of control and, as with the cane toad, its expansion north and south could not be stopped. It could be pierced and stabbed, but it would spring back to life. 'We need crows,' Brunetti said out loud, looked up, and saw Vianello at the door.

'It's the autopsy report,' Vianello said in an ordinary voice, as though he had not heard Brunetti speak. He handed Brunetti a manila envelope and, even before Brunetti nodded to him, took a seat in front of his desk.

Brunetti slit open the envelope and slid out the photos, surprised to see that they were no bigger than postcards. He put them on his desk and removed some sheets of paper, placing them to the side of the photos. He looked at Vianello, who had noticed how small the photos were.

'Economy measure, I suppose,' Vianello observed.

Brunetti tapped the edges straight on his desk and began to look through the crime-scene photos, passing them to Vianello after he had studied each one. Postcard size: indeed, what better postcards for the new Italy? His mind fled to the possibility of an entire new line of tourist posters and souvenirs: the squalid shack in which Provenzano had been arrested, the illegal hotel complexes inside national parks, the twelve-year-old Moldavian prostitutes at the sides of the road?

Or perhaps they could create a deck of playing cards. Bodies? Reduce the size of one of the photos of Guarino and they could begin a deck composed of the bodies found only in the last few years. Four suits: Palermo, Reggio Calabria, Naples, Catania. A joker? And who would that be, filling in wherever he was needed? He thought of the cabinet minister rumoured to be in their pocket – he would do nicely.

A light cough from Vianello put an end to Brunetti's grim flight of fancy. Brunetti handed him another photo, and then another. Vianello took them with increasing interest, all but snatching at the last of them. When Brunetti looked across at his assistant, he saw that his face was grim with shock. 'These are scene of crime photos?' he asked, as if he needed Brunetti's assurance to be able to believe it.

Brunetti nodded.

'You were there?' Vianello asked, though it was not really a question.

At Brunetti's repeated nod, Vianello tossed the photos face up on to Brunetti's desk. '*Gesù Bambino*, who are these clowns?' Vianello stabbed an angry forefinger on to one of the photos, where the toes of three different pairs of shoes could be seen. 'Whose feet are these?' he demanded. 'What are they doing so close to the body if it's being photographed?' He jabbed his finger on the imprints left by a pair of knees. 'And whose are these?'

He shoved the photos around and found one taken from a distance of two metres, showing the two Carabinieri standing behind the body, apparently in conversation. 'Both of them are smoking,' Vianello said. 'So whose cigarette butts are going to be in the evidence bags, for the love of God?'

The Ispettore lost all patience and pushed the photos back towards Brunetti. 'If they'd wanted to contaminate the scene, they couldn't have done a better job.'

Vianello pressed his lips together and retrieved the photos. He lined them up in a row, then switched them around so that they could be read, left to right, as the camera approached the body. The first showed a radius of two metres around the body, the second a radius of one. In both photos, Guarino's outstretched right hand was clearly visible in the bottom left of the photo. In the first photo, his hand lay on a clear field of dark brown mud. In the fourth, a cigarette butt was visible about ten centimetres from his hand. Guarino's head and chest filled the last photo, blood soaked into the collar and front of his shirt.

Vianello could not prevent himself from appealing to the gold standard. 'Alvise couldn't make a worse mess.'

Brunetti finally said, 'I think that's probably it: the Alvise factor. It's simple human stupidity and error.' Vianello started to say something, but Brunetti did not stop. 'I know it would be more comfortable, somehow, to blame it on conspiracy, but I think it's just the usual mess.'

Vianello considered this then shrugged, saying, 'I've seen worse.' After a time, he asked, 'What does the report say?'

Brunetti opened the papers and started to read through them, passing each one to Vianello as he finished reading it. Death had indeed been instant, the bullet having ripped through Guarino's brain before emerging from his jaw. The bullet had not been found. There followed some speculation about the calibre of the gun used in the crime, and it ended with the bland statement that the mud on Guarino's lapels and knees was different in composition and bore higher traces of mercury, cadmium, radium, and arsenic than did the mud under his body.

'"Higher?"' Vianello asked as he handed the papers back to Brunetti. 'God help us,' Vianello said.

'No one else will.'

The Inspector was reduced to raising his hands in a gesture of surrender. 'What do we do now?'

'There remains Signorina Landi,' Brunetti answered, much to the Ispettore's confusion.

22

They met the next day, he and Dottoressa Landi, at the train station of Casarsa, having agreed to split the distance between Venice and Trieste. He paused on the steps of the station, hit by the warmth of the sun. Much in the manner of a sunflower, he turned his face towards it and closed his eyes.

'Commissario?' a woman's voice called from the row of cars parked in front of him. He opened his eyes and saw a short dark woman with black hair step from a car. He noticed first that her hair, cut as short as a boy's, glistened wetly with gel, then that her body, even inside the padding of a grey down parka, was slim and youthful.

He walked down the steps and over to the car. 'Dottoressa,' he said formally, 'I want to thank you for agreeing to meet me.' She came barely to his shoulder and appeared to be in her thirties, though not by much. What makeup she wore had been carelessly applied, and she had already gnawed off most of her lipstick. It was a sunny day up here in Friuli, but her eyes were pulled tight by more than the sun. Regular features, normal nose, a face made memorable because of the hair and the evidence of strain.

He took her hand. 'I thought we might go somewhere and talk,' she said. She had a pleasant voice a bit heavy on the aspirants. Tuscan, perhaps.

'Certainly,' Brunetti answered. 'I don't know this area at all well.'

'I'm afraid there isn't all that much to know,' she said, getting back into the car. When both of them were buckled in, she started the engine, saying, 'There's a restaurant not far from here.' With a shiver, she added, 'It's too cold to stay outside.'

'Whatever you like,' Brunetti answered.

They drove though the centre of town. Pasolini, Brunetti remembered, had come from here, had fled in disgrace, gone to Rome. As they drove down the narrow street, Brunetti thought how lucky Pasolini had been to have been driven out of all of this undistinguished orderliness. How to live in a place like this?

Beyond the town, they drove down a highway, each side lined with houses or businesses or commercial buildings of some sort. The trees were naked. How bleak the winter was up here, Brunetti thought. And then came the thought of how bleak the other seasons would be.

No expert, Brunetti could not judge how well she drove. They turned to the left or right, passed through roundabouts, switched to smaller roads. Within minutes he was completely lost, could not have pointed in the direction of the station had his life depended on it. They passed a small shopping centre with a large optician's shop, then down another road lined with bare trees. And then to the left and into a parking lot.

Dottoressa Landi turned off the engine and got out of the car without saying anything. Indeed, she had not spoken since they set out, and Brunetti had remained just as quiet, busy watching her hands and what little scenery they passed.

Inside, a waiter showed them to a table in a corner. Another waiter moved around the room, which held about a dozen tables, putting down silver and napkins, shifting chairs closer to or farther from the tables. The scent of roasting meat came from the kitchen, and Brunetti recognized the penetrating odour of fried onions.

She asked for a *caffè* macchiato, Brunetti the same.

She draped her parka over the back of her chair and sat, not bothering with the business of waiting for someone to help her. He chose the place opposite her. The table was set for lunch, and she carefully shifted the napkin to the side, placed the knife and fork on top of it, then rested both arms on the table.

'I don't know how to do this,' Brunetti began, hoping to save time.

'What are our options?' she asked. Her face was neither friendly nor the opposite, her gaze level and dispassionate, as though she were a jeweller given something to assess, about to rub it on the touchstone of her intelligence to see how much gold it contained.

'I give one piece of information and then you give one, and then I give another, and so forth. Like laying down cards in a game,' Brunetti suggested, not entirely serious.

'Or else?' she asked with mild interest.

'Or else one of us tells everything they know, and then the other does the same.'

'That gives a tremendous advantage to the second person, doesn't it?' she asked, but in a warmer voice.

'Unless the first person lies, too,' Brunetti answered.

She smiled for the first time and grew younger. 'Shall I go first, then?' she asked.

'Please,' Brunetti said. The waiter brought the coffees and two small glasses of water. The Dottoressa added no sugar to her coffee, he noticed. Instead of drinking it, she looked into the cup and swirled it around.

'I spoke to Filippo after he went to see you.' She paused after that, then added, 'He told me what you talked about. The man he wanted you to help him identify.' Her eyes met his, then returned to the study of the foam on the top of her coffee. 'We worked together for five years.'

Brunetti drank his coffee and set the cup on the saucer.

Suddenly she shook her head, saying, 'No, it won't work this way, will it? My doing all the talking?'

'Probably not,' Brunetti said and smiled.

She laughed for the first time, and he saw that she was really an attractive woman disguised by worry. As if relieved to be starting all over again, she said, 'I'm a chemist, not a policewoman. But I told you that, didn't I? Or you knew it?'

'Yes.'

'So I try to leave all of the police stuff to them. But after all these years, I'm still learning things, even if I don't realize it. Even if I'm not paying attention.' Nothing she had said so far suggested that she and Guarino had been more than colleagues. Then why was she bothering to explain how it was she knew so much about 'police stuff'?

'I'm sure it's impossible not to hear things,' Brunetti agreed.

'Of course,' she said, then her voice changed and she asked, 'Filippo told you about the shipments, didn't he?'

'Yes.'

'That's how we met,' she said in a voice that had moved into a softer register. 'They sequestered a shipment that was going south. This was about five years ago. I did the chemical analysis of what they found, and when they traced it back to where it was picked up, I did the analysis of the ground and water around it.' After some time, she said, 'Filippo was in charge of that case, and he suggested I be transferred to his unit.'

'Friendships have started in stranger ways,' Brunetti volunteered.

Her glance was sudden and long. 'Yes, I suppose so,' she said and finally drank her coffee.

'What was it?' Brunetti asked and at her inquisitive glance, added, 'In the shipment.'

'Pesticides, hospital waste, and outdated pharmaceuticals.' A pause, and then, 'But not on the bills of lading.'

'What did they say?'

'The usual: urban garbage, just as if they were compressed bales of orange peel and coffee grounds from under the kitchen sink.'

'Where were they going?'

'To Campania,' she said. 'To the incinerator.' Then, as if to be sure he understood the full import of what she had said, she repeated: 'Pesticides. Hospital waste. Outdated pharmaceuticals.' She took a small sip of water.

'Five years ago?' he asked.

'Yes.'

'And since then?' Brunetti asked.

'Nothing's changed, except that there's far more of it.'

'Where does it go now?' he asked.

'Some gets burned, some gets put in dumps.'

'And the rest?'

'There's always the sea,' she told him, as though this were the most natural thing to say.

'Ah.'

She picked up her spoon and set it carefully beside her cup. 'It's just like Somalia, where they used to drop it. If there's no government, then they can do what they want.'

A waiter approached their table, and Dottoressa Landi asked for another coffee. Brunetti knew he could not drink another one before lunch and so asked for a glass of mineral water. Not wanting to be interrupted by the waiter's return, Brunetti said nothing, and she seemed glad of the silence. Time passed. The waiter returned and replaced their drinks.

*

203

When he was gone, she asked, leaping from one subject to another, 'He came to ask you about the man in the photo, didn't he?' Her voice had grown calm, almost as if being able to list the things she had found had worked some sort of exorcism.

Brunetti nodded.

'And?'

Well, here it was, Brunetti realized, that moment when he had to call upon his experience of life, personal and professional, and decide whether to trust this young woman or not. He knew his weakness for women in distress – though perhaps he did not know its full extent – but he also knew that his instincts were often correct. She had obviously decided that he was to be the posthumous beneficiary of Guarino's trust, and he saw no reason to suspect her.

'His name is Antonio Terrasini,' he began. She did not react to the name, nor did she ask how he had discovered this. 'He's a member of one of the Camorra clans.' Then he asked, 'Do you know anything about the photo?'

She made a business of stirring her coffee, then set the spoon on her saucer. 'The man who was killed . . .' she began, then gave Brunetti a stricken look and put her hand to her mouth.

'Ranzato?' Brunetti volunteered.

She nodded by way of answer, then forced herself to say, 'Yes. Filippo said he took it and sent it to him.'

'Anything else?'

'No, only that.'

'When did you see him last?' Brunetti asked.

'The day before he went down to talk to you.'

'Not after?'

'No.'

'Did he call you?'

'Yes, twice.'

'What did he say?'

'That he'd spoken to you and thought he could trust you. Then, the second time, that he had spoken to you again and sent you the photo.' She paused, decided to say it. 'He said you were very insistent.'

'Yes,' Brunetti said, and they lapsed into silence.

He saw her looking at her spoon, as if trying to decide whether to pick it up and move it around. Finally, she asked, 'Why kill him?' and Brunetti realized she had agreed to this meeting in order to ask that question. He had no answer to give.

Voices came from the other side of the room, but it was nothing more than a discussion among the waiters. When Brunetti looked back at her, he saw that she was as relieved as he by the distraction. Brunetti glanced at his watch and saw that he had twenty minutes to reach the next train back to Venice. He caught the waiter's eye and asked for the bill.

After he had paid and left some change on the table, they got to their feet. Outside, the sun was stronger, and it was a few degrees warmer. She tossed her parka into the back seat of the car before she got in. Again, the drive was silent.

In front of the station, he offered his hand. He turned to open his door, and she said, 'There's one more thing.' The sudden seriousness of her voice halted Brunetti just as he touched the handle of the door. 'I think I should tell you.' He turned towards her.

'About two weeks ago, Filippo told me he'd heard rumours. There was all that trouble in Naples, with the dumps closed, too many police. So they stopped shipping and started to stockpile the really bad things, or at least that's what he told me.'

'What does "really bad" mean?' Brunetti asked.

'Anything heavily toxic. Chemicals. Maybe nuclear. Acids. It would have to be substances that can be held in containers or barrels. That's what anyone can recognize as dangerous, so they wouldn't risk shipping it when there was trouble.'

'Did he have any idea where it might be?'

'Not really,' she answered evasively, the way an honest person does when trying to lie. His eyes met hers and held them before she could turn away. 'It's really the only place, isn't it?' she said.

Paola would be proud of him, he had time to think, his eyes still held by Dottoressa Landi's. His first thought had been of the short story, though he couldn't remember who had written it. Hawthorne? Poe? The Something Letter. Hide the letter in the place where no one will notice it: among the letters. Just so. Hide the chemicals among the other chemicals and no one will notice them. 'It explains why he was at the petrochemical complex,' he said.

Her smile was infinitely sad as she said, 'Filippo said you were smart.'

23

When he got back to the Questura, Brunetti decided to start at the bottom of the food chain with someone he had not spoken to for some time. Claudio Vizotti was, not to put too fine a point on it, a nasty piece of work. A plumber, hired decades ago by one of the petrochemical companies in Marghera, he had joined the union when he started his job. Over the years, he had risen effortlessly through its ranks, until now he had the responsibility of representing workers in claims against the companies regarding work-related injuries. Brunetti had first encountered him some years before, about a year after Vizotti had persuaded a worker injured in a fall from badly built scaffolding to settle his claim against the company in return for ten thousand Euros.

It had come to light – during a card game in which a drunken accountant from the company had complained about the vulpine behaviour of the union representatives – that the company had actually given Vizotti a total of twenty thousand Euros for his efforts in persuading the worker to settle, money that had somehow failed to make its way either into the hands of the injured worker or into the union's coffers. The word had spread, and since the card game had taken place not in Marghera but in Venice, it had spread to the police and not to the workers to whose protection Vizotti had dedicated his professional life. Brunetti, learning of the conversation, had called Vizotti in for another one. At first the union representative had indignantly denied everything and threatened to sue the accountant for libel and to make a complaint against Brunetti for harassment. It was then that Brunetti had pointed out that the injured worker, a man of irascible temper, now had one leg a few centimetres shorter than the other and was in almost constant pain. He knew nothing about the accommodation Vizotti had made with his employers, but he could very easily learn of it.

At this, Vizotti had turned smilingly tractable and said he had actually been keeping the money for the injured man and had somehow forgotten to pass it on to him: the press of work, union responsibilities, so much to do and think about, so little time. Speaking man to man, he had asked Brunetti if he wanted to take part in the transfer. Had he even winked when he proposed this?

Brunetti had refused the opportunity but told Vizotti to keep his name in mind should Brunetti ever want to talk to him again. It took Brunetti a few minutes to locate the number of Vizotti's *telefonino*, but there was no delay before Vizotti recognized Brunetti's name.

'What do you want?' the union representative asked.

In the ordinary course of events, Brunetti would have chided the man for his incivility, but he decided to take a more liberal stance and asked in a normal voice, 'I'd like some information.'

'About what?'

'About storage facilities in Marghera.'

'Call the firemen, then,' Vizotti shot back. 'That's not my job.'

'Storage facilities for things that the companies might not want to know about,' Brunetti went on imperturbably.

Vizotti had no instant answer to this, and Brunetti asked, 'If a person wanted to store barrels there, where would he put them?'

'Barrels of what?'

'Barrels of dangerous substances.'

'Not drugs?' Vizotti asked quickly, a question Brunetti found interesting but would not pause to consider just now.

'No, not drugs. Liquids, perhaps powders.'

'How many barrels?'

'Perhaps several truckloads.'

'Is this about that man they found out here?'

Seeing no reason to lie, Brunetti said, 'Yes.'

There ensued a long silence, during which Brunetti could almost hear Vizotti plunking down on the scales the possible consequences of lying against those of telling the truth. Brunetti knew enough of the man to know that Vizotti's thumb would be pressed down on the side that held self-interest.

'You know where he was found?' Vizotti asked.

'Yes.'

'Some of the men were talking – I don't remember who they were – and they said something about the storage tanks out in that area. Where the body was.'

Brunetti recalled the scene, the abandoned rust-eaten tanks that served as a background to the body in the field.

'And what did they say about them?' he asked in his mildest voice.

'That some of them look like they've doors now.'

'I see,' Brunetti said. 'If you hear anything else, I'd be . . .'

But Vizotti cut him short, saying, 'There won't be any more.' Then the line went dead.

Brunetti replaced his phone quietly. 'Well, well, well,' he allowed himself to say. He felt enmeshed in ambiguity. The case was not theirs, but Patta had ordered him to investigate it. The Carabinieri had control over the investigation of illegal shipping and dumping, and Brunetti had no authorization from a magistrate to make inquiries, certainly not to make an unauthorized raid. Well, if he and Vianello went alone, it could hardly be described as a raid on to private property, could it? They would be doing nothing more than going back to have another look at the scene of the murder, after all.

He was just getting to his feet to go down and talk to Vianello when the phone rang. He looked at it, let it ring three more times, then decided to answer it.

'Commissario?' a man's voice asked.

'Yes.'

'It's Vasco.'

It took Brunetti a moment to struggle through the events of the last few days, during which he stalled for time by saying, 'Good of you to call.'

'You remember me, don't you?' the man asked.

'Of course, of course,' Brunetti said and, with the lie, memory returned. 'At the Casinò. Have they come back?'

'No,' Vasco said. 'I mean yes.' Which was it, an irritated Brunetti wanted to ask. Instead he waited and the other man explained, 'That is, they were here last night.'

'And?'

'And Terrasini lost heavily, perhaps forty thousand Euros.'

'The other one; was it the same man who was with him last time?'

'No,' Vasco said. 'It was a woman.'

Brunetti did not bother asking for a description: he knew who it had to be. 'How long were they there?'

'It was my night off, Commissario, and the man on duty couldn't find your phone number. He didn't think to call me, so I didn't know about it until I got here this morning.'

'I see,' Brunetti said, fighting the impulse to shout at Vasco or at the other man, or at all men. Controlling this, he said, 'I appreciate your calling me. I hope . . .' He let his voice drift off, since he had no idea what he hoped.

'They might be back tonight, Commissario,' Vasco said, failing to hide the satisfaction in his voice.

'Why?'

'Terrasini. After he lost, he told the croupier he'd come back soon to get it all back from him.' When Brunetti said nothing, Vasco went on, 'It's a strange thing to say, no matter how much you lose. It's not like the croupier's taking your money: it's the Casinò and your stupidity in thinking you can beat it.' Vasco's contempt for gamblers was molten. 'The croupier told one of the inspectors it sounded like a threat. That's what's so strange about it: no real gambler would think that way. The croupier's just following the rules he's memorized: there's nothing personal at all in it, and God knows he's not going to keep the money he wins.' After a moment's reflection, he added, 'Not unless he's very clever.'

'What do you make of it?' Brunetti asked. 'You know how to read these people: I don't.'

'It probably means he's not used to gambling, at least to gambling where he loses all the time.'

'Is there any other sort?' Brunetti asked.

'Yes. If he plays cards with people who are afraid of him, then they'll let him win when they can. A man gets used to that. We get them in here once in a while; usually from the Third World. I don't know how things are there, but a lot of these men don't like to lose and get angry when they do. I guess it's because it never happens to them. We've had to ask a few of them to leave.'

'But he went quietly the other time, didn't he?'

'Yes,' Vasco said, his voice dragging out the word. 'But he didn't have a woman with him. That usually makes winning more important to them.'

'You think he'll be back?'

There was a long silence, and then Vasco said, 'The

croupier thought so, and he's been here a long time. He's tough, but he was nervous about it. These guys have to walk home at three in the morning, after all.'

'I'll come tonight,' Brunetti said.

'Good. But there's no need to get here before one, Commissario. I checked the records, and he's always shown up after that.'

Brunetti thanked him, saying nothing about the woman, and hung up.

'Why can't we just go out there in daylight and have a look?' Vianello asked after Brunetti had explained both calls to him and the need each created to go somewhere during the night. 'I mean, we're police; a murder victim was found there: we have every right to search the area. We still haven't found the place where he was murdered, remember.'

'It's better if no one realizes we know what we're looking for,' Brunetti said.

'We don't, though, do we?' Vianello asked. 'Know what we're looking for, that is.'

'We're looking for a couple of truckloads of toxic waste hidden somewhere near where Guarino was killed,' Brunetti said. 'That's what Vizotti told me.'

'And as I told you, we don't know where he was killed, so we don't know where we should be looking for these barrels of yours.'

'They aren't my barrels,' Brunetti said shortly, 'and they couldn't have taken him a long distance, not out there. Someone would have seen them.'

'But no one did see them, did they?' Vianello asked.

'You can't bring a dead man into the petrochemical area, Lorenzo.'

'I'd say it's a lot easier than bringing in a few truckloads of toxic waste,' the Ispettore answered.

'Does this mean you don't want to come?' Brunetti asked.

'No, of course it doesn't,' Vianello said, making no attempt to disguise his exasperation. 'And I want to go to the Casinò, as well.' Then, unable to stop himself from saying it, he added, 'If this wild goose chase ends before one.'

Ignoring that, Brunetti asked, 'Who'll drive?'

'Does that mean you don't want to ask for a driver?'

'I'd be more comfortable if it were someone we can trust.'

'Don't look at me,' Vianello said. 'I haven't driven more than an hour in the last five years.'

'Who, then?'

'Pucetti.'

24

Fincantieri was working three shifts building cruise ships, so there was a constant stream of people leaving and entering the petrochemical and industrial area. When three men arrived in a plain sedan at nine-thirty that evening, the guard did not bother to come out of his booth: he raised a friendly hand and waved them through the gates.

'Do you remember the way?' Vianello asked Brunetti, who sat in the front seat of the unmarked police car beside Pucetti. The Inspector peered out of the windows on one side of the car, then the other. 'It all looks different.'

Brunetti remembered the directions the guard had given the other day and repeated them to Pucetti. A few minutes later, they came upon the red building; Brunetti suggested they leave the car there and proceed on foot. Vianello, not a little embarrassed, asked them if they wanted anything to drink before they set off, saying that his wife had insisted he take along a thermos of tea with lemon and sugar. When they declined, he added that he had thought to put some whisky in, patting the pocket of his down parka.

The moon was almost full that night, so they had little need of Vianello's flashlight, and he soon put it in his other pocket. The source of the eerie glow that allowed them to see their way was hard to determine: it seemed to come as much from the flaring gas burn-off at the top of a tower not far from them as from the general radiance that slipped across the *laguna* from Venice, a city that had conquered darkness.

Brunetti turned and looked back towards the red building, red no more at night. Distance and proportion were meaningless: they could have been passing the place where Guarino had been found, or they could be hundreds of metres from it. Ahead he saw the hulking outlines of the storage tanks, draughtsmen on this vast, flat plain. Pucetti asked, keeping his voice low, 'If there are new doors, how do we get in?'

By way of answer, Vianello tapped the pocket of his jacket, and Brunetti knew he had brought along his set of burglar tools, scandalous should they be found on the person of a serving police officer. Even more shocking, Brunetti knew, was the skill with which the Ispettore could use them.

Droplets of humidity clung to their coats, and suddenly they were all conscious of the smell. It was not acid, nor was it the strong tang of iron, but some combination of chemical and gas that left a film on the skin and caused a faint irritation to nose and eye. Better not to breathe it; better not to walk in it.

They came abreast of the first storage tank and circled it until they came to a door that looked to have been crudely cut into the metal with a blowtorch. They stopped a few metres short of it, and Vianello cast the beam of his flashlight on the area just in front of the door. The mud there was slick and smooth, frozen and undisturbed since the last rain, some weeks before. 'No one's been in there,' Vianello said unnecessarily and switched off the light.

The next was the same: the mud was unmarked save by the tracks of some sort of animal: cat, dog, rat. None of them had any idea.

They went back to the dirt road and continued towards the third tank. It loomed above them, at least twenty metres high, a menacing cylinder back-lit by the lights of the port of San Basilio in the distance. To its left and right they saw the thousands of lights on the three cruise ships docked in the city across the *laguna*.

From behind them, they heard the dull hum of an approaching motor, and they all moved to the side of the road, seeking a place to hide. They ran towards the third tank and pressed themselves flat against its corroded surface as the sound grew, and grew. A light hit the ground and came towards them at alarming speed, and they pressed themselves harder against the curved metal surface.

The plane passed over them, drowning them in sound. Brunetti and Vianello covered their ears, but Pucetti did not bother. When the plane was past them, leaving them stunned in its wake, they pushed themselves away from the tank and started to circle back towards the door.

Again, standing not far from it, Vianello waved the beam across the mud in front of the door, but this time it revealed an entirely different story: tyre tracks and footprints led to and from the entrance. This door, further, was not a sloppy rectangle cut with a blowtorch and then hastily patched with a few wooden boards nailed together to discourage entrance. It was a proper, curved sliding door, the sort seen on a garage, but not the garage of a private house: the garage of a bus terminal. Or a warehouse.

Vianello went over to study the lock. His light illuminated another one above it, and then a padlock fixed through two metal circles soldered to the door and the wall of the tank. 'I'm not good enough for the top one,' he said as he turned away.

'So now what?' Brunetti asked.

Pucetti walked off to the left, staying close to the metal hull of the tank. He came back after a few steps and asked Vianello for the flashlight, then set off again with it in his hand. Brunetti and Vianello could hear his steps as he circled towards the back of the tank, then the odd clang as he banged something against the side. The sound of his footsteps was suddenly drowned out by the arrival of another plane, which again filled their universe with noise and light, and then was gone.

A minute passed before something approaching silence returned, though motors were audible in the distance and, somewhere, electrical wires hummed in the night air. Then they heard Pucetti coming back, frozen mud splintering under his feet.

'There's a ladder up the side,' the young officer said, unable to contain his excitement: cops and robbers, a night out with the boys. 'Come on; I'll show you.'

He was gone, disappearing around the curve of metal. They went after him and found him standing near the tank, flashlight pointing up the side. When their eyes followed the beam, they saw a series of round metal crossbars, starting about two metres from the ground and going up straight to the top.

'What happens up there?' Vianello asked.

Pucetti backed away, keeping the beam aimed at the point where the ladder reached the top. 'I don't know. I can't see.' Both of them joined him, but they could see nothing, either, save the final crossbar a hand's-breadth from the top.

'Only one way to find out,' Brunetti said, feeling quite bold. He walked back to the tank and reached towards the rungs.

'Wait a minute, sir,' Pucetti said. He came over to them and stuffed the flashlight into Brunetti's pocket, then got down on one knee, then the other, and made himself into a human footstool. 'Step up from my shoulder, sir. It'll be easier.'

Five years ago, Brunetti's masculinity would have scorned the offer. He raised his right foot, but when he felt the pull of cloth across his chest, he put his foot down and unbuttoned his coat, then stepped on Pucetti's shoulder and grabbed the second and third rungs. Easily, he pulled and stepped at the same moment and ended with both feet on the first rung of the ladder. As he started climbing, he heard Pucetti, then Vianello, say something. The sound of scrabbling below drove him up and up again; and he heard a heavy thump below him as a foot banged the side of the tank.

He had watched the first *Spider-Man* film with the kids and had enjoyed it. He could not now shake the feeling that he too was climbing up the side of a building, clinging to the side by virtue of his special powers. He climbed ten more rungs, paused for a moment and started to look at the men below him, but thought better of it and continued towards the top.

The ladder ended at a metal platform the size of a door. Luckily, it was enclosed in a metal handrail. Brunetti crawled on to it and got to his feet, then walked to the far end to leave space for the others. He took out the flashlight and lit the way for them, first Vianello and then Pucetti, as they crawled on to the platform. Vianello got to his feet and gave a stricken look into the flashlight's beam. Brunetti moved it quickly to Pucetti, whose face was radiant. What larks, what larks.

Brunetti turned the light on the wall of the tank and saw that a door with a metal handle stood at his end of the platform. He pressed it, and the door swung open easily on to an identical platform on the inside of the tank. He stepped inside and turned the light back so they could see well enough to join him inside.

Brunetti snapped his fingers: a moment later the sound came back, then repeated itself a few times until it dissolved. He tapped the thick plastic case of the flashlight against the railing that surrounded this platform, and after a moment that duller sharper sound was echoed back.

He shone the light down the steps ahead of them, illuminating the stairway that curved along the inner wall

218

and towards the bottom of the tank. The beam was not strong enough to reach the end of the stairs so they could see only part of the way down: the darkness changed everything and made it impossible to calculate the distance to the bottom.

'Well?' Vianello asked.

'We go down,' Brunetti said.

To assure himself of what he sensed, Brunetti switched off the flashlight. The other men drew in their breath: darkness visible. They knew darkness, the ancients, knew it as people today could only construct it artificially so as to make themselves feel the titillation of fear. This was darkness: nothing else was.

Brunetti switched the light back on and felt the other two relax minimally. 'Vianello,' he said. 'I'm going to give Pucetti the light, then you and I join arms and go down first.' Handing the light to Pucetti, he said, 'You shine it on our feet and follow us.'

'Yes, sir,' Pucetti said. Vianello reached sideways and took Brunetti's arm.

'Let's go,' Brunetti said. Vianello was on the outside, so he kept one hand on the railing, his other arm linked with Brunetti's, just as if they were a pair of frail old pensioners out for an afternoon walk that had suddenly turned out to be more difficult than expected. Pucetti kept the light on the step immediately in front of the other men, following them by instinct as much as by sight.

All of them could see the piles of rust on the steps, and Brunetti, walking down a stairway wide enough for only one person, felt the flakes brushing free from the inner wall and was convinced he could smell them as well. They descended into the Stygian dark, and with each step the stench grew more intense. Oil, rust, metal: it became more invasive as they got closer to the bottom, or else the overpowering sense of being engulfed in limitless darkness made their other senses more acute.

Though Brunetti knew it to be impossible, he thought it was darker than when they had entered. 'I'm going to stop, Pucetti,' he said, so that the young man would not crash into them. He paused, Vianello perfectly in step with him. 'Take a look around the bottom,' he told Pucetti, who leaned against the railing and flashed the light into the darkness below.

Brunetti looked up and saw a dull greyness that must be the door they had used to come in; he was surprised to see they had come more than halfway round the tank. He turned back and let his eyes follow the beam of light: they were still four or five metres from the bottom. In the beam of light, the floor seemed to glisten and sparkle, as from some inner glow or source of light. It was not liquid for, like the mud outside, its surface was composed of stiff whirls and waves: the moving reflection transformed it to a wine dark sea.

A shiver passed down Vianello's arm, and Brunetti was suddenly aware of the cold.

'What now, sir?' Pucetti asked, moving the beam back and forth in an even rhythm, ever farther from them. About twenty metres from them it lit up a vertical surface, and Pucetti allowed the light to move slowly up, as though asking it to climb the face of a mountain. The obstacle, however, proved to be no more than five or six metres high, for the face exposed by the light was the front of an assemblage of barrels and plastic containers: some black, some grey, some yellow. No great effort had been made to stack them neatly or in straight rows. Some of the barrels in the top row leaned tiredly against the ones next to them, and some in the outside rows tilted inwards like penguins huddling in the Antarctic night.

Without having to be told to do it, Pucetti ran the beam to one end of the pile, then moved it slowly back to the other end, allowing them to count the barrels in the front row. When the light reached the end, Vianello said softly, 'Twenty-four.'

Brunetti had read once that barrels contained a hundred and fifty litres, or perhaps it was more. Or less. But surely more than a hundred. He tried to do the numbers in his head, but his uncertainty about the volume, as well as how many rows stood behind the ones they could see, meant that he could not estimate the total more than to say each row contained at least twelve thousand litres.

Not that the number meant anything, not without knowing the contents. After that, they could tabulate the extent of the danger. All of these thoughts, numerical and otherwise, went through his mind as the light played over the façade of barrels.

'Let's have a look,' Brunetti said, keeping his voice down. He and Vianello descended to the bottom step. 'Give me the light, Pucetti.'

Brunetti freed his arm from Vianello's and stepped on to the floor of the tank. Pucetti passed the Ispettore and stepped down, then took another step, and joined Brunetti. 'I'll come with you, sir,' the younger man said, shining the light on to the mud just beneath their feet.

Vianello lifted one foot, but Brunetti put a restraining hand on his arm. 'I want to see how we get out of here, first.' He was conscious of how softly they all spoke, as if to cause an echo might bring peril.

Instead of answering, Pucetti waved the beam of light back up the curving stairs, all the way to the top.

'In case we have to move quickly,' Brunetti said. In the glow from the flashlight, he reached out and took it from Pucetti's hand. 'Wait here,' he said and moved off, his left hand sliding along the wall of the tank. He moved slowly until he found the door and then the inner keyholes of the two locks.

Not too far ahead he saw what he had hoped to see: the horizontal hand-bar of a smaller emergency exit cut into the larger door. Brunetti saw no written warning about an alarm nor any sign that it was wired to one. He pressed down on the bar, and the door swung outward on well-oiled hinges. The air brushed across his face, bringing different smells and a reminder of just how foul the air inside was. He toyed for a moment with the idea of leaving the door propped open, but decided against it. He pulled it closed, and the inner cold and smell returned.

He lit his way back to the others. Before he could say anything, Pucetti stepped closer and linked his arm in Brunetti's, a gesture Brunetti found touchingly protective. Tentatively, arm in arm, they set off, careful of where they trod on the icy surface, pausing after every step to see that their feet were safely grounded on the frozen peaks and crevices of the floor. Caution slowed them, so it took them some time to reach the centre of the front line of barrels.

Brunetti ran the light across them, hunting for something that would disclose their contents or origins. The first three gave no indication of either, though the white skull and crossbones suggested the superfluity of such niceties. The next barrel had traces of white paper where something had been ripped away, leaving two faded Cyrillic letters. The container beside it was clean, as were the next three. Close to the end of the row stood a barrel with a sulphurous green trail leading from under the lid to a patch of dried powder in the mud in front of it. Pucetti released Brunetti's arm and walked beyond the last barrel. Brunetti turned the corner and flashed the light along the side of the rows of barrels. 'Eighteen,' Pucetti said after a moment. Brunetti, who had counted nineteen, nodded and moved back to have a closer look at the corner barrel; he could see an orange label just below the lid. German was not a language he could read, but it was one he could recognize. 'Achtung!' Well, that left little doubt. 'Vorsicht Lebensgefahr.' This one, too, had a leak near the top and a dark green stain in the mud below.

'I think we've seen enough, Pucetti,' he said and turned back to where he thought Vianello was waiting.

'Right, Commissario,' Pucetti said and started towards him.

Brunetti stepped away from Pucetti, called Vianello's name and, when he answered, pointed the beam in the direction of his voice. Neither of them saw what happened. Behind him, he heard Pucetti take a sharp breath – of surprise, not of fear – and then he heard a long slithery noise that he was able to identify only in retrospect as the sound of Pucetti's foot sliding suddenly forward on the frozen mud.

He felt something slam into his back and he had a moment's terror at the thought that it was one of the barrels. Then a thud, then silence, then a sudden cry from Pucetti.

He turned slowly, moving his feet carefully, and pointed the light towards Pucetti's voice. The young officer was on his knees, wiping his left hand across the front of his coat, moaning while he did so. He stuffed his hand between his knees and began to rub it back and forth against the cloth of his trousers.

'*Oddio, oddio*,' the young man moaned and astonished Brunetti by spitting on his hand before wiping it again. He scrambled to his feet.

'Vianello, the tea,' Brunetti shouted and turned to point the light wildly, no longer sure where Vianello was, nor the door.

'I'm here,' the Ispettore said, and suddenly Brunetti had him transfixed in the light, thermos in one hand. Brunetti pulled Pucetti forward and locked his own hand around his lower arm, shoving Pucetti's hand towards Vianello. The young man's palm and part of the back of his hand were covered with traces of some black substance, much of which he had managed to wipe on to his clothing. Amidst the black, the skin was red, in places peeling back and already bleeding.

'This is going to hurt, Roberto,' Vianello said. He raised the thermos above the young man's hand, and at first Brunetti didn't understand what he was doing. But when the liquid spilled out, steaming, he realized that the Ispettore hoped that it would cool at least minimally before hitting the burnt flesh of Pucetti's hand.

Brunetti tightened his grip, but there was no need to do that. Pucetti understood and stood motionless as the tea hit and then splashed across his hand. Brunetti stepped back, the better to keep the light steady on what was happening. The stream fell, leaving a halo of vapour all around it. Time seemed without end. 'Here,' Vianello finally said and handed Brunetti the thermos.

The Ispettore pulled off his parka and ripped a piece of the fleece lining from the inside. He dropped the jacket in the mud and used the ragged strip to wipe between the young man's fingers, as thoughtful and careful as a mother. When he had most of the black goo removed, he took back the thermos and dribbled more tea across Pucetti's hand, turning the hand carefully to see that the liquid went everywhere before running off on to the ground.

When the thermos was empty, Vianello dropped it and said to Brunetti, 'Give me your handkerchief.' Brunetti gave it to him, and Vianello wrapped it around Pucetti's hand, tying it in a knot on the back. He picked up the thermos, pulled the young man to him in a one-armed hug, then said to Brunetti, 'Let's get him to the hospital.'

25

The doctor at the Pronto Soccorso at the Mestre hospital took almost twenty minutes to clean Pucetti's hand, soaking it in a mild cleansing liquid and then in a disinfectant to lower the risk of infection from what was, in essence, a burn. He said that whoever had thought to wash his hand had probably saved it, or at least prevented the burns from being far worse than they were. He slathered on salve and wrapped Pucetti's hand until it looked like a white boxing glove, then gave him something for pain and told him to go to the hospital in Venice the next day, and every day for a week, to have the dressing changed.

Vianello stayed with Pucetti while Brunetti was out in the corridor talking to Ribasso, having reached the Carabiniere after some difficulty. The Captain seemed not at all surprised by Brunetti's account and, when Brunetti finished telling him about Pucetti, replied, 'You're lucky my sharpshooters decided to leave you alone.'

'What?'

'My men saw you drive in and go up the ladder, but one of

them thought of checking the registration. Good thing you used an official car or there might have been trouble.'

'How long have you been there?' Brunetti asked, fighting to keep his voice neutral.

'Since we found him.'

'Waiting?' Brunetti asked, his mind running after possibilities.

'Of course. It's strange they'd leave him so close to where the stuff is,' Ribasso said, offering no explanation. Then he went on, 'Sooner or later, someone has to come for what's in there.'

'And if they don't?'

'They will.'

'You sound very sure about that.'

'I am.'

'Why?'

'Because someone must have been paid to let them stock-pile it there, and if they don't move it, there will be trouble.'

'So you wait?'

'So we wait,' Ribasso answered. 'Besides, we've got lucky. A new magistrate's been assigned to Guarino's murder, and it looks like she might be serious.'

Brunetti, silent, left him to his optimism.

Then Ribasso asked, 'What happened to your man? They told me it looked as if you had to help him to your car.'

'He fell and put his hand down into the mud.'

Hearing Ribasso's sudden intake of breath, Brunetti said, 'He'll be all right. He's seen a doctor.'

'Is that where you are, the hospital?'

'Yes.'

'Let me know what happens to him, all right?'

'Of course,' Brunetti said, and then asked, 'How bad is it in there?'

'You name a chemical and it's in that mud.' After a long pause he said, 'And blood.'

Brunetti allowed an even longer period to pass and asked, 'Guarino's?'

'Yes.' He added, 'And the mud matches what was on his clothes and shoes.'

'Why didn't you tell me?'

Ribasso said nothing.

'You find the bullet?' Brunetti asked.

'Yes. In the mud.'

'I see.' Brunetti heard a door open behind him and saw Vianello put his head out. 'I've got to go.'

'Take care of your man,' Ribasso said.

'What is it, Lorenzo?' Brunetti asked as he flipped his phone closed.

Vianello held out his own *telefonino*. 'It's Griffoni. She's been trying to get you. So she called me.'

'What's she want?' Brunetti asked.

'She wouldn't say,' the Ispettore said, handing the phone to Brunetti.

'Yes?' Brunetti asked.

'Someone called Vasco's been trying to find you, but your phone was turned off; then it was busy. So he called me.'

'What did he say?'

'That the man you're looking for is there.'

'Wait a minute,' Brunetti said. He went back into the other room, where Vianello stood leaning against the wall. The doctor did nothing to disguise his displeasure at Brunetti's arrival. 'It's Vasco. He's there.'

'The Casinò?'

'Yes.'

Instead of answering, Vianello looked at the dull-eyed Pucetti, who sat bare-chested on the edge of the examining table, propping his bandaged hand up with the other. He turned to Brunetti and smiled, 'It doesn't hurt any more, Commissario.'

'Good,' Brunetti said and smiled encouragingly. Then, to

227

Vianello, 'Well?' He held up the phone to show the call was still active.

He watched Vianello consider and then decide. 'See if she can go with you,' he said. 'You'll be less conspicuous. I'll stay with him.'

Brunetti pulled the phone back and said, 'I'm at the hospital in Mestre, but I'm leaving now. I'll be at the Casinò in . . .' he began, paused to calculate the time, and said, 'In half an hour. Can you make it?'

'Yes.'

'Not in uniform,' he said.

'Of course.'

'And have a launch get me at Piazzale Roma. I'll be there in twenty minutes.'

'Yes,' she said and was gone.

Brunetti never understood how she did it, but Commissario Claudia Griffoni was standing on the deck of a taxi waiting at the police landing stage when his car pulled up twenty minutes later. Even had she worn her uniform, it would have been reduced to insignificance, perhaps invisibility, by her dark mink coat. It reached just to the top of a pair of razor-point crocodile-skin shoes with heels so high they made her as tall as Brunetti.

The taxi pulled away as soon as he was on deck and sped up the Grand Canal towards the Casinò. Brunetti explained as much as he could, finishing with what Ribasso had told him about sharpshooters.

When he stopped, she asked only, 'And Pucetti?'

'His hand's burnt; the doctor said it's not as bad as it could have been and his only real risk is infection.'

'What was it?' she asked.

'God knows. Whatever's leaked out of those barrels.'

'Poor boy,' she said with real feeling, though she could be no more than ten years older than Pucetti.

They saw Ca' Vendramin Calergi appear on their left and moved out on to the deck. The driver cut towards the dock, switched into reverse, and brought them to a stop a millimetre from the landing. Griffoni opened her sequined bag, but the driver said only, 'Claudia, *per piacere*,' and offered an arm to help her step on to the dock.

Glad that he had thought to clean his shoes and wipe his coat with one of the hospital's towels, Brunetti stepped on to the red carpet close behind her, took her arm, and walked towards the open doors. Light spilled towards them and warmth engulfed them as they stepped inside: how very unlike the place where he had been with Vianello and Pucetti. He glanced at his watch: well after one. Was Paola asleep or was she awake, perhaps in the company of Henry James, waiting for her legal husband to come home? He smiled at the thought, and Griffoni asked, 'What is it?'

'Nothing. I thought of something.'

She gave him a quick look before they moved off across the courtyard and through the main doors. At the front desk, Brunetti asked for Vasco, who appeared after a very short time, his face unable to disguise his excitement and then, when he saw a different woman with Brunetti, his surprise.

'Commissario Griffoni,' Brunetti said, enjoying the sight of Vasco's badly disguised reaction, which he covered by telling them to come with him and put their coats in his office. Inside, he handed Brunetti a tie and while he waited for him to put it on, said, 'He's up at the blackjack table. He's been here about an hour.' Then, with surprise even greater than that with which he had greeted Griffoni, he said, 'Winning.' It sounded as if that sort of thing were not meant to happen there.

The two commissari fell into step behind Vasco, who decided to take the stairs to the first floor. Everything was as Brunetti remembered it: the same people, the same sense of physical and moral dilapidation, the same soft lighting on shoulders and jewels.

Vasco led them through the roulette rooms and towards the one in which Brunetti had watched the card players. He stopped just before the door and told them to wait there until he was well across the room. He had dealt with Terrasini before and did not want to be seen entering the room with them.

Vasco walked in and made his slow way towards one of the tables, his hands clasped behind his back in the manner of a floorwalker or an undertaker. Brunetti noticed that Vasco's right forefinger was pointing to the table at his left, though his attention seemed entirely directed to another table.

Brunetti looked towards the table, and as he did a man on the near side stepped aside, opening a sightline to the young man who sat on the opposite side. Brunetti recognized the sharp, exaggerated angle of the eyebrows, as though painted there with geometric exactitude. Dark eyes, unnaturally bright and seeming to be all iris, a broad mouth, and dark, gelled hair that brushed past the left eyebrow without touching it. He had a day's growth of beard and, when he raised his cards to look at them, Brunetti saw large, thick-fingered hands, the hands of a labourer.

As Brunetti watched, Terrasini slid a small pile of chips forward. The man sitting next to him tossed down his cards. The croupier took another card. Terrasini shook his head. The man next to him took another card, then threw the others down. The croupier gave himself another card, then he too tossed his cards down on the table and swept the chips towards Terrasini.

The sides of the young man's mouth pulled upward, but it was more taunt than smile. The dealer gave each player two cards – one up, one down – and the game continued. Brunetti glanced up and saw that Griffoni had wandered off to the other side of the room, where she appeared to be dividing her attention between the table where the young man was playing and the one where Vasco had his head bent to hear what was being said to him by a woman in a yellow dress who stood beside him.

Brunetti looked back just as the standing man took another step to the right, broadening the sightline. And he saw Franca Marinello, standing behind Terrasini, her eyes on his cards. Terrasini turned to her, and her lips moved. He tipped his chair back while he waited for the other players to decide what to do. He reached his arm out and wrapped it around her hip, drawing her close to him. Inattentively, as though her hip were a lucky coin or the knee of a saint's statue that brought luck when touched, he rubbed his hand against it: Brunetti could see the cloth of her dress wrinkle under his touch.

Brunetti watched her face. The eyes glanced at Terrasini's hand, then returned to the table. She said something, perhaps calling his attention to the croupier. He removed his arm and let his chair fall forward. Her expression did not change. Terrasini called for a card, which the croupier placed in front of him. Terrasini looked at the card, shook his head, and the croupier turned his attention to the next player.

Terrasini's eyes moved around the table, then slid off in the direction of Brunetti, but by then Brunetti was pulling his handkerchief out of his breast pocket to wipe his nose, his attention elsewhere. When he glanced back at the table, the croupier was sliding more chips in Terrasini's direction.

There was a minor disturbance at the table as the croupier got to his feet, saying something to the players. He gave a small bow and moved behind his chair, and another man in impeccable evening clothes slid into his place.

Terrasini took this opportunity to stand and turn away from the table. He raised his arms and grasped his hands together above his head like a tired sportsman. His motion pulled at the back of his jacket, and Brunetti saw the bottom half of what looked like a brown leather holster just above the left back pocket of his trousers.

The new dealer took fresh cards and began to shuffle them. At the sound, Terrasini lowered his hands and moved closer to Franca Marinello. Casually he ran both palms slowly across her breasts before taking his seat once again. Brunetti saw the flesh around her mouth go dead white, but she made no attempt to move away from the table, and she did not look at Terrasini.

She blinked, and her eyes stayed closed perhaps a second too long. When she opened them, she was looking in Brunetti's direction. And she recognized him.

He thought she might nod, perhaps smile, but she gave no sign of knowing him. Then it occurred to him that she might say something to Terrasini, but she did not move. She could have been a statue, gazing at another statue. After some time she looked back at the cards in front of Terrasini. The game resumed, but this time it was the croupier who finished with the chips in front of him, and so with the next hand, and the next. Then the man to Terrasini's right and then the one to his left won, and then it was again the turn of the croupier.

The chips in front of the young man melted away until there was only one pile, which grew smaller, and then it was gone. Terrasini pushed his chair back and all but jumped to his feet: his chair fell backwards to the floor. He slammed the palms of both hands on to the cloth of the table and leaned forward to shout at the croupier. 'You can't do that. You can't do that.'

Suddenly Vasco – Brunetti had no idea where he had come from – and another man were on either side of Terrasini, helping him stand upright and talking to him in low voices. Brunetti noticed how white were the knuckles of Vasco's right hand and how the cloth of Terrasini's sleeve wrinkled even more than had Franca Marinello's dress.

The three men started towards the door, Vasco leaning down and speaking to Terrasini all the while, his expression friendly and relaxed, as if he and his assistant were helping a client to his water taxi. The woman in the yellow dress moved quickly towards the table, righted the chair and set it back in place. She sat, put her purse in front of her, opened it and took out a handful of chips.

Brunetti saw Griffoni heading for the door, caught her eye, and hurried to join her. Franca Marinello was a few steps in front of them, walking quickly in the direction of the three men, who had reached the door. Still walking, Vasco shot a quick glance back into the room. When he saw the police approaching, he abandoned his smile and hurried the young man down the first ramp of steps. Marinello followed them, accompanied by the low sound of voices from the gambling room.

The men stopped at the first landing, and Vasco spoke to Terrasini, who nodded, head still lowered. Vasco and the other man exchanged a look over the young man's head and, as if they had practised the move many times, let go of his arms at the same moment and stepped away from him.

Marinello pushed past Vasco's assistant and went to stand next to Terrasini. She put a hand on his arm. It looked to Brunetti as if it took him a moment to recognize her, and when he did, he appeared to relax. Seeing the situation defused, Vasco and his assistant started back up the stairs; they stopped before they reached Brunetti and Griffoni, two steps above them.

She bent her head close to Terrasini and said something. Startled, Terrasini looked up at the four people, and Brunetti thought he saw Marinello's lips move as she spoke again. Terrasini's right hand moved so slowly that Brunetti could not believe what he was doing until he saw his hand fumble under the front of his jacket and emerge holding the pistol.

Terrasini shouted, Vasco and his assistant looked back,

then flattened themselves on the stairs. Griffoni moved to the railing, as far from Brunetti as possible, pistol already in her hand. Brunetti took his and pointed it at the slow-moving Terrasini, saying, in a voice he worked to keep calm and authoritative, 'Antonio, there are two of us.' He did not allow himself to consider what would happen if the three of them opened fire in this enclosed space, how the bullets would ricochet against surfaces, hard or soft, until their energy was entirely spent.

As if coming out of a daze, Terrasini looked from Griffoni to Brunetti, then at Marinello and at the two men huddled on the stairs, and then back to Brunetti.

'Put the gun on the floor, Antonio. There are too many people here and it's dangerous.' Brunetti saw that Terrasini was listening to him, but he wondered what it was that made his eyes so dull: drugs, or drink, or rage, or all three. Tone was probably more important than what he said – that and keeping the young man's attention.

Signora Marinello took a small step towards Terrasini and said something Brunetti could not hear. Very slowly, she raised her hand, placed it on his left cheek, and turned his face in her direction. Again, she spoke to him, and put out her hand. Her lips pulled back and she gave a small, encouraging nod.

Terrasini narrowed his eyes, suddenly confused. He looked at his hand, seemed almost surprised to see the gun there, and let his hand drop halfway to his knee. In ordinary circumstances, Brunetti would have approached them, but her presence near the young man kept him at a cautious distance, gun still raised.

Again she spoke. The young man handed the gun to her, shaking his head in what appeared to Brunetti to be confusion. She took the gun with her left hand and transferred it to her right.

Brunetti lowered his own pistol and began to slip it into his

234

holster. When he returned his attention to the people on the landing, he saw Terrasini look at her in astonishment and then pull his right hand back and make a fist. His left hand shot out and grabbed her just at the point where the shoulder becomes the throat, and Brunetti realized what he was going to do.

She shot him. She shot him in the stomach once and then again, and when he was lying on the floor at her feet, she took a step towards him and shot him in the face. Her dress was pale grey and long: the first two shots stained the silk at her stomach, and the third one sprinkled red droplets just above the hem.

In the stairwell, the noise was deafening. Brunetti looked at Griffoni, whose mouth moved, but the only sound he heard was a loud buzz that did not stop, even after Griffoni's mouth closed.

Vasco and his assistant scrambled to their feet, looked down at the landing, where Franca Marinello stood, the pistol still in her hand. They turned and, as one, vaulted up the stairs and through the doors into the gaming room, from which no sound emerged. Brunetti saw the double doors close and vibrate with the force, but still all he could hear was the buzz.

Brunetti looked back at the landing. Franca Marinello tossed the gun negligently on to Terrasini's chest, looked up at him, and said words he could not hear, trapped as he was inside this bell jar of unrelenting noise.

He heard something beside him, something dull and leaden that managed to penetrate the buzz, and turned to see Griffoni approach: it must have been her footsteps on the steps. 'You all right?' Brunetti asked. Griffoni understood and she nodded.

Brunetti saw that Franca Marinello was crouched against the wall, as far as she could be from Terrasini's body, face pressed into her knees. No one had certified that the young man was dead, but Brunetti knew it was a body that lay there, blood seeping on to the marble behind his head.

He was surprised at the stiffness in his knees and at how reluctant they were to take him down the steps. He could feel, but still not hear, his footsteps. Avoiding Terrasini, he knelt on one knee beside the woman. He waited until he was sure she was aware of him near her and then said, glad to be able to hear his own voice, however faintly, 'Are you all right, Signora?'

She raised her head and presented him with her face, never before seen so close to. The tilted eyes looked all the stranger for being so near, and he suddenly noticed a thin scar starting just below her left ear and disappearing behind it.

'Did you have time to read the *Fasti*?' she asked, and Brunetti wondered if this were a sign of shock.

'No,' he said. 'I've had so little time.'

'Pity,' she said. 'It's all there. Everything.' She lowered her head to her knees.

Brunetti found himself with nothing to say. He got to his feet and turned towards a sound from above, again swept with relief that he could hear it. He saw Vasco at the top of the stairs, looking enormous from this angle, like a character in an action film, like a cartoon figure of Conan the Barbarian, like . . .

'I called your people,' he said. 'They should be here soon.'

Brunetti's eyes fell to the top of the head of the silent woman and, on the other side of the landing, the eternally quiet body. Terrasini lay on his back. Looking at him, Brunetti thought of that other corpse, Guarino, and to the terrible resemblance between these two men so quickly, so terribly, stripped of life.

26

After a few minutes' sensation, Vasco managed to calm the people in the gaming rooms at the head of the stairs by telling them there had been an accident. Willing to believe it, they went back to what they were losing, and life went on.

Claudia Griffoni went back to the Questura with Signora Marinello, she also enveloped in a long fur, the same one she had been wearing the night Brunetti first saw her. He waited while the technical crew set up their cameras on the stairs. Two police officers having witnessed the shooting, the technicians did little more than photograph the scene and put the pistol in a plastic evidence bag, then wait for the *medico legale* to arrive.

He called Paola a little before three and told her sleep-fogged voice that he would not be back for some time. After Terrasini was declared dead, Brunetti asked the technical squad if they would take him back with them but chose to stay on deck with the pilot. Neither man spoke; the motor seemed unaccountably low until Brunetti remembered the three shots and the odd dislocation of sound that followed them. He looked at the façades of the buildings they passed, not really seeing them, for he was back on the stairs, watching, and not understanding, what happened.

Franca Marinello spoke to Terrasini and he took out the gun, then she spoke again, and he gave it to her. And then, while Brunetti was looking away, something happened – did she say something? – that maddened him. And then she used the gun. Everything, Brunetti knew, was subject to rational explanation. Cause was followed by effect. The autopsy would determine what substances were in the young man's brain, but at least when Brunetti was watching him, he had been responding to words, not to chemicals.

The launch swung into the Rio di San Lorenzo and pulled up at the dock of the Questura. Brunetti looked into the cabin of the boat and saw the two attendants getting to their feet. Did they talk to one another, he wondered, on their way back from these trips?

He thanked the pilot and jumped off the still-moving boat. He knocked on the door of the Questura, and the night man let him in, saying, 'Commissario Griffoni is in her office, sir.'

He went up the stairs and then followed the beacon of light from her door at the end of the dark hallway. He paused at the door but did not knock. 'Come in, Guido,' she said.

A clock on the wall to the left of her desk told him it was three-thirty. 'If you gave me a coffee, I'd shoot Patta and have you promoted to his job,' she said, looking up, and then smiled.

'They didn't tell us, when we took these jobs, about this part of it, did they?' he said, crossing the room and sitting opposite her. 'What did she say?'

Griffoni ran both hands through her hair in a gesture he had seen her make towards the end of Patta's meetings, a sign that her patience was running short. 'Nothing.'

'Nothing?' Brunetti asked. 'How much time did you spend with her?'

'I brought her back here in the boat, but she didn't say anything except thank you to the pilot, and then to the man who opened the door, and then to me.' She moved her hands towards her head but stopped herself and said, 'I told her she could call her lawyer if she wanted to, but all she said was, "No, thank you. I'd prefer to wait until the morning", like a teenager caught for drunk driving who didn't want to wake her parents up.' She shook her head, either at the comparison or at Marinello's behaviour.

'I told her she could leave if her lawyer came and she made a statement in my presence, but she said she wanted to talk to you. She was perfectly polite – I even liked her – but she refused to say anything, and there was nothing I could do to make her change her mind. I'd ask her, and she'd say thank you but no. It's strange, really. And that face.'

'Where is she?' Brunetti asked, not wanting to enter into that discussion.

'Downstairs, in one of the interview rooms.'

Ordinarily, these rooms would have been called 'interrogation rooms'. Brunetti wondered what made her use the less threatening description, but that was not something he wanted to talk about, either.

'I'll go down,' he said, getting to his feet. He held out his hand. 'Could you give me the key?'

She opened her hands in a helpless gesture. 'The door's not locked. As soon as she went in, she sat down and took a book out of her bag and started to read. I couldn't do it, couldn't lock the door.' Brunetti smiled at her, liking her for her weakness. 'Besides, Giuffrè's down there, and she'd have to go past him if she tried to leave.'

'All right, Claudia. Maybe you should go home and get some sleep. Thanks. And thanks for coming tonight.'

She looked up at him and asked, unable to hide her nervousness, 'Your ears? Are they still ringing?'

'No. Are yours?'

'Not really. But there's a small buzz. It's much less than it was, but a little bit of it's still there.'

'Get some sleep, then go over to the hospital in the morning and tell them what happened. There might be something they can tell you.'

'Thanks, Guido, I will,' she said and reached to switch off her desk lamp. She got to her feet and Brunetti helped her into her coat and waited for her at the door to her office. Not speaking, they went down the stairs together. On the ground floor, she said good-night. Brunetti turned down the corridor towards the single light that came from the door of one of the rooms at the end.

He paused and glanced in, and Franca Marinello looked up from her book.

'Good morning,' he said. 'I'm sorry you had to wait for me.'

'Oh, that's all right. I don't sleep a lot any more, and I had a book with me, so it doesn't matter.'

'But you'd be more comfortable at home, I'm sure.'

'Yes, surely that's true. But I thought you might think it important that we talk tonight.'

'Yes, I think it is,' he said, coming into the room.

As if it were her salon, she nodded to the chair across from her, and he sat. She closed her book and laid it on the table, but he could not see the spine and so had no idea what it was.

She had seen his glance. 'Psellus's *Chronographia*,' she said, placing a hand on the book. Brunetti recognized the author and the title, but no more than that. 'It's about decline,' she told him.

It was late, almost four, and he longed for sleep. This was not the time or the occasion for the discussion of books. 'I'd like to talk to you about the events of this evening, if I might,' Brunetti said soberly.

She turned to the side as if to try to look around him. 'Isn't

240

there supposed to be someone with a tape recorder, or at least a stenographer?' she asked lightly, hoping to make it sound like a joke.

'I suppose there should be, but that can wait until later. I'd like you to speak to your lawyer first.'

'But isn't this a policeman's dream, Commissario?'

'I don't know what you're talking about,' he said, his patience slipping, and he too tired to disguise that fact.

'A suspect willing to talk to him without a tape recorder and without a lawyer?'

'I'm not sure what you're suspected of, Signora,' he said, trying to say it lightly, if only to change the mood, probably failing, he realized. 'And nothing you say has much value, simply because it isn't being recorded or filmed, and so you will always be able to deny having said it.'

'I'm afraid I long to say it,' she said. He saw that she had become serious, even sober, but her face gave no sign of that, only her voice.

'I'd appreciate it, then, if you'd tell me.'

'I killed a man tonight, Commissario.'

'I know. I saw you do it, Signora.'

'How did you interpret what happened?' she asked, as if she were asking him what he thought of a film they had both seen.

'I'm afraid that's irrelevant. What counts is what happened.'

'But you saw what happened. I shot him.'

He felt a wave of tiredness wash over him. He had climbed up and into that storage tank, seen Pucetti's hand, skin hanging off, seen his blood on the bandages. And he'd watched her shoot and kill a man, and he was too tired to endure this talk, talk, talk.

'And I saw you speak to him, and each time he did something different.'

'What did you see him do, then?'

241

'I saw him look up at us as though you'd warned him we were there, and then you said something else and he gave you the gun, and then after you had it, I saw him pull his hand back as if he were going to hit you.'

'He *was* going to hit me, Commissario. Please don't let there be any question of that.'

'Could you tell me why?'

'What do you think?'

'Signora, what I think or don't think doesn't matter, I'm afraid. What matters is that Commissario Griffoni and I saw that he was going to hit you.'

She surprised him by saying, 'It's a pity you still haven't read it.'

'I beg your pardon?'

'The *Fasti*: 'The Flight of the King'. I know it's a minor work, but some other writers found him interesting. I'd like the piece to get the just attention it deserves.'

'Signora,' Brunetti snapped, pushing his chair back and getting angrily to his feet. 'It's almost four o'clock in the morning, and I'm tired. I'm tired of being out in the cold for most of the night and, if you don't mind my saying so, I'm tired of playing literary cat and mouse with you.' He wanted to be at home, warm, in his bed, asleep, with no buzzing in his ear and no provocation of any sort, from anyone.

Her mask gave no sign of how this affected her. 'Well, then,' she said and sighed. 'I think then I'll wait until the morning and call my husband's lawyer.' She slid the book closer, looked him in the eye, and said, 'Thank you for coming to talk to me, Commissario. And thank you for talking to me those other times, as well.' She picked up the book. 'Perhaps it does me good to realize that a man can be interested in me for something other than my face.'

With a final glance at him and something that might have been a smile, she returned to her reading.

Brunetti was glad she had turned her attention away from him. There was nothing he could say to this, no response, no question.

He wished her good-night and left the room and went home.

27

He slept. Paola, about to leave for class, tried to wake him at nine, but she managed no more than to shift him to her side of the bed. Some time later, the phone rang, but it did not penetrate to wherever Brunetti had gone, a place where Pucetti had two good hands, where Guarino was not lying dead in the mud, nor Terrasini on the marble floor, and where Franca Marinello was a lovely woman in her thirties whose whole face moved when she smiled or laughed.

After eleven Brunetti woke, looked out the window and saw that it was raining. He slept again. When next he woke there was bright sun, and for the first moments, Brunetti wondered if he were still asleep and this was a dream. He lay still for at least a minute, and then he pulled one hand slowly from under the covers, happy to hear the rustling of the sheets. He tried to snap his fingers, but all he managed to create was the sound of two fingers rubbing together. But he heard it clearly, with no buzz, and then he shoved back the covers, delighted by the slithery sound of them.

244

He stood, smiled at the sun, and accepted the fact that he needed a shave and a shower, but more than that, he needed coffee.

He took the coffee back to bed with him and set the cup and saucer on the night table. Kicking off his slippers, he got back under the covers and reached over to pull out his old copy of Ovid from the books beside him. He had found it two days ago but had had no time, no time. *Fasti*. What had she said, 'The Something of the King'? He flipped through the table of contents and found it, 'The Flight of the King', for 24 February. He pulled up the covers, shifted the book to his right hand, and took a sip of coffee. He replaced the coffee and began to read.

After a paragraph he recognized the story: he thought it was also told in Plutarch, and hadn't Shakespeare used it for something? Wicked Tarquin, the last king of Rome, driven from the kingdom by the populace at the head of which strode the noble Brutus, outraged by the death of his wife, the fair Lucrezia, who had been driven to suicide by her rape by the even more wicked son of the king, who had threatened to destroy her husband's reputation.

He read the passage again, then closed the book very softly and placed it on the covers beside him. He finished his coffee, allowed himself to slide lower in the bed, and looked out the bedroom window at the clear sky.

Antonio Terrasini, nephew of a Camorra boss. Antonio Terrasini, arrested for rape. Antonio Terrasini, photographed by a man who was later shot to death in an apparent robbery, the photo in the possession of a man who died in similar fashion. Antonio Terrasini, apparent lover of the wife of a man somehow involved with the first victim. Antonio Terrasini, shot to death by that same woman.

As Brunetti looked out the window he moved these people and facts around on the surface of his memory, prodding them here and there with a recalled detail, then shoving one possibility aside to replace it with some new speculation that lined them up in a different order.

He recalled the scene at the gaming table: the man's hand on her hip and the look she gave him then; his hands on her breasts and the way she failed to move away, though her entire body seemed to shrink from him. She had been in profile to Brunetti when she shot him, not that her face was capable of indicating much. Her words, then: what words had lit the man's anger, then quelled it, then set it flaming again?

Brunetti reached for the phone and dialled the number of the home of his parents-in-law. One of the secretaries answered, and he gave his name and asked to speak to the Contessa. Brunetti had learned over the years that the speed with which his call was transferred seemed related to his use of their titles.

'Yes, Guido?' she asked.

'I wonder if I might stop by on my way to work and speak to you,' Brunetti said.

'Come along whenever you can, Guido,' she said.

He turned to look at the bedside clock, amazed to see that it was after one. 'I'll be there in half an hour or so; if that's convenient for you, that is.'

'Of course, Guido, of course. I'll expect you, then.'

When she was gone, Brunetti pushed back the covers and went down to shower and shave. Before he left the house, he opened the refrigerator and found the remains of the leftover lasagne. He set it on the counter, took a fork from the cabinet, and ate most of what remained, put the fork in the sink, pulled the plastic wrap back over the ravaged lasagne, and put it back in the refrigerator.

Ten minutes later, he rang the bell to the *palazzo* and was taken, by some dark-suited person he did not recognize, to the Contessa's study.

She kissed him when he came in, asked if he wanted coffee,

insisted until he agreed, and asked the man who had accompanied Brunetti to bring coffee and biscotti for them both. 'You can't go to work without coffee,' she said. She took her usual place in the easy chair that allowed her to see out over the Grand Canal and leaned over to pat the seat of the chair beside her.

'What is it?' she asked when he sat down.

'Franca Marinello.'

She did not seem surprised. 'Someone called and told me,' she said in a sober voice that grew softer as she added, 'The poor girl, the poor girl.'

'What did they say?' he asked, wondering who had called but unwilling to ask.

'That she was involved in something violent at the Casinò last night and was taken to be questioned by the police.' She waited for Brunetti to explain and when he did not, she asked, 'You know about this?'

'Yes.'

'What happened?'

'She shot a man.'

'And killed him?'

'Yes.'

She closed her eyes, and Brunetti heard her whisper what might have been a prayer, or something else. He thought he heard the word 'dentist', but that made no sense. She opened her eyes and looked at him directly. In a voice that had regained its force, she said, 'Tell me what happened.'

'She was there in the Casinò with a man. He threatened her, and she shot him.'

She considered this and asked, 'Were you there?'

'Yes. But for the man, not for her.'

Again, the Contessa paused a long time before asking, 'Was it this Terrasini man?'

'Yes.'

'And you're sure it was Franca who shot him?'

'I saw her do it.'

The Contessa closed her eyes and shook her head.

There was a knock on the door, and this time it was a woman who came in. She wore sober and formal clothes, though there was no tiny white apron. She set two cups of coffee, a bowl of sugar cubes, two small glasses of water, and a plate of biscotti on the table in front of them, nodded to the Contessa, and left.

The Contessa handed Brunetti his coffee, waited while he dropped in two cubes of sugar, then picked up her own, which she drank without sugar. She set her cup back on the saucer and said, 'I met her – oh, it was years ago – when she came here as a student. Ruggero, a cousin of mine, had a son who was Franca's father's best friend. They were related on the mother's side, as well,' she began, then made an exasperated noise and stopped.

'It doesn't matter, does it, if we're related? When she came here to study, Ruggero's son called and asked me if I'd keep an eye on her.' She picked up a biscotto, but set it back on the plate untouched.

'Orazio said you became friends.'

'Yes, we did,' the Contessa said promptly and tried to smile. 'And we still are.' Brunetti did not ask about this, and the Contessa went on. 'Paola was gone,' she said, then smiled. 'Married to you. It had been years, but I suppose I still missed having a daughter in the house. She's younger than Paola, of course, so perhaps I missed having a granddaughter. Well, a young person.' She paused a moment and added, 'She knew almost no one here and was so terribly shy then; one wanted so much to help her.' She glanced at Brunetti and said, 'Still is, don't you think?'

'Shy?' Brunetti asked.

'Yes.'

'I think so, yes,' Brunetti said, just as if he had not watched Franca Marinello shoot a man to death the previous evening.

At a loss for what to say, the best Brunetti could think of was, 'Thank you for seating me opposite her. I never have anyone to talk to about books. Other than you, I mean.' Then, in justice to his wife, he added, 'Well, the ones I like.'

The Contessa's face brightened. 'That's what Orazio said. That's why I put you with her.'

'Thank you,' he repeated.

'But you're here for work, aren't you?' she asked. 'Not for books.'

'No, not for books' he said, though that was not the entire truth.

'What do you need to know?' she asked.

'Anything you can tell me that might help,' he said. 'You knew this Terrasini?'

'Yes. No. That is, I never met him, and Franca never talked about him. But other people did.'

'Saying that they were lovers?' Brunetti asked, fearing it was too soon to be so direct but wanting to know.

'Yes, saying that.'

'Did you believe it?' Brunetti asked.

Her look was as cool as it was level. 'I don't want to answer that question, Guido,' she said with surprising force. 'She's my friend.'

He thought of what she had whispered before and asked in honest confusion, 'Did you say something about a dentist?'

Her surprise was real. 'You mean you don't know?'

'No. I don't know anything about her. Or about a dentist.' The second part was true.

'The dentist who did that to her face,' she said, adding to his confusion. When his expression did not change, she continued heatedly, 'I could understand if she had shot *him*. But it was too late. Someone already did.' Saying that, she stopped speaking and looked across the canal.

Brunetti leaned back in his chair and put both hands flat on the arms. 'I don't understand any of this.' When her face remained impassive, Brunetti said, 'Please tell me.'

She pushed herself back in her chair, mimicking his posture. She studied his face for some time, as though trying to determine how and what and how much to tell him. 'Soon after she married Maurizio, whom I've known for most of my life,' she began, 'they made plans to go on vacation – I suppose it was a kind of honeymoon. Somewhere in the tropics, I don't remember now where it was. About a week before they were to leave, she started having trouble with her wisdom teeth. Her dentist was on holiday, so some friend from the university told her about one she went to in Dolo. No, not Dolo: somewhere out there. So she went to him and he said that both teeth had to come out. He took X-rays and told her it wouldn't be difficult, that he could do it in his surgery.'

The Contessa looked at him, then closed her eyes for a moment. 'So she went there one morning and he did it, extracted them both, gave her some painkillers and an antibiotic in case of infection and told her she could leave on vacation in three days. The next day she had some pain, but when she called him he told her that was normal and told her to take more of the painkillers he'd given her. The next day it was no better, so she went to see him, and he told her there was nothing wrong, gave her more painkillers, and off they went on vacation. To wherever it was, some island somewhere.'

She was silent for so long that Brunetti finally asked, 'What happened?'

'The infection continued, but she was young and she was in love – they were both in love, Guido. I know that to be true – and she didn't want to ruin their vacation, so she kept taking the painkillers, and when the pain still didn't go away, she kept taking them.'

This time, Brunetti sat quietly and waited for her to go on.

250

'After five days on the island, she collapsed, and they took her to a doctor – there wasn't much in the way of medical attention there. He said there was an infection in her mouth, something he wasn't able to treat, so Maurizio hired a plane and took her to Australia. That was the nearest place where he thought she could get help. Sydney, I think.' Then, absently, 'Not that it matters.'

She picked up the water, drank half of it and set the glass down. 'She had one of those terrible hospital infections. Apparently it had spread from where the teeth had been and gone into the tissue of her jaw and face.' The Contessa covered her own face in her hands, as if trying to protect it from what she was saying.

'The doctors there had no choice. They had to go in and try to save what they could. It was one of those infections that doesn't respond to antibiotics, or she was allergic to them. I really don't remember now.' The Contessa uncovered her face and looked at Brunetti. 'She told me once, years ago. It was terrible to hear her talk about it. She was such a lovely girl. Before it happened. But they had to do so much, destroy so much. To save her.'

'So that explains it,' said a bemused Brunetti.

'Of course,' the Contessa said fiercely. 'Do you think she'd *want* to look like that? For the love of God, do you think any woman would?'

'I had no idea,' Brunetti said.

'Of course you didn't. And no one else does.'

'But you do.'

She nodded sadly. 'Yes, I do. When they came back, she looked like she looks now. She called me and asked to come to see me, and I was overjoyed. It had been months, and all I knew was what Maurizio told me on the phone, that she had been very sick, but he didn't say what. When she called me, Franca told me she had had a terrible accident, and I wasn't to be shocked when I saw her.' Then, after a moment, 'At least she tried to prepare me. But nothing could, could it?' she asked, but Brunetti had no answer to give her.

He sensed that the Contessa was bringing it all back by speaking of it. 'But I *was* shocked, and I couldn't hide it. I knew she'd never want to do something like that. And she was so pretty, Guido: you can have no idea how pretty she was.'

The photo in the magazine had given him an idea, and so he did know.

'I started to cry. I couldn't help myself: I simply started to cry. And Franca had to comfort me. Guido, think about it – she came back like that, and I was the one who broke down.' She stopped talking and blinked her eyes a few times, but she managed to fight back tears.

'It was the best the surgeons in Australia could do. Because the infection had gone on for too long.'

Brunetti cast his attention out the window and studied the buildings on the other side of the canal. When he looked back, tears ran down the Contessa's cheeks. 'I'm sorry, *Mamma*,' he said, quite unconscious of calling her that for the first time.

She gave herself a shake. 'I'm sorry too, Guido, so sorry for her.'

'But what did she do?'

'What do you mean, what did she do? She tried to live her life, but she always had that face and the assumptions people made about it.'

'She didn't tell anyone?'

The Contessa shook her head. 'I told you: she told me, and she asked me not to tell anyone. And until today, I haven't. Only Maurizio and I know, and the people in Australia who saved her life.' She gave a sigh and sat up straighter. 'For there's that to say, Guido: they saved her life.'

'What about the dentist?' he asked, and then added, 'And how did he die?'

'It turned out he wasn't a dentist after all,' she said, voice

252

moving closer to anger. 'Just one of those *odontotechnici* you read about all the time: they start making false teeth, then they set themselves up as dentists and do that until they get caught, but nothing happens to them.' He saw her hands grip tight on the arms of the chair.

'You mean he wasn't arrested?'

'Finally,' she said tiredly. 'The same thing happened to another patient. This one died. So the inspectors from ULSS went in, and they discovered his whole surgery – the tools and the furniture – filled with that hospital infection. It's a miracle he killed only one person and that any of the others survived. So this time someone did go to prison. The sentence was six years, but the trial had taken two – and he was at home for that, of course – so he was supposed to be there for four years, but he was released with the *indulto*.'

'Then what happened?'

'He went back to work, it seems,' she said with a bitterness he had seldom heard her express.

'Work?'

'As an *odontotechnico*, not a dentist.'

He closed his eyes at the folly of it. Where else could something like this happen?

'But he didn't get a chance to hurt many people,' she said neutrally.

'Why?'

'Someone killed him. In Montebelluna – he'd moved there to open a new surgery. There was a break-in and someone killed him and raped his wife.'

Brunetti remembered the case. Two summers ago, a break-in, a murder that was never solved.

'He was shot, wasn't he?' Brunetti asked.

'Yes.'

'Did you ever talk to her about this?' he asked.

Her eyes widened. 'What for? To ask if she felt better because he was dead?' She saw how stunned he was by her question and softened her tone to say, 'I read about it and recognized his name, but I couldn't ask her.'

'Did you ever discuss it – him – with her?'

'Once, just after he was sentenced, I think. At any rate, years ago.'

'What did you say?'

'I asked if she had read about his conviction and that he would go to prison, and she said she had.'

'And?'

'And I asked her what she thought about it.' Without waiting for Brunetti, she went on, 'She said it didn't make any difference. Not to her and not to any of the people he'd injured. And certainly not to the person he'd killed.'

Brunetti considered this for some time and then asked, 'Do you think she meant that she had forgiven him?'

She looked at Brunetti, a long, thoughtful glance. 'She could have meant that,' she said and then added, coldly, 'But I hope she didn't.'

28

Brunetti left soon after that and, standing in the *calle* beside the *palazzo*, called Griffoni at her office, who told him that Signora Marinello had left the Questura that morning in the company of her lawyer. The file, she told him, was downstairs, but she would call him back in a few minutes with Marinello's number. While he waited for her to do that, Brunetti continued towards the Cà Rezzonico stop, from where he could take a vaporetto in either direction.

Griffoni called back with the *telefonino* number even before he reached the *imbarcadero*. Brunetti explained that he wanted to talk to Marinello about the night before, and Griffoni asked, 'Why'd she shoot him?'

'You saw it,' Brunetti said. 'You saw him get ready to hit her.'

'Yes, of course I did,' the other commissario replied. 'But I don't mean that: I mean the third time. He was on the floor, with two bullets in him, for God's sake, and she shot him again. That's what I don't understand.'

Brunetti thought he understood, but he did not say this.

'That's why I want to talk to her.' He cast his memory back to the scene of the killing: Griffoni had been standing against the railing when Brunetti looked at her, so she would have seen the people on the landing below from a different angle.

'How much of what happened did you see?' he asked.

'I saw him pull out the gun, then he handed it to her, then he raised his hand to hit her.'

'Could you hear anything?' he asked.

'No, I was too far away, and those other two were coming up the stairs towards us. I didn't notice him say anything, and her back was to me. Did you hear anything?'

He hadn't, so he answered, 'No,' then added, 'but there's got to be a reason he did what he did.'

'And why she did what she did, I'd say,' Griffoni added.

'Yes, of course.' He thanked her for the number and hung up.

Franca Marinello answered her phone on the second ring and seemed surprised that Brunetti had called. 'Does this mean I have to go back to the Questura?' she asked.

'No, Signora, it doesn't. But I'd like to come and speak to you.'

'I see.'

There was a long pause, after which she said, offering no explanation, 'I think it would be more convenient if we talked somewhere else.'

Brunetti thought of her husband. 'As you like.'

'I could meet you in about twenty minutes,' she suggested. 'Would Campo Santa Margherita be convenient for you?'

'Of course,' he said, surprised at such a modest neighbourhood. 'Where?'

'There's that *gelateria* on the side opposite the pharmacy.'

'Causin,' Brunetti supplied.

'In twenty minutes?'

'Fine.'

She was there when he arrived, sitting at a table at the back.

She stood when she saw him enter, and he was struck anew by the conflict of her appearance. From the neck down, she looked like any casually dressed woman in her mid-thirties. Tight black jeans, expensive boots, a pale yellow cashmere sweater and a patterned silk scarf. Once his eyes rose above the scarf, however, everything changed, and he was looking at the sort of face usually reserved for the ageing wives of American politicians: too-tight skin, too-wide mouth, eyes pulled here and there by the attentions of surgeons.

He shook her hand, again noticing the firmness of her grasp.

They sat, a waitress appeared, and he could think of nothing he wanted to drink.

'I'm going to have camomile tea,' she said, and it suddenly seemed the only possible choice. He nodded, and the waitress went back to the counter.

Not knowing how to begin, he asked, 'Do you come here often?' feeling awkward at having begun with such a stupid question.

'In the summer I do. We live quite close. I love ice-cream,' she said. She glanced out of the large plate glass window. 'And I love this *campo*. It's so – I don't know the right word – so full of life; there are always so many people here.' She glanced at him and said, 'I suppose this is the way it was years ago, a place where ordinary people lived.'

'Do you mean the *campo* or the city?' Brunetti asked.

Thoughtfully, she answered, 'I suppose I must mean both. Maurizio talks about the way the city used to be, but I've never seen that. I've known it only as a foreigner, I suppose you could say, and not for very long.'

'Well,' Brunetti conceded, 'not very long by Venetian time, perhaps.'

Brunetti judged they had spent enough time saying polite things and so said, 'I finally read the Ovid.'

'Ah,' was her response. Then, 'I suppose it wouldn't have

257

made any difference, not really, if you had read it any sooner.'

He wondered what difference it was meant to make, but he did not ask her that. Instead, he asked, 'Would you tell me more about it?'

They were distracted by the waitress's return. She carried a large tray with a teapot and a small jar of honey, along with cups and saucers. She set everything on the table, saying, 'I remembered you like it with honey, Signora.'

'How very kind of you,' Marinello said, her smile in her voice. The waitress left; she lifted the top of the teapot and bounced the teabags up and down a few times, then replaced it. 'I always think of Peter Rabbit when I drink this,' she told Brunetti as she picked up the teapot. 'His mother gave it to him when he was sick.' She swirled the pot a few times.

Brunetti had read the book to the kids when they were small and remembered that this was true, but he said nothing.

She poured out the tea, spooned some honey into hers and pushed the bottle in his direction. Brunetti added some to his, trying to remember if old Signora Rabbit had added honey or not.

He knew the tea was too hot to drink, so he ignored it and asked, choosing not to return to a discussion of Ovid, 'How did you meet him?'

'Who? Antonio?'

'Yes.'

She stirred the spoon around in her cup and set it in her saucer. Then she looked across at Brunetti. 'If I tell you that, then I'll have to tell you everything, won't I?'

'I'd like you to do that,' Brunetti answered.

'Well, then.' She returned to stirring the tea. She glanced up, then back at her cup, and finally said, 'My husband has many business contacts.'

Brunetti was silent. 'Some of them are . . . well, they are

persons who . . . persons he would prefer I knew nothing about.'

She looked to see that he was following and continued, 'A few years ago, he began a collaboration . . .' She stopped herself short. 'No, that's too easy a word, I think; or too evasive. He hired a company run by people he knew to be criminals, though what he was doing was not illegal.'

She sipped at her tea, added more honey, and stirred it around. 'I learned later,' she began, and Brunetti made note of the fact that she did not say how she came to learn whatever it was she was about to tell him, 'that it happened at dinner. He was out with the most important of them: they were celebrating their contract or their agreement or whatever they called it. I had refused to go with him, and Maurizio told them I was sick. It was the only thing he could think of that wouldn't offend them. But they understood, and they were offended.'

She looked at him and said, 'You have more experience with these people than I do, I suppose, so you know how important it is to them that they be respected.' At Brunetti's nod, she added, 'I think part of it must have begun there, when Maurizio didn't bring me to meet them.' She shrugged and said, 'It doesn't matter, I suppose. But one does like to understand things.'

Suddenly, she said, 'Drink your tea, Commissario. You don't want it to get cold.' Commissario, then, Brunetti thought. He did as he was told and drank some: it brought back his youth and being in bed with a cold or the flu.

'When he told them that I was sick,' she went on, 'the man who had invited him asked what was wrong – I had had more dental work that day.' She looked at him as if to see whether he understood the significance of this, and he nodded. 'It was all part of the other thing.'

She drank more tea. 'And Maurizio must have sensed their resentment because he told them more than he should have;

at least, enough for them to understand what had happened. It must have been Antonio who asked about it.' She looked at him again and said in a voice as cold as death, 'Antonio could be very charming and sympathetic.'

Brunetti said nothing.

'So Maurizio told them at least part of what had happened. And then he said something . . .' She paused and asked him: 'Did you ever read the play about Becket and Henry the Somethingth?'

'Second,' Brunetti said.

'So you know the part about the king's asking his knights if no one would rid him of that pesky cleric, or something like that?'

'Yes, I know it.' The historian in him wanted to add that the story was probably apocryphal, but this did not seem the moment.

She stared into her cup and puzzled him by saying, 'The Romans were so much more direct.' Then she continued, as if she had not mentioned the Romans, 'That's what happened, I think. Maurizio told them what had happened, about the fake dentist and what he did, and that he had been in jail, and I suppose he said something about there being no justice in this country.' It sounded to Brunetti as if she were repeating something she had learned by rote or had said – at least to herself – many times. She looked at him and added, in a softer voice, 'It's what people are always saying, isn't it?'

She looked at her teacup, picked it up but did not drink. 'I think that was all Antonio needed. A reason to hurt someone. Or worse.' There was a faint clink as she set her cup back in the saucer.

'Did he say anything to your husband?'

'No, nothing. And I'm sure Maurizio must have thought that was the end of it.'

'He didn't tell you about the conversation?' Brunetti asked, and at her confusion, explained, 'Your husband, that is.'

Her astonishment was complete. 'No, of course not. He doesn't know I know anything about it.' Then, in a much slower, softer voice, 'That's what this is all about.'

'I see,' was the only thing Brunetti could think of to say, though it seemed as if he was seeing less and less.

'Then, some months later, the dentist was killed. Maurizio and I were in America when it happened, but we heard about it when we got home. The police from Dolo came to ask us about it, but when Maurizio told them we had been in America, they went away.' He thought she was finished, but then she added, in a different voice, 'And the wife.'

She closed her eyes and said nothing for a long time. Brunetti finished his tea and poured them both some more.

'It was Antonio, of course,' she said conversationally.

Of course, thought Brunetti. 'Did he tell your husband what he'd done?' he asked, wondering if this was going to become a tale of blackmail, and that was why she had come to the Questura to speak to him.

'No. He told *me*. He called and asked to come and see me – I don't even remember what the excuse was. He said he was one of my husband's business associates' – she said the words with malice. 'I told him to come to the apartment. And he told me.'

'What did he say?'

'What had happened. That Maurizio, at least according to him – Antonio, that is – had made it clear what he wanted to be done, and Antonio had done it.' She looked at him, and he had the feeling she had said everything she had to say and was waiting for him to comment. 'But that's impossible,' she added, trying to sound convinced.

Brunetti let some time pass and then asked, 'Did you believe him?'

'That Antonio had killed him?'

'Yes.'

Just as she was about to answer, the high-pitched noise of a child's delight flew in from the *campo*, and her eyes turned towards it. Not looking at Brunetti, she said, 'It's strange: that was the first time I saw Antonio, but it never occurred to me to doubt him.'

'Did you believe that your husband asked him to do it?'

If Brunetti had expected her to be shocked by his question, he was disappointed. If she sounded anything, it was tired. 'No. Maurizio couldn't have done that,' she said in a voice that tried to stave off doubt or discussion.

She turned her eyes back to Brunetti. 'The most he could have done was talk about it; there's no other way they could have known, is there?' Her voice was painful to hear as she asked, 'How else would Antonio have known the dentist's name?' She waited for some time, then said, 'But Maurizio, no matter how much he might want it to happen, would not ask him do something like that.'

Brunetti said only, 'I see. Did he say anything else when he came to see you?'

'He told me that he was certain Maurizio would not want me to know about it. He started by suggesting that Maurizio had asked them to do it directly, but when he saw – Antonio was not stupid, you have to understand – that I couldn't believe that, he changed the story and said that it might have been no more than a suggestion but that Maurizio had given them the name. I remember: he asked me if I thought there was any other reason Maurizio would have given them the name.' Brunetti thought she had finished, but then she added, 'And the wife.'

'What did he want?'

'He wanted me, Commissario,' she said in a voice that had a savage edge to it. 'I knew him for two years, and I know he was a man with . . .' She left the phrase hanging while she searched for the suitable words. 'With unpleasant tastes.' When Brunetti did not respond to the use of those words, she added, 'Like Tarquin's son, Commissario. Like Tarquin's son.'

'Did Terrasini threaten to call the police?' Brunetti wondered, though that seemed unlikely, especially since he would be confessing to murder if he did.

'Oh, no, nothing like that. He told me he was sure that my husband would not want me to know what he had done. No man, he said, would want his wife to know that.' She turned her head to one side, and Brunetti noticed how tight the skin on her neck was. 'He argued that Maurizio was responsible for what happened.' She shook her head. 'Antonio was not stupid, as I said.' Then, soberly, 'He went to Catholic schools. Jesuits.'

'And so?' Brunetti asked.

'And so to keep Maurizio from learning that I knew what had happened, Antonio suggested that he and I come to an accommodation. That was his word: "accommodation".'

'Like Tarquin's son with Lucrezia?' Brunetti asked.

'Exactly,' she answered, sounding very tired. 'If I agreed to the terms of this accommodation, then Maurizio would never learn that I knew he had told these people about the dentist or that he had given Antonio the idea to do – well – to do what he did. And the name.' She put both hands on the sides of the teapot as if they had grown suddenly cold.

'And so?' Brunetti asked.

'And so, to save my husband's honour . . .' she began and when she saw his response, said, 'Yes, Commissario, his honour, and to let him continue to believe that I respected and loved him – which I do, and did, and shall always do – well, I had one way to ensure that.' She removed her hands from the warmth of the teapot and folded then neatly on the table in front of her.

'I see,' Brunetti said.

She drank more of her tea, thirstily, without bothering to add honey. 'Do you find that strange?'

'I'm not sure "strange" is the right word, Signora,' Brunetti said evasively.

'I would do anything to save my husband's honour, Commissario, even if he *had* told them to do it,' she said so fiercely that two women sitting at a table near the door turned to look at them.

'In Australia, Maurizio was with me all the time. He was at the hospital all day, every day, then in my room when they would let him in. He left his businesses to run themselves and stayed with me. His son called and told him he had to come back, but he stayed with me. He held my hand and he cleaned me when I was sick.' Her voice was low, passionate.

'And then, when it was all over, after all the operations, he still loved me.' Her eyes wandered away, off to the Antipodes. 'The first time I saw myself, I had to go into the bathroom in the hospital to do it: there was no mirror in my room. Maurizio had had them all taken out, and at first, when the bandages came off, I didn't give it a thought. But then I did begin to think about it and I asked him why there was no mirror.'

She laughed, low and musical; a beautiful sound. 'And he told me he had never noticed, that maybe they didn't have mirrors in hospital rooms in Australia. That night, after he was gone, I went down the corridor into the bathroom. And I saw this,' she said, waving a hand under her chin.

She propped one elbow on the table and pressed three fingers against her mouth, staring off at that distant mirror. 'It was horrible. To see that face and not be able to smile or frown or do anything with it, really.' She took the fingers away. 'And in the beginning it was a shock to see the way people looked at me. They couldn't help it: they'd see this and a look of dull shock would appear on their faces, and then, a moment later, I'd see the puritanical disapproval, no matter how hard they tried to disguise or hide it. *"La super liftata"*,'

264

she said and he heard the rage in her voice. 'I know what I'm called.'

Brunetti thought she was finished, but that was not so. 'The next day I told Maurizio what I'd seen in the mirror, and he said it didn't matter. I still remember the way he waved his hand and said, "*sciochezze*", as if this face were the least important thing about me.'

She pushed the cup and saucer away from her. 'And I believe he meant that, and means it still. To him, I'm still the young woman he married.'

'And during these last two years?' Brunetti asked.

'What do you mean?' she asked angrily.

'Has he never suspected?'

'What? That Antonio was my – what do I call him? – my lover?'

'Hardly,' Brunetti said. 'Has he suspected?'

'I hope not,' she said instantly. 'But I don't know what he knows, or if he can let himself think about it. He knew that I spent time with Antonio, and I think . . . I think he was afraid to ask. And I couldn't tell him anything, could I?' She sat back in her chair and crossed her arms. 'It's all such a cliché, isn't it? The old man with the young wife. Of course she'll take a young lover.'

'"And so on both sides is simple truth suppressed,"' Brunetti surprised himself by saying.

'What?' she asked.

'Sorry, something my wife says,' Brunetti answered, not explaining, not knowing himself how he had dredged that up.

'Could you tell me about last night?' he asked.

'There's little to say, really,' she answered, again sounding very tired. 'He told me to meet him there, and I'd got used to obeying him. So I went.'

'And your husband?'

'He's become as accustomed to it as I have, I suppose,' she

said. 'I told him I was going out, and he didn't ask me anything.'

'You didn't get home until morning, did you?' Brunetti asked.

'I'm afraid Maurizio's grown accustomed to that, as well.' Her voice was bleak.

'Ah,' was the only thing Brunetti could find to say. Then, 'What happened?'

She propped her elbows on the table and put her chin on her folded hands. 'Why should I tell you that, Commissario?'

'Because, sooner or later, you are going to have to tell someone, and I'm a good choice,' he said, meaning both.

Her eyes, he thought, grew softer, and she said, 'I knew that anyone who liked Cicero so much had to be a good man.'

'I'm not,' he said, meaning that, as well. 'But I'm curious and, if I can – and within the limits of the law – I'd like to be able to help you.'

'Cicero spent his life lying, didn't he?' she asked.

Brunetti's first response was to be insulted, but then he realized that what he was hearing was a question, not a comparison. 'Do you mean in the legal cases?'

'Yes. He twisted evidence, certainly bribed every witness he could get money to, distorted the truth, and probably used every cheap trick lawyers have ever used.' She seemed pleased with the list.

'But not in his private life,' Brunetti said. 'Perhaps he was vain, and weak, but in the end he was an honest man, I think. And a brave one.'

She studied his face, weighing what he had said. 'The first thing I said to Antonio was that you were a policeman and had come to arrest him,' she told him. 'He always carried a gun. I knew him well enough by then . . .' she began and paused a long time after saying that, as if listening to an echo, then went on, 'to know he would try to use it. But then he saw you – I think he saw you both, with guns – and I told him it

266

was useless, that his family's lawyers could get him out of any trouble he might be in.'

She pressed her lips together, and Brunetti was struck by how very unattractive the gesture was. 'He believed me, or he was so confused he didn't know what to do, so he handed me the gun when I told him to.'

The front door slammed and they both looked in that direction, but it was only a woman with a pram trying to leave. One of the women at the table near the door got up and held the door for her, and she left.

Brunetti looked back at her. 'What did you say to him then?' he asked.

'I told you I knew him well enough by then, didn't I?'

'Yes.'

'So I told him I thought he was gay, that he fucked like a fag, and that he probably wanted me because I didn't really look like a woman.'

She waited for his response, but Brunetti made none, and she said, 'It wasn't true, of course. But I knew him, and I knew what he'd do.' Her voice changed, all emotion long since leached from it, and she said with a detachment that was almost academic, 'Antonio had only one reaction to opposition: violence. I knew what he'd do. So I shot him.' She paused, but when Brunetti remained silent, she went on, 'And when he was on the ground, I realized I might not have killed him, so I shot him in the face.' Her own face remained immobile as she said this.

'I see,' Brunetti finally said.

'And I'd do it again, Commissario. I'd do it again.' He was tempted to ask her why, but he knew she was now incapable of stopping herself from explaining. 'I told you: he had unpleasant tastes.'

And that was the last thing she said.

29

'Well,' Paola said, 'I'd give her a medal.' Brunetti had gone to bed soon after dinner, saying he was tired, not explaining why. Paola had come to bed some hours later, had fallen instantly asleep, only to be awakened at three by a sleepless, motionless Brunetti lying beside her, his memory chasing after everything that had happened the day before. He went over his conversations with the Contessa, with Griffoni, and then with Franca Marinello.

It took him some time to tell all of this, his voice interrupted every so often by the sound of bells from different parts of the city that neither of them paid any attention to. He could explain, theorize, try to imagine, but his memory kept swirling back to that phrase she had sought, and found: 'unpleasant tastes'.

'God above,' Paola had said when he repeated it. 'I don't know what it could mean. And I think I don't want to know.'

'Would a woman let something like that go on for two years?' he finally asked, knowing as he spoke that he had sounded the wrong note.

Instead of answering, she switched on her bedside lamp and turned towards him.

'What's the matter?'

'Nothing,' Paola said. 'I just want to see the face of a person capable of asking a question like that.'

'What question?' asked an indignant Brunetti.

'Whether a woman would *let* something like that go on for two years.'

'What's wrong with it?' he asked. 'The question, I mean.'

She slid down a bit and pulled the covers over her shoulder. 'To begin with, it assumes that there is something like the female mind, that all women would react in the same way in those circumstances,' she said. Abruptly, she propped herself up on her elbow and said, 'Think about the fear, Guido: think about what has been happening to her for two years. This man was a murderer, and she knew what he had done to the dentist and his wife.'

'Do you believe that she felt she had to sacrifice herself to keep her husband's illusions about himself intact?' he asked, feeling quite virtuous in doing so and in phrasing it the way he did. He tried, but failed, to keep himself from going on and asked, 'What sort of a feminist are you, to defend something like that?'

For a moment, even though she opened her mouth to speak, Paola found it difficult to find the words. Finally she said, 'Look at the pulpit from which this sermon comes.'

'What's that supposed to mean?'

'It isn't *supposed* to mean anything, Guido. But what it *does* mean is that you are not, especially in this matter, allowed to present yourself as a paladin of feminism. I will allow you a lot, and I will allow you at other times and in other circumstances to be a paladin of anything you like, even of feminism, but not now, not about this.'

'I don't know what you're talking about,' he said, though he feared he did.

She pushed back the covers and sat up, facing him. 'What I'm talking about is rape, Guido.' Then, before he had the chance to say anything, she said, 'And don't give me that look, as if all of a sudden I'm a hysterical woman, afraid that any man I smile at is going to jump out of the wardrobe, or that I assume every compliment is the prelude to an assault.'

He turned away and switched on his own lamp. If this was going to go on a long time – and he now suspected it would – he might as well be able to see her clearly.

'It's different for us, Guido, and you men simply don't want to see that or you can't see it.'

She paused after that and he took the opportunity to say, 'Paola, it's four in the morning, and I don't want to listen to a speech, all right?'

He feared that would inflame her yet it seemed to do just the opposite. She reached aside and put a hand on his arm. 'I know, I know. All I want you to do is try to see it as a situation in which a woman consented to sex with a man with whom she did not want to have sex.' She thought for some time, then added, 'I've spoken to her only a few times. It's my mother who likes her – loves her, really – and her judgement is good enough for me.'

'What judgement did your mother make about her?' he asked.

'That she wouldn't lie,' Paola said. 'So if she told you she did this unwillingly – and I think "unpleasant tastes" is enough to suggest it was – then it's rape. Even if it went on for two years, and even if her reason was to protect her husband's sense of himself.' When his expression did not change, she said, in a much warmer voice, 'You work around the law in this country, Guido, so you know what would have happened if she had gone to the police and if any of this had ever been dragged into the courts. What would happen to that old man, and to her.'

She stopped and looked at him, but he chose not to answer and chose not to object.

'Our culture has very primitive ideas about sex,' she said.

To lighten the mood, Brunetti said, 'I think our society has very primitive ideas about a number of things.' But as soon as he said it, he realized how firmly he believed this and so it did little to cheer him.

And that was when she said it: 'Well, I'd give her a medal.'

Brunetti sighed, then shrugged, then reached aside to turn off the light.

When he felt the pressure, he noticed that her hand had never left his arm. 'What are you going to do?' she asked.

'I'm going to go to sleep,' he said.

'And in the morning?' she asked, switching off her light.

'I'll go and talk to Patta.'

'What will you tell him?'

Brunetti turned on to his right side, though to do so, he had to pull his arm free of her hand. He rose up and pounded his pillow a few times, then pulled himself over so that he could put his left hand on the inside of her arm. 'I don't know.'

'Really?'

'Really,' he said, and then they slept.

The newspapers latched on to the story and would not let it go. They sank their teeth into it and shook it, for it had just what their public loved: wealthy people caught in apparent misbehaviour; the younger wife caught with the lover; violence, sex, and death. On the way to the Questura, Brunetti saw again the photo of the young Franca Marinello; in fact, he saw a number of photos of her and wondered how it was possible that the press could have found so many and so soon. Did her university classmates sell them? Her family? Friends? When he got to his office, he opened the papers and read through the story as it was presented in all of them.

Amidst the tumble of words, there were more photos of

her at various social functions during the last few years, and speculation was rife about what would have driven an attractive young woman to have tampered with – they drew themselves short of talking about 'God's gift', limiting themselves to 'her natural appearance' – in order to end up looking the way she did. Various psychologists were interviewed: one of them said she was a symbol of a consumerist society, never satisfied with what it had, always looking for some symbolic achievement to validate its worth; while another, in *L'Osservatore Romano*, a woman, saw it as a sad example of the way women were driven to attempt any means to make themselves younger or more attractive so as to compete for the approval of men. Sometimes, the psychologist said, with badly disguised glee, these attempts failed, though that failure seldom served as sufficient warning to those still willing to pursue the evanescent goal of physical beauty.

A different journalist speculated about the nature of Franca Marinello's relationship with Terrasini, whose criminal past was splattered across the pages. They had become a well known couple, it was said by a number of unnamed people, and had been seen at the best restaurants in the city and often at the Casinò.

Cataldo, it seemed, had been selected to play the role of the betrayed husband. Entrepreneur, former city councillor, well regarded by his fellow businessmen of the Veneto, he had ended his former marriage of thirty-five years in order to marry Franca Marinello, a woman more than thirty years his junior. Neither he nor Marinello was available for comment, nor had a warrant been issued for her arrest. The police were still questioning witnesses and waiting for the results of the autopsy.

Brunetti, one of the witnesses to the crime, had certainly not been questioned, nor, it turned out when he phoned both Griffoni and Vasco, had they. 'And who the hell is supposed to be questioning us?' he could not stop himself from asking out loud.

He closed the papers and, realizing it was nothing more than a gesture of protest and, as such, self-indulgent and meaningless, tossed them into the wastepaper basket – and felt better for having done it. Patta did not come in until after lunch, but when he arrived Signorina Elettra phoned Brunetti, and he went downstairs.

Signorina Elettra was at her desk and said, when he came in, 'I see I didn't find enough about her, or about Terrasini. Or I didn't find it soon enough.'

'You've read the papers, then?'

'I looked at them and found them more disgusting than usual.'

'How is he?' Brunetti asked, nodding towards Patta's door.

'He's just finished speaking to the Questore, so I suspect he'll want to see you.'

Brunetti knocked on the door and went in, knowing that Patta's mood usually had a one-note overture. 'Ah, Brunetti,' the Vice-Questore said when he saw him. 'Come in.'

Well, it was more than one note, but they had all been in a minor key, so that meant a subdued Patta and that meant a Patta who was up to something and not certain about whether he could get away with it and even more uncertain about whether he could count on Brunetti to help him with it.

'I thought you might like to speak to me, sir,' Brunetti said in his most deferential voice.

'Yes, I do,' Patta said expansively. He waved Brunetti to a seat, waited until he was comfortable, and said, 'I'd like you to tell me about this incident in the Casinò.'

Brunetti was growing more and more uneasy: a civil Patta always had that effect on him. 'I was there because of the man, Terrasini. His name had come up' – Brunetti thought it best not to mention the photo Guarino had sent him, and Patta would never be curious enough to ask – 'in my investigation into Guarino's death. The chief of security at the Casinò called me and told me he had come in, so I went over. Commissario Griffoni came with me.'

Patta sat, all but regal, behind his desk. He nodded and said, 'Yes. Go on.'

'Soon after we came in, Terrasini had a sudden losing streak and, when it looked like he might cause trouble, the head of security and his assistant intervened and started to take him downstairs.' Patta nodded again, understanding so well how important it was that trouble be removed quickly from the public eye.

'He had been at the table with a woman, and she followed them.' Brunetti closed his eyes, as if reconstructing the scene, then continued. 'They took him to the bottom of the first flight of steps, and I suppose they judged he wasn't going to give them any trouble because they let go of his arms and waited to see if he had cooled down. Then they started up the steps, back to the gaming rooms.'

He looked at Patta, who liked it when people did so when speaking to him. 'Then, for no reason I can understand, Terrasini pulled out a pistol and aimed it up at us, or at the two security men – I don't know which.' This was certainly true enough: he had not known whom Terrasini was pointing his gun at.

'Griffoni and I both had our guns in our hands by then, and when he saw them he must have changed his mind, because he lowered his and gave it to Signora Marinello.'

Brunetti found it encouraging that Patta seemed not to find it unusual that Brunetti should refer to her formally like this. He went on. 'Then – it was only a few seconds later – he turned to her and raised his hand as if he were going to hit her. Not slap her, sir, but hit her. He had his hand in a fist. I saw that.'

Patta looked as if he was hearing a story with which he was already familiar.

'And then she shot him. He fell, and she shot him again.' Patta asked nothing about this, but Brunetti said, anyway, 'I don't know why she did that, sir.'

'Is that all?'

'That's all I saw, sir,' Brunetti said.

'Did she say anything?' Patta asked, and Brunetti prepared to answer, but Patta specified, 'When you spoke to her in the Casinò? About why she did it?'

'No, sir,' Brunetti answered honestly.

Patta pushed himself back in his chair and crossed his legs, showing a sock blacker than night and smoother than a maiden's cheek. 'We have to be cautious here, Brunetti, as I think you can understand.'

'Of course, sir.'

'I've spoken to Griffoni, and she confirms your story, or you confirm hers. She said exactly what you did, that he gave her the gun and then pulled his fist back to hit her.'

Brunetti nodded.

'I spoke to her husband today,' Patta said, and Brunetti disguised his astonishment with a small cough. 'We've known one another for years,' Patta explained. 'Lions Club.'

'Of course,' Brunetti said, filling his voice with the admiration of non-members. 'What did he say?'

'That his wife panicked when she saw that Terrasini was going to hit her.' Then, with a confidentiality that allowed Brunetti a one-day membership in the old boys' club, Patta said, 'You can imagine what would happen to her face if anyone hit it. It might fall apart.'

Brunetti's stomach clenched with rage at the words, but then he realized that Patta was entirely serious and spoke literally. A moment's reflection forced him to accept the fact that Patta was also probably right.

Patta went on, 'And when he was on the ground, she saw his hand start to move towards her leg. Her husband told me that's what made her shoot him again.' Then, to Brunetti directly, he asked, 'Did you see it?'

'No, sir, I was looking at her, and I think the angle was wrong, anyway.' That made no sense, but Patta wanted to believe what he had been told, and Brunetti saw no reason to prevent that.

'That's exactly what Griffoni said,' Patta volunteered.

Some imp of the perverse urged Brunetti to ask, 'What did you and her husband decide, sir?'

Patta heard the question but not the words, and answered, 'I think what happened is pretty clear, don't you?'

'Yes, sir. I do,' Brunetti answered.

'She felt threatened and she defended herself the only way she knew how,' Patta explained, and Brunetti was suddenly sure he had said the same to the Questore. 'And this man, Antonio Terrasini – I've asked Signorina Elettra to find out about him, and once again she has done so with remarkable speed – has a criminal record filled with violence.'

'Ah,' Brunetti allowed himself to exclaim, then asked, 'And so the possibility of criminal charges?'

Patta flicked the idea away as though it were a fly. 'No, that's certainly not necessary.' Then, switching to the mode of pathos, the Vice-Questore went on, 'They've certainly suffered enough.' Presumably, her husband was the other part of that plural, and Brunetti thought how true his words were. They had.

He got to his feet. 'I'm glad this is settled, then,' he said.

Patta graced Brunetti with one of his rare smiles, and Brunetti was struck, as happened each time he smiled, by how very handsome the man was. 'You'll write a report, then, Brunetti?'

'Of course, sir,' Brunetti said, filled with the uncharacteristic desire to do his master's bidding. 'I'll go up and do it now.'

'Good,' Patta said and pulled some papers towards him.

Upstairs, Brunetti remembered his missing computer but could not bring himself to care much about it. He wrote an account, neither brief nor long, of what had happened in the Casinò two nights before. He confined himself to describing what he had seen, making reference to Franca Marinello in a passive way, as the person who had followed Terrasini down the steps and to whom he had handed his gun. She became active, in Brunetti's account, only when Terrasini raised his hand to her, and then Brunetti described her response. He made no mention of having seen her speak to Terrasini, nor did he mention her asking him about Ovid, nor yet did he refer to his meeting with her in the *gelateria*.

As he was writing, his phone rang and he answered.

'It's Bocchese,' the chief technician said.

'Yes,' Brunetti said, still writing.

'They just emailed me the autopsy reports on that guy who got shot in the Casinò.'

'Yes?'

'He had a good deal of alcohol in his blood, and something else they can't identify. Might be Ecstasy, might be something like it. But something. They're doing more tests.'

'And you?' Brunetti asked. 'You find anything?'

'They sent me the bullets, and I had a look. The guys in Mestre had already sent me the photos of the bullet they took out of the mud in that tank in Marghera. If it's not a match, I'm going to retire and open an antique shop.'

'Is that what you're going to do when you retire?' Brunetti asked.

'No need to,' the technician answered. 'I know so many people in the business by now that I don't have to bother with a shop. That way, I don't have to pay taxes.'

'Of course.'

'You still want me to check on that, what was he, that guy with the trucks in Tessera?'

'Yes, if you can.'

'It'll take a couple of days. I'll have to nag them to send me the photos of the bullets.'

'Keep at it, Bocchese. It might be something.'

'All right, if you say so. Anything else?'

There was the dentist, Brunetti knew, and his still unsolved murder. If the police found a link between his death and the gun, then they would have a link between Terrasini and the dentist, wouldn't they?

'No, nothing else,' Brunetti said and replaced the phone.

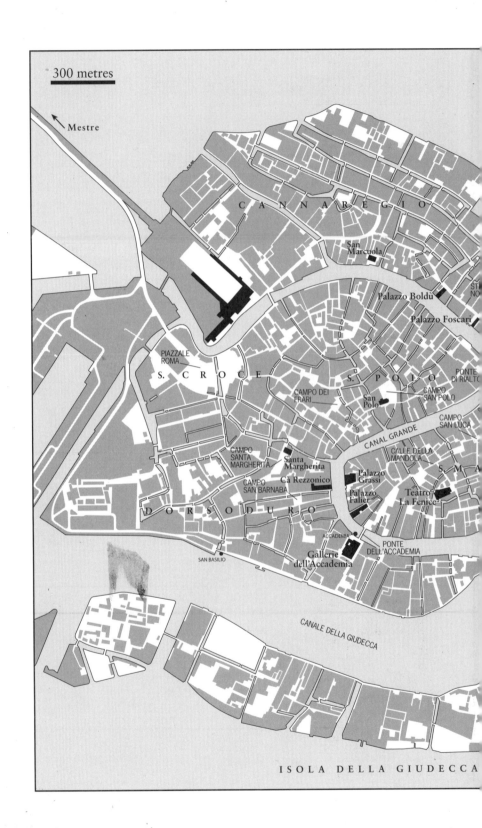

300 metres

Mestre

CANNAREGIO

San Marcuola

Palazzo Boldù

S. NO

Palazzo Foscari

PIAZZALE ROMA

S. CROCE

S. POLO

PONTE DI RIALTO

CAMPO DEI FRARI

San Polo

CAMPO SAN POLO

CANAL GRANDE

CAMPO SAN LUCA

CAMPO SANTA MARGHERITA

Santa Margherita

Ca Rezzonico

CAMPO SAN BARNABA

CALLE DELLA MANDOLA

S. M A

Palazzo Grassi

Palazzo Falier

Teatro La Fenice

DORSODURO

ACCADEMIA

SAN BASILIO

Gallerie dell'Accademia

PONTE DELL'ACCADEMIA

CANALE DELLA GIUDECCA

ISOLA DELLA GIUDECCA